Death Of An Emmet

Ian Searle

The characters portrayed in this story are all fictitious.
Any resemblance to real persons, living or dead, is
completely coincidental. The settings described are also
largely invented, although parts of St Mary's are
identifiable. There was no university based in Chichester
in 1980, though Sussex University, I believe, may have
had a branch there. And I certainly know of no red light
district in that elegant and lovely city.

First published in 2019 by CompletelyNovel.com

ISBN 9781787233720

Contents

Cover picture: Hugh Town, St Mary's, Isles of Scilly by Andrew Roland. Dreamtime.com

Prologue

In the grey light of dawn, the tumble of boulders betrayed only a hint of form at the foot of the cliff. Monochrome shades suggested smoothness and roundness on a larger than human scale. Jack Matthews, steering his small boat with the casual ease of long experience, headed for his crab pots with hardly a glance at the shoreline. But there was a darker patch where there should have been the faintest gleam of the approaching day on the top of one of the boulders, and it caught Jack's eye. He turned towards it.

It was too large to be a dead cormorant. Jack cut the outboard motor and drifted the boat expertly to bump gently against the rocks. Stepping ashore with the painter in his hand, he reached the spot with two swift strides and looked down on the body of a man. It was above the high-water mark. The body lay on its back, eyes open, very dead.

Jack noted the dark stain on the front of the sweatshirt and the bloodied dent high on one temple. Then he turned back to his boat, and abandoning the round of his crab pots, he headed for the beach and Sergeant Roberts' police house.

Chapter 1

The sound of birds and the gentle surge of the small waves below him were all that disturbed Thorn's tranquillity. This was the third time he had played this course and he still felt a sense of wonder as he placed his ball on the tee. Space on the island was limited, so this, the second of the nine holes, was perched like an eagle's eyrie on a small, rocky peninsula at the end of a short ridge that dipped in the middle. The green, 200 yards away, was on the same level, and to the right. To reach it he simply had to drive over the curving gap – not a very difficult shot, but impressive, for between the tee and the fairway the cliff dropped sheer to the sea some 80 feet below and rose again, equally sheer on the other side. Thorn was not a particularly enthusiastic golfer, and his motive in driving his hire car out to this course at seven in the morning was not to enable him to play without queuing so much as to enjoy the silence and the solitude. As he straightened up, therefore, he stood for a moment and looked about him, savouring the view, before taking a club from his bag. The placid, green curve of the links before him was broken by the appearance on the skyline of a small, moving object which bobbed up and down, grew slightly larger and taller, and was too symmetrical to be a bird. It was a hat and, since its owner was heading across the fairway, towards the path and the promontory upon which he stood, there was little Thorn could do but wait. Beneath the hat a head appeared. It was too far off still to distinguish the features, but Thorn no longer needed to do so, for the shape of that hat was now as clear and familiar as it was unwelcome. It was a policeman's hat.

There was only one policeman in Scilly, Sergeant Roberts. Scilly (winter population 2000, summer population, including visitors, 10,000), was wonderfully law-abiding. Thorn had been well aware of that fact when he decided to visit. This was the kind of community one only remembered wistfully on the mainland, where the village policeman on his bike greeted everyone as a friend, and grew his vegetables on the allotment like everyone else. Everyone knew Sergeant Roberts, the visitors by sight, at least, and the islanders on first name terms. What he was doing on the golf course at seven in the morning Thorn could only guess at, but he felt his heart sink at the sight of this well-built, confident figure striding ever closer. He waited.

The policeman crossed the fairway and came on. He had spotted Thorn by now and he headed straight for him. By the purposeful stride Thorn knew this was not some casual meeting. Still he waited. Roberts reached the path but did not stop. He came steadily on as far as the tee where he stopped at last.

"Morning, sir," he said.

"Good morning, Sergeant. Were you looking for me?"

"Yes, sir." He frowned, as though looking for a way to state his business. "You are Detective Superintendent Thorn, are you, sir?"

"I am when I'm at work," admitted Thorn warily.

"Well, sir, I... There's been... I've had a phone call from the Deputy Chief Constable in Exeter. He'd like to speak to you urgently."

"I'm on holiday, Sergeant."

"I know, sir, but this is very urgent."

"What's it about?"

8

"If you don't mind, sir, I think it would be better if you rang Exeter and found out."

"So, you know what it's about?"

"I've got my car at the clubhouse."

"It's all right, Sergeant, so have I."

Roberts seized the handle of the golf trolley and set off back down the path. Thorn followed without speaking. He was annoyed at the brusque interruption of his holiday, the more so because the call came not from his own boss, but from the Deputy Chief Constable of a force with which he had no connection. The matter was hardly likely to be anything to do with York, his home town, nor could it any longer, he thought with a sudden, sharp pain, be anything to do with his family. He made himself concentrate on his surroundings.

Sergeant Roberts' police house was a small, granite cottage with a lean-to garage on one side and a small office on the other. Thorn followed the sergeant inside and sat down on the visitors' side of the desk, Roberts called Headquarters and, after a moment's wait, was put through. He handed the receiver to Thorn and discreetly left the office.

"Detective Superintendent Thorn?" The voice was crisp, military.

"Speaking."

"I'm Stonehill, Deputy Chief Constable. Has Sergeant Roberts told you what this is about?"

"Not a word," said Thorn, deliberately omitting the word "sir".

"Good. Now it was sheer chance that we heard you were holidaying on St Mary's. I hope you will agree to help us out."

"Help you out, sir?"

"Yes, we are stretched over capacity at the moment because of this international conference being staged at Torquay. We've had warning of possible terrorist activity and we've had to assign just about all our uniformed men and most of our CID men to cover that. We have absolutely no one to spare to send to St Mary's. Since you are there, and you are clearly a very experienced senior officer, I have already taken the liberty of phoning your Chief Constable – you know he came to you from behind this very desk, I suppose? – and he is happy to lend you to us, if you agree."

"You want me to help out at Torquay?" Thorn was puzzled.

"Good heavens, no; on St Mary's, of course."

"I'm sorry, sir," said Thorn, "I don't understand. What has the conference at Torquay got to do with a peaceful little holiday island?"

"Nothing whatsoever. We want you to run an enquiry into the suspicious death that happened this morning."

Thorn thought for a moment. "What suspicious death?" he asked.

"The Sergeant has all the details, and he'll fill you in. I told him not to, until I'd spoken to you."

"Do I have a choice, sir?"

"You could say no; you are on leave and this isn't your patch, I know. But you would be helping us enormously and you could get things moving quickly; the Sergeant is a very capable man, but this is out of his league. It would take us at least six hours to organise another investigating officer, to get him out there by plane. And I have been told you can extend your leave once this case has been cleared up."

The door opened, and the Sergeant came in with a tray. It contained a pot of hot coffee, a plate of croissants, butter and marmalade. It smelled delicious. An attractive woman, neat, dark-haired, held the door open and closed it behind her husband.

"Very well, sir" said Thorn into the phone.

"Good man," said Stonehill. "Look forward to hearing from you."

"Welcome aboard, sir," Roberts smiled briefly. "Breakfast?"

"Where's the body?" asked Thorn, impatient.

"It's all right, sir. I know I am single-handed, but we do have things organised. The body is at the foot of the cliff at Purley Head. It won't be disturbed until you've been there; I've got three of my coastguard pals standing watch. I've asked Dr Cooper to report here so we can go out with him. I've also asked Phil Gurnard. He's the chap that runs the photography shop in Well Street. I've asked him to come out to Purley Head in half an hour. You've got time to have a bite to eat."

"Right," said Thorn. "Who is the victim, do we know?"

"One of the visitors, an unpleasant sort of chap, called Lambert. He was last seen leaving the Pirate at about 11 o'clock last night. His body was found by Jack Matthews, a local man who was collecting his crab pots round that bit of the coast at about 5.30 this morning. He came straight here, and I went back with him to take a look for myself. It looked as if he'd fallen over the cliff, probably because he'd had a skinful last night. His head was badly bashed in, so it could have been just the fall."

"So," Thorn pressed him as he helped himself to a second croissant, "What turns this into a suspicious death?"

"That's down to me at the moment."

Thorn looked at him sharply. "Why?"

"If someone slips and falls over a cliff, he is likely to fall forwards or sideways, not backwards. Take a look at the traces of mud and grass on his shoes and trousers."

"Is that all?"

"Oh, no, sir. At the point where the man fell over the cliff there is no grass near the edge anyway. What's more, I'm not at all sure, until the doctor has had a look at the body, but I couldn't state definitely that it was the fall that killed him. His head has been bashed in, it's true, but there's blood on the front of his sweatshirt and there is a bruise – I went so far as to lift the sweatshirt and T-shirt – which looks at first as though it might have been caused by a sharp stone. Only the cliffs round there, and the small boulders at the bottom, aren't exactly sharp, you see. And I thought the wound in his chest wasn't just a rough bruise. I might be wrong, but it looks suspiciously like a stab wound."

"In that case, Sergeant, I hope you're right; I shan't take kindly to losing part of my leave if you're proved wrong."

The outside door opened and an untidy man in need of a haircut came in. He wore shapeless, grey trousers and an old jacket over a roll-neck sweater. He pushed a pair of glasses back in position in what seemed to be a habitual gesture, and looked at the two men at the desk.

12

"What's the problem, Bill?" he asked. Thorn, who found voices were very important when he was assessing character, thought this man sounded at ease and confident. His voice was a pleasant baritone and the question suggested curiosity.

"Come in, Doctor," said Roberts. "This is Detective Superintendent Thorn."

"I've seen you out and about," said Cooper, proffering a hand. "So, you're here on business, are you?"

"So it would seem," said Thorn, taking the outstretched hand. "Glad to meet you, Doctor. Let's go; the sooner we get out to the scene the better."

"What scene?" asked Cooper, with a slightly puzzled smile.

Thorn looked at Roberts. "There's a body on the rocks at Purley Head, Doctor," the Sergeant explained. "One of the visitors."

"Right," said the doctor. "Forgive me if I seem a little thick, but why does the accidental death of a tourist warrant attention from a detective superintendent?"

"Call it professional curiosity," said Thorn, heading for the door. Cooper pulled a wry face and turned in the same direction.

Purley Head was a truly beautiful spot, a mere ten minutes' drive from the police station. Roberts parked at the point where the narrow road, after skirting the beach beyond the small town, and rounding the headland, began to curl back inland, turning northwards. To the east there was no hedge or border, but the beach gave way to a rising cliff of broken granite blocks, surrounded by grass and scrub, which stretched seaward several hundreds of yards, before it rose to a spectacular summit. A path led from the road towards the point. The three men left the car and took the path in single file, Roberts leading.

"The body is just round the point," he said over his shoulder.

The path divided. The right fork continued towards the foot of the cliff, and Thorn could see it climbed very little, perhaps ten or twelve feet above the reddish-stained rocks that marked the high-water mark. The left fork turned sharply and disappeared behind a small ridge of sand, covered in tussocks of wiry grass, and presumably it led up to the top of the cliff. Roberts took the right fork. For the next few minutes the going was easy, but as the cliff above them grew taller and began to bend northward again, the tumble of polished boulders grew lumpy, the stones themselves no longer the size of footballs, but three or four feet in diameter, and the footpath disappeared. It now became a matter almost of scrambling over and between these huge masses of granite. Thorn had already noticed the curious formations this ancient stone had taken over countless thousands of years, formations to which fanciful men had given picturesque names like "Skull Rock" and "the Elephant."

At last, as they all climbed onto a huge slab, now out of sight of the road and close to the most seaward point of the Head, Thorn saw beyond Roberts' shoulder, the figure of a man in dark trousers and jersey, who stood looking towards them.

"Ray Collins," said Roberts, "coastguard."

"What about…?"

"Two more up top," Robert anticipated the question. "They said they'd rope off the cliff edge for me…for us."

Thorn grunted, surprised. The man seemed to have his wits about him.

In a matter of minutes, they reached the spot. Collins eyed the stranger with suspicion then, when Roberts explained who he was, with mild distrust. The dead man lay in ungainly death, partly in a cleft between two huge boulders. Thorn saw at a glance that Roberts' earlier comments were true: there were no small stones here, and all the surfaces he could see were smooth and rounded like the bald heads of mouldering giants. The dead man was in his late 30s or early 40s, he would guess. He wore a loose and expensive sweatshirt which was stained with blood and showed marks where he had slid across lichen-covered stones. He wore jeans and good shoes. The toes of the shoes and the front of the trouser legs were, indeed, clean but, at the angle the body was lying it was possible to see something of the back of the same trouser legs and they were marked and streaked with grass stains.

Thorn stood aside and asked the doctor to examine the body but not to move it for the moment. "I want some photographs first," he explained. Cooper made no comment but knelt awkwardly by the dead man and began a careful examination of the head, then, as Roberts had done earlier, he lifted the sweatshirt and eased back the tee-shirt beneath. He looked long and hard at the livid, bloodstained bruise just below the heart.

"Well?" Thorn looked down at the doctor.

"Look for yourself." Cooper held the tee-shirt while Thorn peered at the bruise. The blood had clotted near the centre of the mark, but it had clearly leaked from a horizontal cut about half an inch long. "I can't be sure until I do the PM, but I'd guess this puncture reached the heart, hence all the blood. A shallow cut would not have bled so much. This has been pumped out."

The coastguard, standing a short distance away, but watching with interest, caught the implication immediately. "So, it wasn't the fall as killed him," he said.

"Don't talk to anyone about this," Thorn said quietly.

"We may live in the back of beyond here," said Collins, "but we're not completely stupid."

"I didn't say that," Thorn blundered on. Then, catching a glimpse of Roberts, he stopped, because the sergeant was shaking his head in warning. "What I meant was that we'll have to wait for the post-mortem to be sure."

The sound of boots scrambling over the rocks in the direction of the path announced the arrival of another member of the party. It was the photographer.

Phil Gurnard was a stocky man. He wore heavy walking shoes, and thick, shapeless trousers which disappeared under a short, waterproof coat which seemed almost entirely made of pockets. Three quarters of his face was covered with a luxuriant, red beard and moustache. Those parts not covered were brick red, the result of hours of exposure to the elements of a skin which refused to turn brown. The eyes were bright blue. The smile of greeting on his face faded as he approached the group of men and perceived the twisted body on the rocks, but he said nothing, just nodding to each man in turn, a little more hesitantly in Thorn's case.

"Who is it?" he asked, then, stepping closer, answered his own question. "Oh, it's that chap as was staying at the Smuggler's. What happened? Fell off the cliff, did he?"

"You've got it," said Roberts. "Could you take a few pictures for us, Phil? We'll want pictures to show how and where he fell, and close-ups of the injuries."

"Take pictures of absolutely everything," Thorn chimed in, "including his clothes. And when you've finished that, join us up on the top and take a few shots of the ground where he probably fell over the cliff."

"What's your interest in all this, then, me 'andsome?" asked Gurnard.

"This is Detective Superintendent Thorn, Phil," the Sergeant explained.

"I see," said the photographer, who clearly didn't.

"Once Mr Gurnard has finished down here," said Thorn, "can we get the body back to where ever the PM is to be done?"

"If you're going up top," said the coastguard, "tell young Colin to nip back to the coastguard station and get a stretcher, and phone Eddie Long."

"Eddie Long?"

"He's got a Citroen he uses as an ambulance," explained Roberts. "He can collect the stretcher from the path and take it back to the morgue."

"Good," Thorn was satisfied. "Can I just repeat, please, will all of you not talk about this until we know more about the circumstances?" No one replied, but all looked as though they were being asked a silly question. "And will you be doing the PM yourself, Doctor?"

"I suppose so," replied Cooper.

"In that case, I'd like photographs of the body without the clothes, particularly of the injury to the chest. Clothes in a sealed plastic bag, please. Can you take the pictures at the morgue, Mr Gurnard?"

17

Gurnard, his camera already half assembled on a convenient boulder, nodded.

"Right, Sergeant, let's get up to the top."

"You'll still want this area sealed off somehow, won't you, sir?"

"Sorry, yes. That goes without saying, though how you're going to do it, I don't know."

"We'll manage," said Collins. "If we can protect wrecks, I daresay we can manage the scene of a murder."

"No one has said it was murder," Thorn said sharply.

"No, that's right, no one said so- yet," agreed Collins.

Thorn turned away abruptly and headed back towards the path. Sergeant Roberts followed. This time when they reached the fork in the path, they took the upper level, and began to climb through the scrub and thin sand covering the rock towards the headland. The view was spectacular and Thorn, who had been here once before, looked down and out to sea. There was next to no wind, but there was still a long swell to remind the watcher that the movement of this alien element was not the result of coastal breezes, but of Atlantic gales halfway to America. As they climbed, the view back down the path was of the small town, crowded on the isthmus between the two uneven bulges of the island, turning it into an irregular egg-timer shape. Beyond that the sea, greener and shallower, then came the narrow slot between the islands, across to Samson and Bryher. Ahead, the path led them over the granite, like an unevenly laid terrace, the cracks between filled with scraps of green, weedy plants, clumps of sea pinks, coarse gravel. The ground at the edge of the cliff had been eroded for some five or ten yards in this way, so that the grass cover resumed several feet to the left of the path. It took nearly fifteen minutes to reach Purley Head, roped off and guarded by two more coastguards.

Roberts took a few minutes to pass on the information and messages, which sent the young Colin off to the coastguard station half a mile away along the northern cliff. Thorn ducked under the rope and made his way carefully to the edge of the cliff, keeping close to the rope until he reached the point from where he looked down the sheer face of the rock. Below him and slightly to his left he saw the doctor, the coastguard and the burly figure of Gurnard as he crouched with his camera near the body. Thorn estimated the dead man must have fallen at a point, some ten or fifteen feet from the spot where he stood. He looked carefully at the ground ahead of him, not moving until he had made a thorough visual check of the area. Roberts was right; there was no trace of grass anywhere near the edge. One careful step at a time he edged towards the fatal spot, scrutinising every inch. There was nothing, nothing, that is, until he thought he detected the faintest trace of scraping, but how recent that was he could not judge. He turned away from the edge and moved with great deliberation still, directly towards the path. Once more he stopped as he thought he saw very faint, parallel lines on the stone about six inches apart. There was nothing more until he reached the path. He stopped.

He looked up and saw Roberts, motionless by the rope, watching him. Again, he was surprised; the Sergeant had once more acted, perhaps instinctively, exactly as he would have wished, not following him with brutish curiosity, to trample on the very ground he wanted to inspect.

"Anything, sir?" he asked.

"Not much. There might be scrape marks here. He may have been attacked here and thrown over."

19

"Test the grass the other side of the path," Roberts pointed. "I was thinking, sir, suppose he came up here to meet someone. Suppose it was at night. They'd need a landmark." He looked to his left. A solitary, tall stone stood, surrounded by grass, a short way from the path. Keeping to the landward side of the path that anyone would follow from this stone to the cliff edge, the two men slowly approached the stone itself, eyes down. They found the tracks; two straight lines which had bruised grass as though someone had dragged a body towards the cliff.

"We'll have photographs of this, too," said Thorn.

At the base of the stone there was a narrow patch of bare earth, suggesting it was a resting place for many people who climbed up here. There was a little litter on the ground, cigarette ends, matches, a couple of crisp packets.

"Damn!" said Thorn, "we should have brought some evidence bags to put samples in."

Roberts grinned and pulled from his pocket a handful of small, plastic, freezer bags. "Thought these might be useful," he said.

"Sergeant," said Thorn, "I think we may be able to work together."

By the time they had collected as much of the rubbish as they could find in the near vicinity of the stone, young Colin was on his way back, and a little later their hirsute photographer appeared. Thorn gave him his instructions, watched him work for a few minutes, and asked when he could expect the results.

"Give me a few hours," said Gurnard "It's just a bit harder these days, now everyone wants colour. A lot of people use this new-fangled digital photography, but I don't like it myself. If I had my way, I'd use black-and-white: it has more character, I think."

Well, Thorn said to himself, beggars can't be choosers. He'd have to make do with whatever Gurnard provided.

Back at the police station, the two men sat in the office. Thorn stared moodily out of the window at the wide harbour, beyond which rose the westerly cliff and the golf course.

"Sorry to spoil your leave, sir," Roberts interrupted.

Thorn acknowledged the remark with a nod. He wasn't at all sure his leave had been ruined simply because it had been interrupted. The familiar buzz of activity, requiring his full concentration, might well be a better therapy than idling the days away and allowing his thoughts to return constantly to his own maudlin preoccupations. He had secretly been dreading the return home in three days' time, to a home full of memories and a double bed which was too big for him on his own, and where his hands reached out in the morning to find emptiness.

"Aren't you staying with Mrs Bennett, sir?"

"Yes, I am."

"Well, I was thinking, how long are you booked in for? She's usually pretty full."

"Until Saturday."

"It might prove difficult finding somewhere to stay after that. There aren't usually many vacancies in the summer. We can put you up here, you know, sir; you'd be more than welcome. And Tina's a good cook. She'd be glad to have you. You could move in tonight, if you wanted to; it would be more convenient for you, being on the job, like. Come and go as you like, sort of thing."

"Perhaps you ought to ask your wife before you suggest it."

"I already have, sir."

"When?"

"When I went out to get your coffee this morning."

"Before you knew we had a case?"

"Oh, I knew we had a case, sir, as soon as I saw the grass stains on that poor bastard's heels."

"Yes, you were right, Sergeant. Good thinking."

"So, you will be wanting the room upstairs?"

"Why not? It would be very convenient as you say, and your wife may as well have my expenses as Mrs Bennett."

"So, what's the next move?"

"What do we know about the victim?"

"His name, Matthew Lambert, and his holiday address, the Smuggler's Arms, and the impression of one or two who have met him, that he was an unpleasant sort of chap, a fairly heavy drinker."

"Right. We'd better start there, then. Better check him out on the computer. Set the wheels in motion, will you, Sergeant, and I'll get back to Mrs Bennett and start sorting out my things."

It was a matter of a few minutes' walk. As he walked, Thorn reflected that it might well be good to get back in harness. Roberts gave every appearance of being as intelligent copper, whose local knowledge could be very valuable. Without him, he was sure, the job would be much more difficult; the islanders were suspicious of "foreigners".

Packing took half an hour. Mrs Bennett, who had been paid for the full week, was not fully convinced by Thorn's explanation that he had orders to work at the police station, and needed to stay there. In vain he tried to persuade her that his early departure was not in any way a criticism of her cooking or her guest house. She wished him goodbye a trifle frostily. Thorn told her he would come back again and stay with her for another holiday in the future, and would certainly recommend her to anyone thinking of visiting the islands. Mrs Bennett sniffed. "You'd better warn them to give me six months' notice, at least. I don't have room for casual visitors, Mr Thorn."

"Of course," he said, backing away. "Thank you very much for all you've done." He turned and headed for his new digs.

Chapter 2

The Smuggler's Arms was a small pub that catered for the tourist. Situated in the centre of the town, it was a convenient place for visitors to drop in for a pint. At the back there was a small, paved area with a dozen tables, topped by large parasols, where you could sit and sip your ale and gaze over the water towards Tresco. Inside, the decor was disappointingly modern, and the walls and the fake beams were festooned with articles better left at the bottom of the sea or on the boats which fished there, glass floats, nets hung with little reason on the walls, lanterns, old firearms, including a large blunderbuss which no self-respecting smuggler would own.

Thorn followed Sergeant Roberts inside and looked gloomily round. The place was busy. The food he saw in front of some of the customers in the bar looked surprisingly good and Thorn realised he was hungry. The two men found a dark corner and sat down. Roberts had already eaten one of his wife's pasties and was content to sip a pint while his companion ate bread and cheese.

"So, no records," mused Thorn.

"Not under the name of Lambert, anyway. I can try again when we have fingerprints."

"Good idea. Have we got his home address yet?"

"No, sir, I was thinking we'd look for that here when you've finished. We'd better try to find his next of kin, too. You never know, he might even be married, though I think he was here on his own."

Behind the bar the landlord was kept busy. Thorn watched him out of habit. He took the orders efficiently but unsmilingly, saying little except to state a price or to take the next order. He was a strong, well-built man, fit -

looking, and he was helped by a more cheerful barmaid, equally efficient. The two of them moved swiftly about, avoiding each other as they rang up the money in the till with the practised skill of ballet dancers, without exchanging a word.

Behind the bar a door led to the private quarters. It opened, and a woman appeared, spoke to the man for a moment. He scowled, then shrugged, and went to the till and counted out a number of notes and handed them over. The woman took them and went back through the door. Thorn looked quizzically at his companion.

"Thora Jefferies," he said. "The landlord's wife."

"She must have been quite a looker in her time."

"I daresay you're right, sir. Not my type, I'm afraid. If this place was called the George and Dragon, some people would say it was pretty appropriate; his name's George."

" Finish your beer, Sergeant, and you can introduce me to Mrs Jefferies."

Roberts managed somehow to speak to the landlord without being overheard. He introduced Thorn, told Jefferies that Lambert had met with an accident, and they would have to have a look at his room. Jefferies gave Thorn an aggressive look and nodded. Thorn led the way out of the building to the side door and rang the bell. Mrs Jefferies opened the door, and Roberts explained again.

"This is not a convenient moment," she said. She was reluctant to let them in. On Roberts' insistence she stepped aside.

The hallway was strangely opulent. It was carpeted thickly in red and looked as though it had never been stepped on. The wall angled away to the left where the stairs rose. The doors gleamed with white paint and the handles shone like gold. And while the hallway felt somehow at odds with Thorn's expectation of the publican's flat, Mrs Jefferies herself seemed also to strike a false note, for she wore clothes which were simple but of quality – well-cut trousers, well-made Italian shoes, and a blouse of silk which fitted her to perfection. She was quite tall, almost on a level with him. On her manicured hands she wore several rings, Thorn noted, and there was the glint of a gold bracelet on her left wrist. Her hair was thick and long but styled with a high degree of art to frame her face and partly to conceal the thinning, drying texture of the skin at the temples. She was, Thorn imagined, about fifty years old, but she wore her age extremely well. Her face, with its wide cheekbones, hollow cheeks, straight, fine nose, and great, grey eyes, was now handsome rather than beautiful, but could never be plain, and must surely once, have been lovely. Yet the eyes were hard and unfriendly.

"Mrs Jefferies," Thorn said, "I believe you have a Mr Lambert staying here."

"Yes. He's not here at the moment."

"We know that, Mrs Jefferies. I'm afraid there has been an accident and Mr Lambert has been killed."

"Killed?" One hand went to her throat. It was a theatrical gesture. Thora Jefferies' face showed very little emotion at the news.

"I'm afraid so," Thorn confirmed. "I'm Superintendent Thorn and I'm helping Sergeant Roberts with the usual, routine enquiries. May we take a look at Mr Lambert's room?"

"Oh no, I can't let you in there at the moment."

"Indeed? Why not?"

"I haven't cleaned it as yet."

"That won't matter, in fact it's all to the good," said Thorn, but he was a little disconcerted at the thought of this elegantly dressed woman busying herself with domestic cleaning. He would have expected her to employ a chambermaid.

"I really do object to having strangers tramp about in my flat, especially when they want to poke about in the room of a guest. Anyway, I'm sure Mr Lambert did not stay in his room last night, because the bed hasn't been slept in, but I haven't tidied."

"That's quite all right, Mrs Jefferies," Thorn insisted. "Now, which is his room?"

Mrs Jefferies turned and led the way upstairs. The impression of richness persisted. On the low windowsill at the turn of the stair stood a bowl of fresh flowers. And suddenly Thorn realised what it was that had been nagging at his mind: this was the first time he had ever been inside licensed premises where the smell of the taproom did not pervade the rest of the house.

Lambert's room was at the back of the building, and overlooked the harbour. It was a double room with a bathroom en suite, and fitted with the same, rather impersonal neatness as an international businessman's hotel. Only the room had been lived in by an extremely untidy guest. Clothes were strewn on the floor and the bed. Two crumpled newspapers lay beside them. On the bedside table a half-empty beer can stood next to one which had been emptied and squashed in the hand. There were ashtrays by the bed, and on the dressing table, which served as a desk as well, and the ashtrays were full of cigarette stubs.

Mrs Jefferies was still standing in the doorway behind the two men. Thorn, having taken in the contrasting, sordid scene inside the room, turned to her.

27

"Thank you, Mrs Jefferies, we'll just poke around a bit on our own for a while. Perhaps we can have a word with you later."

"I don't think I'll be able to tell you very much." Her look remained hostile. She turned and made her way silently towards the door along the landing which Thorn guessed must lead to the private sitting room. He closed the bedroom door and looked at Roberts.

"What's known as a rum do, eh, sir?" said the Sergeant.

"Rum indeed," agreed Thorn. "But, if you don't mind, Sergeant, I prefer to look and think and compare notes later. For the moment, let's look round for papers and information. You realise the dead man didn't have his wallet with him; either that or it was stolen?"

They began a methodical examination of the rest. Lambert's wallet was in the drawer of the bedside table. Thorn opened it. He found £100 in notes, a couple of credit cards, a packet of condoms, and a driving licence. There were also two receipts for articles of clothing he had bought recently. At least they now had an address. He put the contents back and took a note of the address on the licence. There was nothing else of interest except a cheque book in the name of M.L Lambert, but no cheques had been drawn for the past two weeks.

Leaving the untidy room, Thorn called, "Mrs Jefferies?" A door opened. She stood on the threshold, mouth closed in a firm line, and waited for Thorn to speak.

"We're finished in here, thank you," he said. "Can we ask you a few questions?"

Not replying, she stood waiting.

"How long has Mr Lambert been here?"

"He arrived on the twenty-first."

"And today is July 6, so he's been here a fortnight."

"I suppose so."

"Did he book in advance?"

There was, he thought, the slightest hesitation, then she said, "No, we don't advertise. We have enough work to do just running the pub without bothering with bed-and-breakfast. Mr Lambert turned up one day and asked if he could stay. He said he hadn't booked anywhere and was worried he couldn't get into any of the usual places. We do sometimes help out."

"So, you agreed to let him stay?"

"Yes."

"How did he pay? In advance?"

Again, momentary hesitation. "He paid in cash. Three weeks in advance."

"I see. Did he eat here?"

"Not always. He seemed to be out a lot. I don't know where. He just paid for his room here."

"Did he talk much about himself?"

"I told you, he just had a room here."

"Did he ever bring anyone back?"

"I don't think so, he might have done. I suppose."

"And what time did he go out yesterday?"

"Oh, he had breakfast as usual, then went out. That would be mid-morning, say 11 o'clock."

"And do you know when he got back?"

"Not for sure. I didn't see him. My husband and I were both working in the bar last night. It's Jenny's night off. Mr Lambert had his own key to the flat. He may have been back when we closed up."

"What time was that?"

"By the time we'd washed up and cleaned through, it would be about 1 o'clock in the morning."

"But you don't know for sure if he came back last night at all?"

"Not for sure, no. And we are so tired by the time we finish, we sleep very well, but…" She paused.

"But what, Mrs Jefferies?"

"Well, I can't be sure, but I think I might have heard him coming in or going out, and I think – only think – that was some time after we'd gone to bed. It may have been nothing. I might even have dreamt it."

"Did your husband hear anything?"

"I don't know. You'll have to ask him."

As though on cue there was the sound of the door to the bar opening and closing. The woman made no move and the two policemen turned to face the stairs. Silently, George Jefferies climbed to meet them.

"Still here," he observed.

"George," said his wife quietly, "Mr Lambert has been killed."

"You didn't say killed," Jefferies sounded accusing as he looked at the policemen. "You said it was an accident."

"Did we?" said Roberts innocently.

"What happened?"

"He seems to have fallen over a cliff last night."

"Drunk, was he?"

"We don't know yet," said Thorn. "Look, your wife isn't sure, but she thinks she might have heard Mr Lambert moving about, possibly going out in the small hours, about 1 o'clock or shortly after. Did you hear anything?"

"No, didn't Thora tell you? I sleep like a log."

"So, when did you see him last?"

"Me? Let me see… The day before yesterday. I think. Monday. He looked in the bar at lunchtime. He seemed to be looking for someone."

"And did he find this person?"

"Shouldn't think so, not in the Smugglers', anyway."

"I see. Now does either of you have any idea how he spent his time on St Mary's?"

Neither of the Jefferies answered at first. Then George said, "He wasn't a friend, Inspector. He was just a visitor who had our spare room for a few weeks. He didn't tell us where he was going or what he did, nor did we ask."

"Didn't he give you so much as a hint? Surely, if he had breakfast here, drank in your bar, he must have passed the time of day, given some idea how he had spent his time."

"We have other things to do than gossip to our customers," said Jefferies. "And I believe he spent more time in the Pirate than he did in the Smuggler's. So one of our regulars let drop one evening."

"Didn't you find that a bit strange?"

"None of my business."

"So, there's nothing much you can tell me about Mr Lambert?"

"No,"

Thorn let the silence hang a little. Then he said, "We'll be in touch. Meanwhile, Mrs Jefferies, I'd be grateful if you'd leave the room exactly as it is for the moment – for a couple of days, that is. We'll be back to sort out his effects."

"I must clean it!"

"No. I'm sorry. It's just routine, you understand. And he had paid until Saturday, hadn't he?"

There was no answer. The two policemen left.

"Well, sir?"

"Let's drop in at the Pirate. Let's see if we can trace some of his drinking cronies there."

They walked in silence for a while. The little street was busy, and Thorn was filing his thoughts and impressions. The Jefferies were a strange couple, hardly the stereotype of the jovial hosts. The man never smiled, was uncommunicative, the woman hostile, overdressed, and far removed from the usual image of a warm, friendly publican's wife: he imagined her behind the bar, probably disapproving of the slopped beer and the vulgar jokes. No, as a barmaid she would leave much to be desired. There was a joke there somewhere, he told himself. And that flat! It, too, was odd. Even more odd was the thought of Thora Jefferies agreeing to let her pristine room to a stranger who happened to turn up without booking; a stranger who stayed with them for two weeks without giving any hint of how he spent his time. She seemed more likely to want references from anyone who thought himself good enough to tread on her deep-pile carpet.

They turned into a narrow street, which led to the beach about thirty yards further on. There were no pavements here, and the cottages on either side were uniform, two-storeyed, with small windows set into unpainted, granite walls, unpretentious places, once the homes of fishermen, close to the harbour and their boats.

An inn sign was fastened to the wall between two, bedroom windows at the far end of the street. Under layers of varnish it portrayed a stylised head with eyepatch and red kerchief. Beneath it was a skull and crossbones, and underneath that, in simple, black lettering, Thorn read "The Pirate."

The door of the pub was open. The two men entered. A large, red-faced man with a small, pointed beard was facing the door. "Afternoon, Sergeant," he said cheerfully, "you're a bit late. I was just locking up for the afternoon, as soon as I've thrown old Percy out."

Percy was evidently a regular. He was a small man, shrunken with age. He wore an old hat, and in the low light of the room his eyes seemed to twinkle in deep sockets. He grinned. "See yer later, Ben," he said and walked to the door.

"If you wanted a drink now, it'll have to be tonight. I'm off out to the back to put me feet up for an hour." He stood smiling, waiting.

"Sorry, Ben," said Roberts. "This is an official call."

"Sounds ominous," said Ben, still with a smile, which suggested the easiest of consciences. "I'll just lock up then, and you'd better come through to the back with me."

He seemed to have accepted that Thorn was with the Sergeant. He shot the bolts on the front door and led the way back through to his private quarters, lifting the flap in the bar to let the policemen through, and switching off the lights as he followed them into a small sitting room. It was comfortably furnished as a bachelor's home. By the fireplace were two easy chairs. The television set with video recorder sat in a corner. Against the wall there was

33

a cloth-covered table with two upright chairs. In another corner, in an alcove, there was a rolltop desk, closed, and above it a set of bookshelves full of books, some hardback, some paperback. There were several about military history.

"Sit down, then," said the publican, taking his place in his favourite chair by the fire. Thorn sat opposite, leaving Sergeant Roberts to pull a chair out from the table.

"Ben, this is Superintendent Thorn," began Roberts.

"Blow me down," exclaimed Ben, "so that's it, a policeman! I couldn't work out what line of work you were in. I've seen you around in the last few days. You been in for a drink, haven't you?"

"Thorn nodded.

"So, what are you doing here then? Come to keep an eye on old Bill here? Been fiddling his expenses, has he?"

"No, Mr Jacobs, I'm on holiday."

"Ben, call me Ben. So, if you're on holiday, why are you calling this a duty visit?"

"Well, I *was* on holiday. Now I've been roped in to give Sergeant Roberts a hand."

"Why is that exactly, then? Something to do with the body old Jack found this morning?"

"You're well informed." Thorn was surprised.

"Jack came in for a quick drink this morning. Said as how he needed one. It's not every day as you finds a body on the beach. I think he half expected a couple of free pints on the strength of it."

Thorn grinned. "Did he get them?"

"Lord love us, no! Cornishmen don't give drinks away, boy. I think he might have wangled one out of one of the emmets in the bar, mind you."

"Well, you're right," Thorn admitted. "It is about the body Mr Matthews found."

"And how do you think I can help 'e? You'm surely not going to suggest as I dumped the poor sod there, are you?"

"No," said Thorn.

"Who was it, anyway? Jack said it was a visitor. Didn't know his name, like, but said he'd been in here a few times."

"His name was Lambert, Matthew Lambert. He was staying at the Smuggler's Arms."

"Bloke in his early forties? Surly sort, tallish, wore expensive -looking pullovers?"

"That sounds like him."

"He's been in the Pirate a few times in the past couple of weeks. Drinks quite a bit – beer."

"Did you know he was staying at the Smuggler's?"

"Oh, yes, we know more about you visitors than you realise, I expect. It's like wearing a uniform, you see, it's easy for us to pick out the visitors, easier than it might be for you to pick us out. We all know each other. After all, we're here in the winter, when the islands are ours. In the season we amuse ourselves by watching all your comings and goings."

"That's what we are counting on."

"Why? What's the poor bugger done?"

"Nothing as far as we know."

"Then why all these questions?"

Thorn frowned. "It's an unexplained death," he said. "So, it's a matter of routine."

Ben leaned back in his chair and puffed at a pipe he had just started. He looked at the detective cynically over the bowl. "He's been done in," he said. "That's what you're saying, is it?"

"I'm not saying anything of the sort."

"Whatever you say, then."

"What we'd like to know, if you can help us, is whether Mr Lambert met anyone in the bar last night."

"No. He came in on his own and drank on his own. On the other hand, I reckon he came here to meet someone or maybe to follow 'en at least."

"What makes you say that?" Thorn's interest quickened.

"Well, he was a bit of a morose sod. He's been coming in here pretty well every night and sitting, drinking at one of the tables by the window. Then, a couple of nights back, he was at the bar, ordering another beer, when he caught sight of someone in the snug. You can see through to the snug, because the bar's at the corner, you see."

"You mean he saw someone he was going to meet?"

"Now hang on, boy; not so fast. I didn't say that, now did I? I said he caught sight of another customer in the snug. I'm pretty sure he didn't expect to see him. Or maybe he did, I don't know. He didn't go in after him to say hello. I'd have said the bloke he saw wasn't one of his best friends, not by the look he gave him. No, I think it gave him a bit of a shock. He looked hard and long at the man in the snug. I left him standing at the bar and went and served the one who gave him the fright."

36

"Can you describe the other man?"

"Oh yes. Tallish, about forty, clean shaven, with short, fair hair cut tidily, like a military haircut, fairly tanned, wore a sweatshirt, dark blue with a map of the islands on it; they sell 'em in all the shops in the High Street. He's staying up at the caravan site. Had a woman with him, his wife, I suppose. Good looker, about the same age, dark-haired, short, bit of a curl to it. She'd be about five feet six. Still got a bit of a figure, but not thin, if you know what I mean. She is the way I like 'em, with a bit of meat on 'er."

"What about last night, Ben?" Roberts chipped in. He had been making notes, Thorn realised. Indeed, he suddenly realised that all day. so far, he had been taking notes without being asked. Thorn was so used to working with his own Detective Sergeant that he had not thought to instruct Roberts, who was, after all, just a uniform man with a country beat.

Ben poured some hot water in the pot to warm it and stood in the doorway to the kitchen with pot in hand. "Last night the couple from the caravan park arrived first. I'd just served the man when Lambert turned up. He didn't go to the table where he usually sat, and he didn't stay all that long. I sort of thought he stayed at the bar to try and watch the snug without being seen himself. He didn't stay long, though, not like normal. I reckon he left at about 10 o'clock."

"What about the man in the snug?"

"Stayed until about eleven. He and his wife left before the rest of the gang from the campsite."

"And that's the last you saw of Mr Lambert?"

"Yes."

"Well, thank you. You've been very helpful."

They left the Pirate by the back door and headed back to the police station. There were, reflected Thorn, almost too many things to follow up. He began to regret the backup he would normally expect in his own manor, it would not be easy to cope with just one assistant, however willing and seemingly intelligent Sergeant Roberts was. Simply writing up the report would take up a lot of time, and if this was indeed a murder, as he felt sure it was, he needed to pursue the enquiry as quickly as possible. He was very well aware that most murders are solved within the first 36 hours or not at all.

Seated at a desk once more, he began to map out the course of the enquiry so far. Following his usual practice, he made a large, diagrammatic chart on which he entered times first, beginning at the approximate time of the murder – between 1 am and 5:30 am – and worked backwards, leaving space for information to be entered hour by hour, and day by day. As the enquiry continued, he would pin photographs of the victim and add all details which could be relevant at the time the incidents occurred. Eventually, he knew, the entire wall would be taken up with what appeared to be little more than graffiti in variously coloured felt-tipped pens. Roberts kept a discreet silence but began to write up the notes from his notebook.

It was far too early to expect the photographs, and the doctor was a GP, who would only be able to attend to the examination of the dead man when he had given his attention to his living patients.

He looked at Lambert's home address, taken from the driving licence in his wallet. It was in Chichester. He rang Chichester and asked for a CID man to call at the address to discover what he could. When he had scribbled half a dozen pages of notes, he began to get restless. Waiting for others to produce the information he needed was the part of detective work he always found tiresome.

"I'm taking a walk up to the caravan site," he told the Sergeant. "I'm going to have a word with the couple who gave our man such a turn in the pub."

"Right, sir, Tina usually has a meal ready about sevenish, if you're back by then. I think it's a casserole or something, so it won't spoil."

The afternoon was wearing on. Day trippers were wending their way down to the quay where the passenger ferry from Penzance, the Scillonian, was waiting to sail. They had the tired look of a day well spent relaxing. It seemed to Thorn a long time since he had wheeled his golf trolley onto the first tee.

It was a short walk to the caravan site. The entrance was through a farm gate. All the vans were static; the boat would not bring vehicles. Thorn made his way to the farmhouse. It was a fine but simple, modern building of dressed stone. A neat sign led him towards the side door, marked "Reception." He went in. It was a small room, furnished with three armchairs and a small table on which there were neatly displayed brochures advertising attractions on the Islands and on the mainland in Cornwall. On the counter on one side of the room was a bell push and, reminding Thorn of the "Drink me" labels in Alice in Wonderland, a small notice, "Please ring." He did so.

In a few minutes a door opened, and a young girl appeared.

"Good afternoon," said Thorn. "I'm looking for a couple who have hired one of your vans."

"Yes, sir?"

Thorn produced his warrant card. "I'm working with Sergeant Roberts."

"Who is it you're looking for?"

Thorn repeated the description given by Ben in the Pirate.

"That'll be Mr and Mrs Clapton," said the girl. "I don't know if they're in at the moment, but they're in number 16. It's at the end on the right."

Thorn thanked her and walked down the field. One or two people were coming and going between the vans and the toilet block at the far side of the field. Others were coming back from a day on the beach. Here and there people were relaxing on camp chairs or on inflatable mattresses. One or two looked up and nodded as he passed.

He reached number 16. The door was open. Inside he could see a woman in a simple summer dress, busy at a small sink. A man in a tee-shirt and shorts spoke to her with a laugh and put an arm round her bare shoulders and gave her an affectionate hug. She leaned her head momentarily against his. Thorn coughed. They turned and looked at him with mild surprise. "You looking for something?" the man asked.

"Yes, Mr Clapton."

"That's me," the man replied. "What can I do for you?" He was just a touch wary.

"My name is Thorn. I'm a policeman."

"Police? I thought there was only one policeman here."

"Usually there is. I'm giving him a hand." He took out his warrant card and held it up. "Can I come in?"

He was used to the change in demeanour which the word "police" always seemed to produce. The couple now looked at Thorn suspiciously.

"What's the problem?" asked the man.

"I'm making enquiries about a visitor who has been staying on the island for the past two weeks. I think you might know him."

"What's his name?"

"Lambert," said Thorn, "Matthew Lambert."

The result was immediate. "What about him?" The man asked, his face hardening. The suspicion turned into plain hostility. "What's he been up to?"

"So, you do know him?"

"Of course we do," said the man.

"May I ask in what capacity you know him?"

The woman answered. "Matthew Lambert is my husband," she said.

Chapter 3

Caravan number 16 was identical to all the other vans. It was divided into a living area and a double bedroom. It was surprisingly spacious.

"Mrs Lambert," Thorn began, when they were all three seated inside, "I'm afraid I have some bad news."

"If it's about Matt, it would be. The day he does something you could describe as good news, everybody will be completely gobsmacked." She spoke with a Derbyshire accent, and the word sounded neither odd nor funny.

"Your husband has met with an accident, Mrs Lambert. I'm afraid he's dead."

"Dead?" She turned to Clapton, looking at him as if asking for an explanation of the word. "How can he be dead?"

Clapton put an arm around her and held her close. He said nothing.

"Perhaps a cup of tea would be a good idea," Thorn suggested.

Clapton did not move. "You can see the kettle," he said. "Go ahead."

Thorn did so, filling the kettle and setting it on the lighted gas.

"Did you know your husband was on the island?" he asked.

The woman looked intently at Clapton who, in his turn, did not take his eyes from her face. "We caught sight of him last night outside the Pirate," he said.

"You didn't speak?"

"Are these questions necessary?" Clapton asked.

"Yes, I'm afraid they are, Mr Clapton. Did either of you speak to Mr Lambert last night?"

"No," said Clapton. "He was walking away from the pub and he turned the corner into the High Street and disappeared. We turned right at the end of the street to come this way."

"How long have you been here on St Mary's?"

"Three weeks." Clapton was taking over the conversation, answering for the woman.

"And had either of you seen Mr Lambert during that time before last night?"

"No."

"What kind of accident was it?" Mrs Lambert changed the line of questions.

"He fell, Mrs Lambert, he fell from a cliff. He probably died immediately." There was no need to tell her more at this point.

"Been drinking, had he?" Clapton's tone was hardly sympathetic. The woman, as might be expected, looked shocked now; shocked but not unduly distressed. Her reaction was more like apathy. She sat listlessly in the circle of Clapton's arms.

The kettle came to the boil, but neither of them made a move, and it was Thorn himself who got up to make the tea. While he hunted for the wherewithal to do so, he kept a discreet eye on the couple. They whispered together briefly. Thorn poured three cups of tea and put them down within reach.

"We don't know very much about what happened as yet," Thorn said. "We only know he fell off the cliff sometime last night."

"To tell you the truth, Superintendent," the woman said, "I feel more relieved than sorry."

"Really? Can I ask why, Mrs Lambert?"

"Our marriage ended a year ago," she explained. "But not before I had suffered too many beatings at Matt's hands, or fists, I should say. I finally managed to escape a year ago and hide out in a refuge. After that I got an injunction. I didn't want to see him again ever, and legally he wasn't supposed to pester me."

"No divorce?"

"He wanted to fight it; I couldn't be bothered to push it. Better to wait two years and claim breakdown of the marriage by dint of two years apart."

"What about you, Mr Clapton? Did you know him?"

"Yes. I've known Matt Lambert about fifteen years."

"How did you meet?"

"We were in the Marines together."

"Oh?"

"Marine Commandos, in fact. I reckon Matt just couldn't settle to civvy street, and that's what made him drink, and maybe it's why he turned violent."

"When did he leave the Marines?"

"Three years ago; the year before I did."

"And how long have you been married, Mrs Lambert?"

"Five years."

"Well," said Thorn, "I'm sorry to bring you such news. I must also ask you if you can come down to the police station tomorrow morning."

44

"What for?" asked the woman.

"We need a formal identification of the body, I'm afraid. Will you do it, please?"

She turned to her lover, gave him a look in which Thorn read horror tinged with panic.

"I'll come with you," promised Clapton.

"Good." Thorn got up. "We can complete the formalities then. Before I go, just for the record, can I have your permanent address or addresses and your full names, please?"

Both gave him their names and an address in Chichester. He left them huddled together, staring after him as he strode off towards the gate and back to the police cottage.

He found Roberts and his wife sitting comfortably, watching television.

"Any luck, sir?" asked Roberts.

"Yes, indeed, Sergeant. The lady in question turned out to be Mrs Lambert."

"Is she now?"

"She's coming in tomorrow morning to identify the body. We'll get a full statement then, and we'll interview Mr Clapton at the same time."

"That's the boyfriend, is it, sir?"

Thorn nodded. "Mrs Roberts," he asked, "have I got time for a quick wash and brush up before we eat?"

"Yes, of course, Superintendent. I hope you're hungry. And please call me Tina."

Twenty minutes later Thorn took his place at the table where Tina served a splendid coq-au-vin while her husband uncorked a bottle of Italian wine.

"Tina's father imports the stuff," he explained. "So, we get a very good deal; none of your rubbish."

In spite of his hunger, Thorn ate slowly, savouring the food. It was most definitely in a different league from Mrs Bennett's. Tina watched him covertly, waiting until he complimented her and she looked almost relieved that he approved.

"How long have you been here?" asked Thorn

"Seven years now," Roberts answered.

"Have you never thought about promotion? What about going for inspector?"

"Definitely not," said the Sergeant. "It would mean moving. This way I can do a good job in one of the most attractive places in the UK. I like the islands and they like us, don't they, Tina?"

Tina nodded. "We wouldn't want to live anywhere else," she confirmed.

"No children?"

"Twins," said Tina. "They're almost grown up now, though; eighteen, and both of them up-country at college." She looked at the mantelpiece where there were two photographs of a boy and a girl, taken some time ago, no doubt, while they were still at school, a dark-haired girl with dancing eyes, and a face full of laughter, and a more solemn looking boy.

"You must be very proud of them," said Thorn, but his throat felt dry and he reached for his wine glass.

"How about you, Superintendent?" asked Tina with a look of pert interest. "I suppose you are married?"

"I'm a widower," he said

"That's sad," said Tina. "And have you any children?"

"No," said Thorn, but the word was gall in his mouth.

There was a silence. Tina got up and cleared the dishes away, returning with some confection which tasted sweet and fruity with a hint of Curaçao.

Roberts announced Tina would be going out for the rest of the evening. It was the night for her choir practice, he said. It would, observed Tina, give the men the chance to discuss the case in comfort instead of in the office.

When she had gone, Roberts poured them both a drink and they settled in easy chairs.

"Right," began Thorn, "what do we know so far?"

"Quite a lot, and not very much," Roberts replied. "If you don't mind waiting a moment, I'll collect my notes from next door." He went to the office and returned with the neatly typed notes he had taken all day. "I typed them up while you were at the campsite," he explained.

Thorn took a clean sheet of paper and made notes of his own. He began to see what Roberts meant. They knew the name of the dead man, his address, and that he was an ex-marine commando, who had been violent towards his wife. They knew he had come to the islands two weeks ago, a week after his wife had arrived with her lover. He seemed to have arrived in the high season, without booking in advance, which is why he had taken a room at the Smuggler's Arms. He was not without money, since he had paid in advance and in cash. No one so far had suggested how he spent his time on St Mary's, nor why he was here. He appeared not to have known of his wife's presence until he chanced to see her in the snug of the Pirate, the evening before his death.

As for his last evening, he had been seen in the Pirate, but had left early, maybe at about 10:30. Half an hour later Clapton and Mrs Lambert had seen him walking towards his lodgings, where his landlady thought he was in his room until after midnight, when he had gone out again. Sometime after that he had been killed on Purley Head, and his body dragged and thrown over the cliff.

A phone call from Chichester CID gave a few, sparse details; Matthew Lambert worked as a security guard in the city. He lived in a bedsitter. His landlady said he always paid his rent but kept himself to himself. He spent most evenings out of the house, mostly in local pubs, but had no close friends that anyone knew about. His employers and co-workers could add little; he did not talk much, had a few strong opinions about such things as divorce, foreigners and the IRA, and he had not much of a sense of humour.

Later in the evening the doctor called. "Not much doubt about it," he confirmed. "Death was caused by a stab wound to the heart. The head injuries certainly occurred after death. I'd put the time of death at about 2 am."

"Had he been drinking heavily?"

"Judging by the state of his liver, I'd say he was a regular drinker. Last night he'd probably had 3 pints or so. Difficult to say whether that would make him drunk, but I'd guess that he was used to drinking more than that in one go."

"Any sign of sexual activity?"

"No."

"Anything else?"

"No. I rather imagine he'd been in a bit of a fight. Probably his assailant on the cliff, of course; his knuckles showed signs of bruising as though he'd swung a punch or two on target. Can't be sure, of course. I'll give you a full, written report tomorrow."

"Thanks, Doctor," said Thorn.

The two policemen looked each other in the eye.

"A good grilling for Mr Clapton tomorrow, sir?"

"Seems favourite at the moment," agreed Thorn. "But we're still very much in the dark. If Clapton is telling the truth, and they didn't speak to Lambert, was Lambert waiting outside the Pirate when they left? If he's lying, did they arrange to meet on Purley Head and if so, why at 1:30 in the morning? Neither of the two had any reason we know of to conceal their meeting."

"We need to know more about how he spent yesterday."

Thorn nodded agreement.

"You want me to do a bit of house-to-house, sir? See if we can trace his movements during the day? It shouldn't be too hard to do."

"Yes, that's number one priority. I'll get on with the preliminary interviews with Clapton and Mrs Lambert. It's a damned nuisance not having at least one more policeman: I shan't be able to take statements properly until you're back."

With a couple more glasses to help, the two men made a formal record of the enquiry so far. Tina got home from her choir practice to find the two men half asleep before the fire.

Chapter 4

When Thorn came downstairs the following morning, the Sergeant had already left.

"People are up and about early here," Tina explained, as she gave Thorn his breakfast. "He wanted to catch some of them before they left their houses. He could just as easily find them on the island as at home, I suppose, but he's probably thinking some of them will be out in their boats on a day like this."

It was indeed a splendid, summer's day. Not, thought the Superintendent, the kind of day to be spent mulling over death and men's wickedness, nor, he said to himself as he took his place at the office desk, a day to spend indoors. He had to interview Mrs Lambert and her lover, however, even if it could be no more than an informal business with no witness. While he waited, he would make one or two telephone calls.

First, he called the Deputy Chief Constable to give a preliminary account of his first day. It brought a satisfied grunt down the line. Thorn carefully broached the subject of more help, possibly the transfer of at least one CID man to help investigate. The response was a prevarication: it was appreciated that assistance was needed, but the security conference was putting immense stress on both uniformed and plainclothes officers; perhaps, once the result of the inquest was known... And did Thorn's request for help imply he was not satisfied with Sergeant Roberts? No, he said, firmly, it did not. Then perhaps he should carry on until matters became a little clearer.

A call to the coroner next, requesting him to agree to adjourn the inquest: yes, that would be all right.

He had hardly replaced the receiver when the door opened and Phil Gurnard came in, carrying a very large envelope. It contained about fifty photographs. Thorn examined them with care, while Gurnard peered eagerly and anxiously at him.

"Good," said Thorn, "these will do me nicely."

He was particularly interested in photographs taken on the cliff edge. The marks of the dead man's heels showed clearly, but the rock was dry and there was no way of finding other footprints. As requested, Gurnard had also taken shots of the dead man's naked body. They revealed nothing new, but the bruise and stab wound looked uglier than they had in life.

Gurnard, assured that his work was acceptable, and that he would be paid for it, left. Thorn added a photograph of the body in situ to his wall display.

Clapton and Mrs Lambert turned up together. Thorn rang the doctor to tell him he wanted Mrs Lambert to make a formal identification of the body. Surgery should be ended, said Cooper, by ten thirty. If Thorn were to bring Mrs Lambert to the surgery then, he would take them both to the morgue.

There was time to make a start on the interviews. Tina Roberts was quite imperturbable and readily took Mrs Lambert into her sitting room to chat easily about her stay in Scilly, while the Superintendent began to question a reluctant Clapton. Clapton's attention wandered from time to time to the closed door of the sitting room. Thorn caught him looking in fascinated horror at the photograph he had just pinned up, surrounded as yet by a large array of blank paper.

"I don't know why you want another interview," remarked Clapton testily. "We've already told you neither of us spoke to Matt Lambert last night or at any other time since we arrived here."

"It does seem rather extraordinary to me," said Thorn, "that Mr Lambert should come all this way from Chichester, see his wife in the snug at the Pirate, and make no attempts to speak to her."

"Brenda has an injunction to stop him approaching her."

"Of course, she told me yesterday."

"He wouldn't risk it unless he was drunk."

"And was he?"

"He didn't look it," said Clapton. "When he walked away from us, he was walking steadily enough."

"What I don't understand," Thorn persisted, "is why Matthew Lambert should come here at all, if it wasn't to see Mrs Lambert."

"Oh, that's simple," Clapton was eager to explain. "The islands were his old holiday haunt. He always used to come here for holidays even before he married Brenda."

"Are you suggesting he came here on holiday and happened to stumble across you and Mrs Lambert?"

"Well, it makes sense, doesn't it? Matt knew these islands years ago. He and Brenda came here on their honeymoon. It isn't surprising he decided to come back for another visit any more than it's surprising we did the same. Brenda loves it here and I thought it would be a good idea to get away from Chichester for a break: she's had a tough time recently."

"And you had no idea Matthew Lambert was on the island?"

"No."

"And you insist you didn't speak to him at any time last night?"

"We did not."

Thorn tried a new tack. "I take it Lambert was aware you were living with Mrs Lambert?"

"Oh yes."

"When did your relationship with Mrs Lambert begin?"

"What the hell does that mean?"

"Before or after her marriage breakdown?"

"I don't see that's any of your business."

"In this kind of enquiry," Thorn said grimly, "everything and anything is my business."

"What kind of enquiry are you talking about?" Clapton sounded extremely suspicious.

"Mr Lambert died in suspicious circumstances," said Thorn. "Quite possibly his fall was not an accident."

Clapton rose angrily. "Are you saying you suspect me of murdering him?"

"I'm in no position to suggest any such thing, Mr Clapton. My job is to find out exactly how and why Matthew Lambert met his death that night. If, as you say, you had no contact with him, then you have no reason to be alarmed or even worried."

"That depends on whether you have the brains to take in the facts," Clapton retorted. "I said we didn't speak to him; you don't seem to believe me."

"What I personally believe or disbelieve is neither here nor there, Mr Clapton. My work is concerned with evidence and evidence is based on proof. Even if I believe Matthew Lambert came here by chance, saw you and Mrs Lambert by chance, and had enough self-control not to speak to either of you, at the moment I have no evidence to that effect and no witnesses."

"Brenda will tell you the same thing."

"Of course she will."

At this Clapton swore violently. Thorn said nothing but waited for him to calm down. The ex-marine stood behind the chair on which he had been sitting. His hands gripped the back as he glared belligerently. When Thorn remained silent, Clapton's hands slowly loosened their grip and the look on his face changed from fury to resignation, almost hopelessness. He straightened and walked over to the window to stare out over the harbour, where the bright sunshine danced on the waves and the pure colours of the little boats moored there turned it into a child's picture. After a while he began to speak.

"I first met Matt Lambert fourteen years ago," he began. "He'd already done a year when I joined up for a twelve-year stint. We had a lot in common then: I suppose you could say we were both tearaways. Neither could settle to a job and Matt wasn't quick to accept discipline, either. For the first couple of years we were both fairly indisciplined, and I don't like to think how many times we were in the rattle for one thing or another." He smiled at the memory and came back into the room. "I don't know how much you know about the Marines," he said, "but if you've got too much energy, they can always find ways of using it. We both found ourselves volunteered for all the difficult and high-risk courses. That's how we came to do the commando training."

"So, you are both trained in unarmed combat?"

"Is that another bit of your so-called evidence?"

"No, I was just thinking, if Lambert was skilled in unarmed combat, whoever it was attacked him the night before last – supposing, of course, that someone did – he either didn't know what a risk he was taking, or must have taken him by surprise, or…"

Clapton's eyes narrowed as he caught Thorn's drift. He nodded slowly. "Or was someone at least as well drilled in combat techniques as he was?" He completed the sentence. Thorn made no comment.

"If I had wanted to tackle Matthew Lambert and kill him," Clapton said, "don't you think I'd have used a knife? Why depend on my fists?"

Was this, Thorn wondered, remembering the wound in the dead man's chest, an extremely clever double bluff? "What if," he asked, "this unknown assailant didn't meet Lambert with the intention of doing him in, but was provoked into anger and violence by something he said or did?"

Clapton shrugged, unable to counter this.

"Go on," said Thorn. "You were saying how you got to know Lambert."

Clapton sat down and lit a cigarette. "Matt came from Chichester," he said. "I went back there with him on leave once or twice, when I had nowhere better to go. I didn't have a home; I grew up in care. About six years ago he met Brenda. I think she fancied him because he was tough and knew how to handle himself. He fell for her and they got married a year later. I was his best man."

"Where did they live?"

"They had married quarters at first and I visited them there often. But you know what it's like when your oppo gets tied up like that, it's not the same as it used to be. Matt wanted to have it both ways: married, with Brenda at home keeping the home fires burning, and free for a run ashore with the lads. It doesn't work either way; wives don't stand for that sort of thing these days. A married friend is different from one that isn't married. Things started to go wrong between them after about a year. One day I happened to call round at their quarters and found Brenda nursing a black eye. I felt sorry for her – I had liked her from the beginning, and I had a go at Matt when I saw him later. He'd been drinking, and he accused me of having it off with his wife. We didn't have a fight then because he was half cut, but we never really got on after that."

"And your affair with Mrs Lambert?" insisted Thorn.

"That didn't begin until much later. When Matt left the Marines two years ago, Brenda wrote to me, asking me to go and stay with them. In her letter she said she thought Matt would find it difficult to settle into civvy street and maybe, if I was around, I could help him for a week or two and he might find it easier. It all sounds pretty thin now, as I realise, but I believed it at the time, maybe because I already had a soft spot for her, and this was an excuse to see her again. I hadn't seen a lot of her after the first year of their marriage because they gave up their married quarters, and Brenda moved back to Chichester. When I got to Chichester, it didn't take long to discover the real reason: Brenda was scared of Matt, and hoped I might provide her with protection, at least for a while. I suppose I did, too. I was always just that little bit stronger than he was, and not quite so frequently drunk with it, so, when he turned violent, I told him to lay off or he'd have to deal with me. I told him that if he ever laid into Brenda, and I got to hear of it, I'd be back and give him a hiding."

"It didn't work though," Thorn suggested.

"No. It kept the peace, like a nuclear deterrent, for about three months, then I got a phone call one night from Brenda. I had just been posted and I couldn't do anything about it, because I was sailing in the morning on a three-month assignment. I felt rotten, advised her to go to the police. I couldn't contact Matt."

"So, what happened?"

"She stuck it for another eight or nine months, then she left him one night and went to a refuge for battered wives. That was sometime after I got back to the UK. "

"What about your threat to Lambert?"

"When I got back from overseas, I caught up with him and gave him a going over, but it didn't help much. He waited until I was out of reach, then took it out on Brenda again. I didn't make the same mistake twice."

"And you and Mrs Lambert?"

"I told her to divorce him, but she wasn't bothered overmuch about that so long as he kept away from her. She took out an injunction and, as soon as I got out of the service, she came to live with me. By then both of us knew how we felt."

"What about Lambert's reaction?"

Clapton made an obscene gesture. "That to his reaction!" he said. "There wasn't anything he could do. I was there now to protect Brenda, and there was the injunction as well. We never had anything to do with him."

"Didn't you ever bump into him by chance? Chichester isn't that big a place."

"I suppose we saw him from time to time, if we happened to be in the same pub or shopping or something, but we ignored each other. If our eyes met, we just looked daggers at one another. We didn't speak."

It was Thorn's turn to get up from the desk and walk over to the window. He stood for a while watching the tourists at the quay climbing down into the waiting boats which would take them to the out-islands.

"You still insist that you didn't speak to Matthew Lambert on the night he died?" he repeated without turning.

"That's what I said."

"And his presence on the island at the same time as yours was no more than a coincidence?"

"It is, as far as we are concerned. I can't speak for Matt. But if he'd been here more than a day or two without speaking to me, (there's no injunction to stop him doing that), it doesn't seem very likely he came here to spy on us, does it?"

If Clapton was telling the truth, Thorn admitted, it was a valid point, but it was a big if.

"Very well, Mr Clapton," he said, "you have been very helpful. I'm afraid I'll have to see you to make a formal statement including everything you have told me, when Sergeant Roberts is available."

"Can we go, then?"

Thorn looked up at the clock on the wall. "You can go if you wish, but Mrs Lambert will have to come with us to the clinic to identify her husband's body, and afterwards I have to ask her some questions."

"Can't the questions wait at least?"

"I'm afraid not, but let's see how Mrs Lambert feels. I repeat, there's no need for you to wait, Mr Clapton."

"I'll stay all the same for Brenda. She'll wants me there."

Thorn found Brenda Lambert talking happily still to Tina. When he told her they were about to make the identification, she looked apprehensive and pale, but her jaw was set in determination.

It took only a few minutes to walk to the small clinic. Thorn found himself looking at this tiny town through different eyes. As a visiting tourist he had seen it as a picturesque place, full of men, women and children with no aim but that of enjoying themselves. Now, in his professional capacity, the picture book quality was relatively unimportant, and he was beginning to explore the town as a network of human relationships, with its visible and hidden loves and hates, its satisfactions and its envy, its mundane happiness and its sadness.

There were no patients in the waiting room at the clinic, but when Thorn introduced himself to the receptionist, she asked him to wait until the doctor had finished his last consultation of the morning. They all three sat down before the piles of dated, women's magazines, and a pile of glossy magazines to do with cars.

The door to the consulting room opened at last and a young woman was ushered out. She was crying. Although she was dressed rather drably in a dark skirt and blouse, and the handkerchief she held to her face hid her features, the long, auburn hair, the arch of the eyebrows and the curve of her cheekbone and jaw suggested a beauty not easily concealed. She had evidently just been given some bad news.

Cooper greeted them. "Sorry to keep you waiting," he said, "but poor Sarah was upset, and it took longer than anticipated. The morgue is this way." He led the way out of the waiting room and along a corridor in the brick building. Clapton insisted on accompanying Brenda Lambert.

It was a small morgue. There were three stainless steel doors in the wall which contained the storage chambers. Cooper stepped forward and seized the handles of one. Clapton held Brenda Lambert close. The doctor lifted the sheet sufficiently to reveal the face of the dead man. Brenda Lambert shuddered and drew in her breath, bit her lip, nodded. "Yes," she said quietly, "it's him, Matt."

Outside in the corridor, where the doctor handed Thorn a sealed, plastic bag containing the dead man's clothes, Thorn asked if she was prepared to return to the police station with him to answer a few more questions.

"Can't it wait?" Clapton asked angrily yet again.

"Do you feel up to it, Mrs Lambert?" Thorn asked, ignoring him.

"Yes, I'd rather get it over with." She looked at Clapton, "I'll be all right, love." And she put a reassuring hand on his arm. "Why don't you go and get yourself a drink somewhere?"

At first he argued, but Brenda Lambert had spirit, Thorn decided. Having married a bully, she wasn't going to let a protective partner dominate her in his turn. Reluctantly Clapton left the two of them as they returned to the office and Mrs Lambert said she'd find him down on the quay when she had finished.

Thorn found a note on the desk when they got back. "Interesting morning," it read, "you are busy, so I'll report back about 1 o'clock. Tina knows where to find me, if you need me urgently. WR."

"Sit down, Mrs Lambert," he said. "I'm sorry to put you through that ordeal, but it is one of the legal requirements."

"It's all right, Superintendent," she was calm. Perhaps the sight of her dead husband had laid to rest the fear which must have dogged her for several years. "What do you want to know?"

Thorn began by asking her to tell him in her own words of her meeting with, and subsequent marriage to Lambert. The details tallied with those supplied by Clapton. It was clear in the telling that the dead man had become a terrifying bully when he drank, which was frequently, and that the situation had become intolerable. Clapton's threats had not deterred Lambert, since they could not be followed through while he was at sea. Instead, it led to accusations of infidelity and to even greater violence, but it was administered by a man with training, so that injuries, though painful, left few visible marks. The black eye was an exception.

"At least," Thorn commented sympathetically, "there were no children."

"No, in the end that was a blessing, I suppose."

"Suppose? You'd have liked children?"

Brenda Lambert's composure gave way to a look of despair. "I'm not sorry there were no children of that marriage," she said, "but I would have liked children in the future. Peter – Peter Clapton – wants to marry me. We were going to wait until two years were up. I wanted us to have children"

"And you can't?"

"One of the injuries Matt gave me put me in hospital. It means I can no longer conceive."

"Did you ever make a formal complaint against him?"

She laughed bitterly. "How would I prove it? And besides, the damage was done."

"Did you tell Mr Clapton?"

"Not at the time."

"But he knows now?"

"When we decided to live together. I felt I had to tell him. It wouldn't be fair on him, not knowing. He loves kids."

Thorn fell silent, digesting this information. The picture of Matthew Lambert which was emerging was not a very pretty one, but he must have been either very lucky or very clever to have survived as a violent man without acquiring a police record.

"Can you describe in detail how you and Mr Clapton spent the evening before last?"

The account she gave again tallied in every respect with Peter Clapton's. They had eaten in the caravan, then made their way to the Pirate, where they spent a couple of hours in the snug. There were other caravanners in the bar at the time. They had had a pleasant evening, leaving at about 11 o'clock. Since it was fine, they decided to walk on past the caravan site and go for a stroll around the Garrison, the old fortified, southern part of the island. Their plan had been abandoned, however, because, when they came out of the pub, they had been shaken to see Matt Lambert a little way up the street. He had seen them, as they emerged.

"What was he doing?"

"What do you mean?"

"Was he walking towards the pub or away from it?"

She hesitated. "He – he wasn't doing either," she said. "He was just standing there, looking in our direction."

"Could he have been waiting for you?"

Again, a slight hesitation, then, "I suppose he could have been," she said. "But…" She stopped, and thought, trying to puzzle it out.

"But…?" Thorn prompted.

"Well, he knew he couldn't speak to me without breaking the injunction, so what would have been the point? And he didn't: we turned and walked away. Matt turned left at the top of the street, back towards the town. We went the other way."

"And did you go for your walk?"

"No, the evening was spoiled as far as we were concerned. I'd all but forgotten about Matt over the past three weeks here. Seeing him unexpectedly like that –," she broke off with a shudder.

"Mrs Lambert," Thorn said, "I asked Mr Clapton this question, which I must also put to you; don't you think it a coincidence that your estranged husband should turn up on St Mary's, apparently for a holiday, just when you chose to come here too?"

"Not really," she replied. "Matt used to come here years ago. It was a favourite place for him years before I met him. I'm not sure why Peter and I decided to come here: it's where Matt and I spent our honeymoon five years ago. It could have been a mistake, although I love the island. We decided more or less on the spur of the moment to take a break. I knew the caravan site. We rang up on spec, and there you are."

"Did you and Mr Lambert spend your honeymoon on the same caravan site?"

"Oh no! Matt always booked into a hotel for visits here. They're pretty expensive, and I sometimes asked him why he wasted money on accommodation. It was understandable on honeymoon, perhaps, but he said he always used a hotel in the past."

"Was that out of character?"

"Well, he didn't throw his money around exactly."

"So, why do you think he was staying at the Smuggler's?"

"Was he? I've no idea. Perhaps he couldn't get a booking anywhere else."

Thorn frowned. "When you turned right at the end of the street," he resumed, "did you go straight back to the caravan?"

"Yes. As I said, I felt depressed after that, and we went straight back. We talked for a bit, had a drink and went to bed."

"And stayed there?"

She looked surprised. "Yes, of course."

"Neither of you left the caravan at any time during the rest of the evening or night?"

"No."

"Thank you, Mrs Lambert. I'm sorry again you have had to go through this ordeal. As I told Mr Clapton, I shall have to ask you both to make a formal statement to the Sergeant in the next day or two."

A little bewildered, she stood up and, picking up her handbag, walked to the door. He watched her from the doorway as she went to meet Clapton. He felt sorry for her, this small woman who had suffered at the hands of the dead man, and who had come to St Mary's to forget, only to be reminded in a sudden and dramatic way of past suffering, and of the blight it cast on her future. Life deals us all heavy blows, he thought.

Tina Roberts tapped on the door and looked in. "Would you like some lunch?" she asked.

"That depends on your husband, I'm afraid. I don't know what he has dug up for us."

"He came back ten minutes ago," said Tina. "I knew you were interviewing Mrs Lambert, so I sent him off to the Pirate for a quick drink before lunch. He said he'd be back in half an hour. It's only a salad."

"Fine, I'll join him there," said Thorn, and headed for the pub. It was good to be out in the sunshine again instead of viewing it from the office window. Like everything else in Hughtown, the Pirate was only a minute's walk away, but it was a pleasant walk. He found Roberts in the bar, chatting over a pint to some of the locals.

"What are you drinking, sir?" Roberts asked.

Half an hour later, feeling refreshed in body by the cool drink and refreshed in mind by the bantering chat at the bar, Thorn returned with the Sergeant to the police cottage. They got back to work after lunch. Before he asked Roberts to report, Thorn moved everything off the desk and opened the bag containing Lambert's clothes. There was nothing very remarkable about any of it. The sweatshirt, with the bloodstain on the front, was a moderately expensive one, sold locally. Shirt, trousers, underclothes were all from Marks and Spencer. The shoes were good quality. There was, however, something snagged in one shoe. Thorn looked at it closely and asked Roberts if he had a pair of tweezers. The Sergeant found a pair in the first aid box, and Thorn carefully retrieved a small piece of green stone which was lodged in the crease between the tongue and the welt. It was only a few millimetres long, flat on one side, round on the other. The flat side had the traces of a black adhesive. Neither of the two men could identify it.

"Probably unimportant," Thorn decided, but he put it into a small bag.

Roberts had indeed been busy, talking to everyone who might have seen or heard what had happened in the Pirate that evening. The stories were consistent. Lambert had come into the pub, into the public bar, and had left rather quickly, and his wife and Clapton had left the snug half an hour later.

"That's where it gets interesting," said Roberts. "I was talking to Mrs Brewer, who lives in a cottage in Church Street, just round the corner from the Pirate. She was going to bed that night when she heard a bit of a disturbance outside."

"What kind of disturbance?"

"An argument, she says. She's used to holiday-makers making a bit of a noise on their way back to the caravan site. Doesn't like it, of course. She has complained.."

"Hang on," Thorn interrupted. "Are you saying it was an argument in the street between the road from the Pirate and the caravan park?"

"Absolutely," Roberts said with the triumphant air of one playing a trump card.

"And you're going to tell me she didn't bother to look out, aren't you?"

"That's the even better news," said Roberts. "She did. She looked out of the window and down into the street. She says she saw two men and a woman. The woman was standing back against the wall, keeping out of the way, and she got a good look at the two men right in the middle of the road. They sound like Clapton and

Lambert. And her description of the woman fits Mrs Lambert."

"Well done, Sergeant," Thorn said quietly.

"What did Mr Clapton have to say, sir?" Thorn told him, "That looks like it then, doesn't it, sir?"

"Not quite, Sergeant. Let's not be too hasty. The fact that the two men were probably involved in an argument and a bit of a scuffle at 11 o'clock doesn't explain how Lambert came to be pushed over the cliff at 2 o'clock in the morning."

"According to Mrs Brewer," Roberts said, "the woman intervened in the fight. She says the two men exchanged a few punches, but they seemed to be hitting each other in the body, not in the head. That would explain why Clapton doesn't look bruised about his face. The woman shouted at them to stop. They did, she says, but one of them was still shouting 'I'll get you, you bastard!' And they both looked very angry when they set off in opposite directions. Maybe they agreed to meet again later."

"Maybe." Thorn looked doubtful

"It all seems to hang together, sir, surely. We only have Mrs Lambert's word that Clapton didn't leave the caravan. I've been up to the caravan site asking questions there. Nothing definite, but since their van is on the end of a row, he could have slipped out some time after midnight without being seen."

Thorn grunted, clearly sceptical. "I'll grant you Clapton had a motive for the killing: I'll admit he had the opportunity, but it still seems improbable that he would arrange a rendezvous in the middle of the night. What for?"

67

"But why did the two of them lie about speaking to Lambert?"

"It's a good question," Thorn agreed, "but not telling the truth is not the same thing as admitting to murder."

"Pity we haven't got a witness on Purley Head."

"We need more evidence."

"Of what?"

"I don't know." Thorn pondered a little. "It's just possible we're on the wrong track altogether. If Clapton wanted to kill Lambert, why come all the way here? And I believe them when they say they weren't even aware Lambert was on St Mary's until they saw him that night. I suppose, if they got involved in a violent fight, in a state of anger, it might have finished in a death, but it seems illogical for an unplanned encounter and quarrel to be stopped by Mrs Lambert, after which the two men make an appointment, like a duel or something, and for that to end in death. In all this it was Mrs Lambert who was the real victim of her husband's violence. I'll admit that Clapton must be truly angry on her behalf, but..."

"If Clapton didn't kill Lambert, who did?"

"I don't know. Perhaps he did. But I have a feeling in my bones there's more to it. Who else did Lambert know on the islands? He'd been here several times before. Did any of the locals have reason to kill him?"

Roberts looked nonplussed. "Some of the locals have a reputation for making as much money out of visitors as possible," he said, "but I don't think many of them would kill for it."

"I know, but there's something very odd about all this. If Lambert had been killed as a result of that fight, it would make sense, but for him to arrange to meet Clapton after a chance encounter in the pub…? We need to do a lot more digging, Sergeant, a lot more. Make a few more enquiries about who knew Lambert from previous visits. Can you check out the more expensive hotels where he used to stay? And I think I'll have another word with the Jefferies at the Smuggler's Arms; they are an odd pair and I get the feeling they were economical with the truth. Who came up with the name Smuggler's Arms, by the way; since when do smugglers have a coat of arms?"

Roberts laughed. "It was the idea of the company up-country who bought the place. It used to be the Admiral Benbow."

"Ah," Thorn said, "and they were responsible for the phoney interior, I suppose?"

Roberts nodded. "What about Clapton, sir?"

"What about him?"

"We've caught him out in a lie."

"True. He still has to make a formal statement. We'll tax him with it then, and we'll do the same with Mrs Lambert. For the moment he's not going anywhere."

It was proving to be a busy day. Thorn strolled down to the beach to clear his head before turning back to the Smuggler's Arms. As he often did, he found himself reflecting on the nature of his job. This idyllic place, full of carefree visitors and seemingly uncomplicated islanders, was deceptive: some visitors came here to heal deep wounds, the locals nursed their own in private. And the disturbing image swam into his mind of the lovely girl in the clinic, weeping as she left the surgery. He sighed and turned towards the town.

Chapter 5

Back at the Smuggler's Arms Thorn found both the Jefferies at work in the bar He tried to get them to leave what they were doing to talk to him, but they made the excuse that they were simply too busy. Perhaps, then, they could come down to the police station, in the morning, say? Neither of them seemed particularly daunted at the prospect, and neither of them could invent a plausible excuse. In vain Thorn explained that all he really wanted was an informal chat. He had to be content to wait.

His visit would have been completely wasted – indeed, he thought, it still might be – but for a chance discovery which had no relevance to his enquiry. As he stood at the bar of the pub, and tried to engage George Jefferies in conversation, as difficult and awkward as a cub reporter trying to get a definite statement of facts from a politician, the private door opened and an elegant, dark-haired girl of about twenty appeared briefly. She was well dressed and resembled Mrs Jefferies closely. Seeing her two parents were busy, she hesitated a moment then returned whence she came.

"Your daughter?" asked Thorn.

"Yes."

"Does she live with you?"

"She's home for the vacation."

"I see," Thorn said. "When did she arrive?"

"This morning," Jefferies replied, still sparing with information..

"And where is she at college?"

"Chichester."

Thorn's ears pricked up at this. He sipped thoughtfully at a beer while Jefferies watched him from beneath beetling browns, waiting for the next question. It came: "Why Chichester?"

"Why not?"

"No reason why not. It seems a bit of a coincidence, that's all."

"Coincidence?" Jefferies seemed to have no idea what Thorn was alluding to, or perhaps he was fishing for information himself.

"Lambert came from Chichester."

"Oh yes, now you come to mention it, I remember seeing it in the register."

"Didn't you comment on the coincidence?"

"No."

"How long has your daughter been at university, Mr Jefferies?"

"Two years."

"I see."

The conversation died. Thorn decided to leave it until the Jefferies were formally interviewed. He finished his pint and left with relief. Even the beer tasted flat.

At the police station Roberts greeted him with news of a phone call from Chichester CID. Would he call back?

"Hello, sir." It was an Inspector Clegg. "You are enquiring into the life and crimes of one Matthew Lambert, I believe."

"Yes, Inspector. What have you got for me?"

"Well, it may be nothing, sir, but you never know. Lambert worked as a security guard for a firm called City Safe, as perhaps you already know."

"So your man told me yesterday."

"But did he tell you that Lambert had been involved in an attempted hold-up two months ago?"

"How was he involved?"

"He was the driver of the van which was ambushed. A car pulled out and blocked the road in front of him, while another two, armed men tried to get Lambert and his mate, a man called Clough, to unlock and hand over the money in the back."

"But they didn't?"

"No, Lambert let in the clutch and accelerated away, ramming the car in front of them. He smashed his way through, but the car driver was killed. He will probably have to face charges of manslaughter – or would have, I should say."

What about the armed men trying to hold them up?"

"They got away, I'm afraid."

"Thanks, Inspector."

"Any use to you?"

"I don't know. Probably not. But thanks for the information. Good luck with your enquiries. Any hope of finding them?"

"Well, we do have a couple of witnesses. And, of course, we soon discovered who was driving the car. That's our best lead really, it was a young local lad, name of McNab. He had an older brother, Jock, and we reckon they were in it together. The descriptions could tally, although they were wearing balaclavas."

"Sounds hopeful."

"There's one other thing, sir."

Thorn made encouraging noises.

"There's every chance it was an inside job."

"Lambert? Surely not, if he actually killed one of them."

"Could be, or it could be his mate or anyone else at the depot."

"Why?"

"Well, it was a regular, wages run to a local factory. They used a different route every week and it was decided only one hour before the run. They couldn't know for sure where to make the ambush unless they had been given the information."

Thorn thanked Clegg again and put the receiver down pensively. There might be absolutely no connection between the attempted robbery and Lambert's death. Wage snatches were relatively common and security vans were obvious targets, so it was not entirely surprising that a security guard should find himself a victim or otherwise involved in a crime of this kind. It was a high-risk job. In any case, since the ambush had failed, it was hard to see how Lambert could remain any kind of serious threat to the attackers, McNab and company. It was surely very unlikely that McNab would want to pursue Lambert to Scilly for such a reason, especially since he might well realise Chichester CID would be interested in his whereabouts.

On reflection, Thorn was inclined to discount the information as irrelevant, except for one niggling thought: the relationship between the driver of the car and the man who had seen Lambert drive straight into it could be crucial. Not knowing McNab, Thorn had no way of ascertaining how strongly he would feel about the death of his brother. Would he be so angry that he might pursue Lambert in search of revenge? The doubt persisted and it would, he knew, give him no rest.

He picked up the phone again and asked for details of McNab senior to be faxed to him. They arrived shortly afterwards, with a photo taken three years previously at the beginning of his last stretch. It was villainous enough to appear mildly comical, like a man dressed to look like a convict rather than the genuine article. It lacked only a striped suit with arrows all over it. He got Roberts to make a couple of photocopies, one of which he took later to the Pirate and showed to Ben Jacobs.

"'Ansome-lookin' sort of chap, isn't he?" observed the publican. "And do you know, Superintendent, I reckon as I seen him in the Pirate in the past day or two."

Thorn's excitement was kept concealed, but, he thought to himself, perhaps this was one of those moments when a sudden flash of light heralds the dawn of understanding.

"Exactly when?" he asked.

Ben thought a bit. "Two days ago," he said. "Tuesday."

The day before the murder: "Since then?"

"No. Only the once."

"Is he still on the island?" Thorn asked Roberts as soon as he got back to the office. "And, if he is, where is he staying?" He was beginning to feel more and more strongly the need of more men simply to do the legwork. Small though St Mary's was, to call at all the guesthouses, hotels and bed-and-breakfast places, even on the one island could take a couple of days.

"Maybe we'd do better to start by asking at the harbour and the airport," Roberts suggested. "That way we might find out if he's left the islands already, and finding out where he stayed wouldn't be quite so urgent."

"You take the harbour," said Thorn, thinking once more this self-styled village policeman was brighter than most, "You know the boatmen. I'll nip up to the airport."

The airport was little more than a grassy field where the few fixed-wing aircraft landed, and a small, concrete apron for the helicopter. The offices, check-in desks, waiting rooms, were all contained within a smart, brick-built building. There were no hangars or repair facilities here; all servicing and repairs were carried out on the mainland. Thorn was there in a matter of minutes. He showed the photograph of McNab to the girl in the little buffet. She was busy selling cups of tea and sandwiches. He also showed it to the man who checked tickets for the helicopter. There was no joy from the girl, but the man thought he remembered McNab. He frowned as he concentrated on the caricature-like portrait.

"He's been through here in the past few days," he said at last, "I recognise the face all right. He's got a red beard"

"When you say the past few days," Thorn probed, "do you mean yesterday?"

The clerk frowned again. "No. No, I'm sure it wasn't yesterday," he said.

"Think," urged Thorn. "Was he coming or going?"

The man closed his lips in a tight line and blew air into his cheeks, trying to remember. He shook his head in perplexity.

75

"Got it!" He announced in triumph. "He flew in four days ago by helicopter, he took the minibus into town."

"Has anybody else been on duty?"

"Doing this job, you mean? No."

"And you haven't seen him on his way out?"

"No."

"You're sure?"

"Yes." He nodded, pleased to have remembered after all.

Thorn drove back into town and waited for Roberts to return to the office. He had to wait some time. When the Sergeant came in, his evidence was inconclusive. "No one has seen the man," he said. "I tried the ticket office in town first, to see if he bought a ticket for the Scillonian. No luck there. But you can buy your tickets on the boat, and she sailed this morning, not long ago. The boatmen on the quay wouldn't have remembered him among the foot passengers for the Scillonian: they're only concerned with their own passengers to and from the out-islands. In any case most of them hadn't got back from their own trips. He might still be on the island, but there again, he might just as easily be back on the mainland. We can contact Penzance and get someone to meet the Scillonian this evening, of course. But our man may even have gone back yesterday or the day before."

Roberts rang Penzance and asked for someone to meet the boat just in case. There was nothing else they could do: Chichester had already circulated a picture and details of McNab.

All things considered, the McNab business left Thorn frustrated. It could be a mare's nest. Then again, it could be the key to the mystery. Now he was mixing metaphors: Roberts, sensing his mood, said nothing.

The Scillonian docked in Penzance at 8:30. At 9 o'clock the phone rang. Roberts listened, grunted, put down the receiver. "He wasn't on the boat tonight," he said.

"What time does the airport close?" asked Thorn.

"Half an hour ago." Roberts was surprised. "You didn't expect him to fly back tonight, did you, Sir?"

"No," said Thorn impatiently. "I left instructions they were to call me if McNab tried to buy a ticket or board a plane. No, I want to get to Chichester to check things out personally."

"You really think McNab's our man, do you, sir?"

"I just don't know, Sergeant. I wish I did. I need to look into it, that's all I know."

"The helicopters are usually fully booked at this time of the year," Roberts warned. "You might just get on the first one at 7:30 in the morning. Otherwise I doubt you'll find room."

"If not, I'll have to try to get on a plane," Thorn said. "If I get a train at the other end, let's see how soon I can be in Chichester."

Doing something, Thorn felt less frustrated. Once more he rang Chichester and warned them he would be following up his own enquiries there. There was nothing more to be done before morning except to ring the DCC and, once he had reported his findings to date, tell him of his intention to visit Chichester. The news was received was no more than mild interest.

His own plans now made for the next day or two, Thorn discussed as fully as possible with Roberts the routine enquiries he could continue to pursue on the island.

"Let's hope you turn up something definite in Chichester, sir," Roberts said. "I'll contact you there if there's anything obviously important here."

Thorn was in luck: there were two empty seats on the early morning helicopter. The aircraft rose noisily into the air, tipping forward as the nose headed out over the cliff towards the sea. Looking down on the islands spread beneath him, still not fully awake, Thorn saw the small fields in which grew the spring daffodils, now a weedy green, the grass on the bluffs near the uncultivated parts of St Marys, the smoothly eroded granite, the small pleasure craft in clear, shallow bays, and then the helicopter was over the waves. Far below the rippled surface baffled the eye by its lack of scale until Thorn realised a tiny, white sliver of light was the outspread wings of a gull. By the time the roaring machine was flattening the grass by the helipad on the mainland, 30 miles away, Sergeant Roberts and his wife, Tina, were sitting down to a large breakfast.

In the train on the first leg of his journey, Thorn was thinking how the trail seemed to lead back to Chichester. Since it was Lambert's home town, that was not to be wondered at entirely. However, the choice of Chichester by the Jefferies girl was one of those coincidences which always made him uncomfortable. Not that he was totally sceptical about coincidences, but their introduction into a murder enquiry was, to put it mildly, irritating. The art of detection, as opposed to the routine, mechanical pursuance of enquiries, aimed at checking facts, depended on the ability or gift of spotting connections and relationships. Coincidences were relationships lacking a true causality; they produced in the mind the illusion of causality and that could waste time and energy, for it had to be checked, just in case there was a real link. He would have to investigate this further complication, then.

As he travelled eastward the weather deteriorated. The sunshine of the early morning gave way to cloudy skies and a greyer light which deadened contrast until, as they left Reading and neared London, it began to rain. Thorn took a taxi to change stations. Traffic clogged the wet and noisy streets. He looked out on the crowds. They bustled along the pavements under their umbrellas, their faces grey and unhappy. His own spirits sank. Depression began to settle on him, and he saw himself as a tired, middle-aged man, all alone in the world. He had left behind on St Marys Bill Roberts and Tina, who lived a happy life in exile from all this. Maybe they had made the right choice, when they settled for an island life in a community where they were known and liked. Already they would have forgotten him, though they would welcome him back, no doubt; he was incidental to them. He was not merely incidental, but a downright nuisance to Chichester CID where he would not be welcome, even though they would have to accept him temporarily. And, as he boarded the train at Victoria which would take him to his destination, his face assumed the same grey tension as he had observed in the streets of London.

It was late by the time he got to Chichester. He made his way to the police station by taxi and tracked down Inspector Clegg. He explained he wanted to visit City Safe and talk to the manager as well as to Clough, Lambert's mate at the time of the attempted robbery. Meanwhile he would appreciate a look through the files. Clegg was a big man with an open manner. He had a wide face in which steely blue eyes looked tired, but laughter lines at their corners made him appear approachable. He had a mobile mouth which could be smiling and friendly, or it could set into a firm line of determination or even aggression. To Thorn's relief he showed no resentment at being asked to give his time to help.

"Have you had anything to eat?" he asked.

"I had a snack on the train."

"There's a decent pub round the corner," Clegg suggested. "I could do with a bite to eat myself. And it'll take you an hour or so to read through the files."

By the time they had eaten, Thorn's depression had eased a little. He warmed to this big man. Back in Clegg's office, he familiarised himself with the names and statements, before he examined the map which showed the route of the security van. He checked over details of the McNab brothers, Sandy and Jock. Finally, at 11 o'clock in the evening, he let Clegg direct him to a hotel, where he soaked for a while in a hot bath and went to bed.

For the next two days Thorn was accompanied much of the time by Clegg, an arrangement which occasionally irritated, but mostly pleased him, since it saved a great deal of time. He learned little of substance. City Safe seemed as efficient as most security firms. Its employees were all bonded, which suggested that Lambert had at least appeared to be trustworthy when he had been first employed. Clough, his mate on the day of the ambush, was guarded in his opinions. Thorn got the impression that Clough did not much like Lambert, though the dislike was personal rather than professional. Lambert's tastes were for drinking and for women, in fairly equal proportions. He had been quite often abrasive in style, though he was not generally a great talker, but after working closely with the man for nearly three years, Clough felt he knew him reasonably well.

"Do you think he could have given details of the route to McNab?" asked Thorn.

"It doesn't make sense," replied Clough. "He could have done it, of course: he had time to get out and make a phone call. But if he did, why would he drive straight into the car?"

It seemed logical. Thorn left City Safe and made his way to Lambert's digs. The landlady was co-operative. Thorn breathed a sigh of relief when he did not need a search warrant and spent more than an hour examining the contents of the room. Under the bed there was a small, wooden box, a little larger than a shoe box. It was locked, and Thorn had not brought Lambert's keys with him. He took the box away with him. It could contain evidence which Clegg might use: he decided to take it to Clegg and break into it later. He found an address book in the dressing table drawer which he examined with interest There were several addresses in Scilly, including guesthouses and the Smuggler's Arms. Struck by a sudden suspicion, Thorn looked for "Jefferies" in case Lambert had the Jefferies' daughter's number or address: nothing. There were six or seven other local telephone numbers with girls' names. Thorn took the book back to Clegg, too, and asked him to have them checked out. Clegg's help was again invaluable when it came to the matter of visiting Lambert's bank. The manager was at first very reluctant to divulges anything, then relented. For a security guard Lambert had been doing exceptionally well. He lived comfortably, but seemed never to have been in debt.

"I'm a little puzzled," Thorn observed. "I understand Mr Lambert's salary was paid directly into his account."

"That is so," said Nash, the bank manager, an ordinary-looking man in a dark suit.

"There seems to be no record in his cheque-book of any withdrawals just before his holiday. Perhaps he used plastic."

Nash glanced down at the account which he held in his hands. "No," he said, "Mr Lambert made no withdrawals since he paid in a considerable sum more than three weeks ago." He made a few, quick calculations. "It rather looks as though he was paid his normal month's salary at that time, plus a further month's holiday money. He didn't draw any of it."

Thorn and Clegg exchanged glances. "Are there any other extraordinary or large deposits over the past three months?"

Another quick check, then, "No. He only appears to have banked his normal salary."

Outside, the two police officers got into the car. "Lambert had one hundred pounds in cash in his wallet," mused Thorn. "Where did it come from? And according to Mrs Jefferies, he paid three weeks in advance at the Smuggler's Arms in cash."

"A win on the horses?" suggested Clegg. Both men grinned: neither believed it.

"I need you to apply for a court order to get a copy of Lambert's statements."

"My pleasure," Clegg agreed.

At Thorn's request Clegg also agreed to investigate further the McNab family. It would not be easy, since the two brothers originated from Glasgow and had merely lived in digs in Chichester. They lived separately and had come to the attention of the police in the course of a number of petty crimes, the latest of which, before the robbery attack, had been robbery with violence in which Jock had been implicated, had been sentenced to four years and had been released after two. Whether the brothers were close, whether they had any kind of dealings with Lambert, were matters for further investigation and could take a long time to resolve.

With the aid of a screwdriver they forced the lock of the wooden box. It contained letters, all bearing a foreign stamp. There were over a hundred. Thorn pulled out one at one end of the box. It was addressed to Lambert at an address which was clearly a military base in Singapore. The writing ws large, childish. Inside the letter was written by a child, a Chinese girl, who wrote to 'Dear Uncle' and was a thank you letter in poor English. Thorn replaced it, and pulled out another, nearer the middle. This was also addressed to 'Uncle', but the English was more correct and the handwriting neat. It was largely a report of how the girl was doing at school. It was going to take some time to read all the letters, and they would probably be of no help in his enquiries, but Thorn was a thorough man. Clegg was agreeable to his taking the box back to Scilly with him

Meanwhile, Thorn made one further call, this time at the college, where he managed, with a certain amount of charm and the use of his warrant card, to discover the name of the Jefferies' daughter, Penelope, and her address in Chichester. She shared a flat with two other girls. He called. According to her flatmates, Penny was a clever, hard-working student, and "a bit of a snob at times". She had one or two boyfriends but none of them remotely resembled Lambert, and neither of her fellow-tenants had ever seen him. Thorn stayed long enough to drink a cup of coffee, and found he enjoyed the company of these young people, but the domesticity of the scene reminded him of his now dead daughter, Alice, not much older than these two girls, and the memory plunged him once more into a black mood. He left, trying to fight off the despair he had been learning to combat. It seemed to ensnare him like sticky strands of some giant spider's web. He walked furiously in the rain round a park for an hour before returning to Clegg's office. Clegg looked at him, saw the wet clothes, and recognise the look in Thorn's eyes. He turned to the filing cabinet and took out a bottle from which he poured a stiff drink.

"Thanks," said Thorn, taking a large gulp.

"Any luck?" The voice was even, without expression. It was, Thorn knew, merely a signal: if he wanted to talk, he could.

"No. I'll tell you about it sometime." He finished the drink in one. "There's nothing more I can reasonably attempt here," he said. "Thank you for all your help. I'll keep in touch. I'll get back to the hotel and see if I can organise an overnight train to Penzance."

"I'll book it, if you like," Clegg offered. "I'll phone you at the hotel when it's all arranged."

"Thanks," Thorn hesitated and then. "Really thanks," he repeated. Inwardly he knew Clegg for what he was, a fellow sufferer who had known pain at some time and could recognise his. No need to explain. But Thorn knew one day he would come back: he would explain then. He turned.

He showered, packed methodically, waiting for Clegg's call. He tried to sort out the evidence as best he could as he waited, scribbling in a notebook while he the rain wept on the window. When the phone rang, it was to tell him the train for London left in fifty minutes and that reservation had been made on the sleeper from Paddington. No need to think for himself this time then. He paid his bill and left.

Chapter 6

Thorn slept fitfully on the train and was in a poor temper by the time he reached Penzance. Clegg had somehow managed to book a seat on the 10:30 helicopter, leaving him enough time to look for breakfast. He ate alone in a café in Market Jew Street in the centre of the town before finding his way to the heliport

The rain and clouds were now left behind in the east, and the sun shone. Thorn climbed into the aircraft for the short flight and tried to ignore the noise of the rotors, as the helicopter lifted off and climbed over the shoreline. It cut inland again beyond Mousehole, and moved slowly westward. Below him the small fields and gently sloping countryside slumbered in the sunshine. But Thorn's spirits did not lighten at this spectacle of peace. Instead, he was thinking sourly how greedy, ill-disciplined men like Lambert could spoil even the age-old tranquillity of such a scene. Why had such a man come to the islands? Why had his stupid behaviour led to his death? Why had he ended his life at the foot of the cliff, and thus set in train this relentless search for his killer, dragging Thorn thereby into a grubby life he had much rather not known about?

The fact was that Thorn's compassionate leave had been a grievous necessity, a necessity which had been rudely ignored when he had been pulled into this business. The sudden, alarming return of his depression yesterday had reminded him of that fact. He hoped he could continue with the case without too serious a consequence for himself and his peace of mind.

To his discomfiture, Roberts failed to meet the aircraft, and he boarded the minibus instead for the short journey to town. Tina was in the kitchen when he arrived at the cottage. Her husband had been called out by Cooper urgently, ten minutes before he was due to set off for the airport. There had been some serious trouble at the Treduggan farm in Penwarden Valley, where Roberts suggested Thorn should follow him. Tina knew no details. Refusing the proferred cup of coffee, Thorn got detailed directions and left.

Considering the miniature scale of the islands, the interior was exceedingly mysterious. Small lanes met and crossed between Cornish hedges which concealed the broader view. One mile from town Thorn would have been lost without the instructions from Tina, and, although he knew he had only to step out of the car and climb up on the stone hedge to see as far as the cliff's to west and east, all the time he was at the wheel he might have been in the depths of some much further-flung landscape.

The lane turned downhill and veered left. The hedges petered out at the bottom of a shallow valley, Penwarden no doubt, where a clump of scrubby trees leaned darkly over a tumbledown farmhouse. There appeared to be no telephone line leading to the house. The old roof had been built of thick slates like heavy slabs of stone, and these were now deeply embedded in a layer of cement. Weeds grew in the cracks of the chimney-stack. The woodwork had not seen fresh paint for at least thirty years, and the brooding upstairs windows were grimy and framed in cracked and rotten wood, split, dark, neglected. A broken wall of stone blocks separated the road from the untended front garden. A muddy track led round the further end of the wall towards the back of the building and equally dilapidated sheds and a dairy.

Roberts' vehicle was parked outside. Thorn pulled up behind it and walked as far as the front door. It was ajar. He pushed it open on groaning hinges and entered.

"In here, sir," the voice came from a door on his left. The small entrance hall opened directly onto a staircase, and rooms lay on either side. The stairs were covered with a threadbare carpet which had lost all its colour and was of great age. Bending his head below the low door frame, Thorn went into the living room.

Roberts was standing on one side of the stone fireplace in which an unlit, cast iron range absorbed the light as a sponge soaks up water. Opposite him, in an old rocking chair, sat a man. He was grey-haired and in his fifties. Above his heavy boots he wore corduroy trousers, and a heavy, twill shirt without a collar, of the kind Thorn had not seen for more than twenty years. Unmoving, he sat in the wooden chair, bent forward, elbows on the arms, his face hidden in big, rough hands.

Roberts did not speak, but pointed upstairs. Thorn turned and made his way slowly to the first floor. There were two doors at the top of the stairs. The one on the right led into a double room in which Thorn saw an old bed, roughly made, and men's clothing, littered about on pieces of furniture. He turned to the other room. Opposite the door there was a small dressing table, from the bottom of which a gingham cloth hung to the floor. Above the dressing table, strewn with odd jars and bottles and a hairbrush, there was a cheap, circular mirror. In it Thorn's attention was seized by the image of a young woman, lying on the bed behind the door. Eyes open, she seemed to be staring at him in terror, but she made no move, and Thorn realised with heart-stopping shock, that she had not seen him; the eyes were unseeing, like the shining black eyes of a dead rabbit, and they would never see anyone again.

He stepped into the room and looked directly at the girl. She was wearing a simple cotton nightdress which made her look almost like a child, but even beneath this simple covering her body was voluptuously developed. Thorn guessed she must have been about twenty. The terror in her eyes was the more shocking because the face was also otherwise beautiful in its youthful clarity of line, and because of the livid bruises on the smooth neck, made, Thorn realised at once, by the hands of her killer.

His training overrode his personal reaction. Thorn stared at the body and its situation so as to record a visual memory. While one part of his brain worked automatically and dispassionately, a stronger, deeper and quite uncontrollable sense of utter outrage welled up and threatened to overwhelm him. He closed the girl's eyes and his own turned dark with anger. This, he knew, was the girl he had seen leaving the doctor's surgery just the other day, but in his mind's eye another image tried to superimpose itself, the image of his own daughter's body, lying on wet tarmac, a picture which gripped him in an agony of guilt in those few moments before he had passed out. Once again pictures of the crystallised windscreen and the underside of the car, with its wheels still spinning, spinning, blinding him for a moment, until he wrenched his attention back.

It was with heavy heart that he looked round the tiny bedroom. He found nothing of any interest to him, no dramatic note, no diary, not even some indication of a healthy, developed individuality. The wardrobe contained just a few dresses, two or three skirts, a few simple blouses. There were no soft toys to suggest a sentimental attachment to childhood, and no make up to suggest an attempt to embrace womanhood. There were no photographs, simply a faded, nineteenth century print of a girl in a garden, and an embroidered text, "There's No Place Like Home."

He returned to the sitting room. "Where is Cooper?" he asked. His face had set into a still mask of anger and indignation, barely suppressed.

"He's gone to fetch someone to look after the livestock. He should be back directly. I told him we'd wait."

"What happened?" Thorn jerked his head, not trusting himself to refer to the sight seen upstairs in words.

"The Lord giveth and the Lord taketh away." The voice came from behind the horny hands of the farmer as he sat in the rocking chair. Still he did not move. "She had to be punished. She had turned herself into a trollop, a Jezebel, a harlot. If her mother had still been alive, it would have killed her with the shame. A daughter of mine!"

"Mr Treduggan?" Thorn was unsure of the name. Roberts nodded to confirm it. "What happened?"

"She stole out to meet 'im at night. I heard 'er, you see, I heard 'er. I heard 'er creepin' out, tryin' to deceive me, off to meet 'er fancy man, she were."

"How do you know where she was going, Job?" This time it was Roberts asking the question.

"I followed 'er, didn't I? Walking off into the night; no shame, none at all. She were goin' to meet 'im up on Purley 'Ead, it was, in the dead o' night. 'Men love the darkness rather than the light, because their deeds are evil'."

At the mention of Purley Head Thorn's attention was even more acute. "And when was this?" he asked quietly, as though making a threat. Roberts looked at him sharply, hearing in his tone a note of menace he was unaccustomed to.

"Wednesday."

The night of Lambert's murder! The coincidence was too great.

"Who killed your daughter, Mr Treluggan?" Again, the note of menace, the barely suppressed anger.

"I 'ad to," said Treluggan. "She was a slut. She disgraced us. All these years I've strived to live a godly life. I have worshipped the Lord and done his will, and this is how she repays me! We couldn't go on after that, not the same way. She couldn't atone for 'er sin. She didn't even want to. Better she should die than bring more disgrace on us."

"Have you cautioned him?" asked Thorn, his voice thick with disgust, and Roberts detected a tremor in it.

"Yes, sir."

Thorn, his fists clenched, span on his heels and left. He strode across the road to the opposite side. To his right there was a five-barred gate. He walked over to it and gripped the top rail so tightly that his knuckles showed white. The skin at his temples was stretched tight, and his eyes burned deep in their sockets. His face had taken on the appearance of a mask in which an observer could have seen a mixture of anger, frustration, disgust and pain. He stood thus, staring across the flower-filled meadow, unseeing, for several minutes. He breathed deeply, as his demons came to haunt him. He was unaware of the birdsong, of the warmth of the gentle breeze, of the soft green of the grass before him. He failed to notice the car which crunched its way down the lane to halt behind him, or the sound of the slammed door, followed by the doctor's footsteps.

"Thorn!" He turned to face Cooper, who stopped in his tracks, disconcerted by the look on Thorn's face. "Are you all right?"

Thorn pulled himself together. He nodded. "Was it you who found her?" he asked, his voice was still unnaturally harsh.

"Yes. It's a bad business. I'd asked her to come to the surgery and see me. She was upset, she'd got herself pregnant. I told her to come back and see me yesterday. I knew she wouldn't be able to talk sensibly to her father. He's one of those religious fanatics who holds so-called principles more important than his own flesh and blood. She didn't come back, and I thought I'd better call."

The doctor in his turn leaned on the gate for support, its rough wood keeping him in touch with reality, while he relived in memory the events of the morning.

"Job didn't answer the door. I knocked twice then looked through the window. He was sitting by the fire in the rocking chair. I let myself in. At first, he didn't answer me when I spoke to him. It seems he had been sitting there all night. He'd found out she'd had an affair, you see. He strangled her. He's not really sane."

Thorn's anger was under control now, but only just. Cooper looked directly at him. "You look awful," he said. "You must have seen worse than this in your time, surely."

"Yes, I suppose you might say that."

"Superintendent," said Cooper, "are you sure you're all right?"

"I'll cope," said Thorn. "Let's get on with it, shall we?"

It was two hours later that Thorn locked the door of the farmhouse and drove back to the police station and the concerned care of Tina Roberts. Treluggan had been accommodated in the solitary cell, and Bill Roberts was already hard at work typing up his account of the morning's dismal discovery. Sarah Treduggan's body was now stored in the mortuary next to that of the man who had perhaps been her lover.

Thorn's personal feelings were a complication which confused him deeply. He knew, absolutely now, that he was not really ready, not yet recovered from the trauma of the accident; in such a state of mind, he was not a truly fit person to conduct a murder enquiry, perhaps two murder cases. As a professional, he should withdraw now. He knew he was too personally involved. His own guilt, which he might have been able to come to terms with in time, was turning into a wild, vehement hatred for this other father, who had killed his own daughter. He felt no compassion for him, nor could he withhold judgement.

Both Tina and her husband saw at once the change in him. Neither of them understood it, but both of them kept silent at the sight of his dark face, with its barely hidden violence. And Thorn made no attempt for a long time to speak to either of them, except to give Roberts perfunctory orders. He sat at the desk and stared out of the window at the harbour. He had been sitting thus, without speaking, for nearly an hour, when Roberts left the small table at which he was working and returned with a large glass full of brandy, which he put down at Thorn's elbow. Thorn picked up the glass and drank.

"Tell me about the dead girl," he said.

"There's not much to tell," said Roberts. "She was a quiet, pleasant enough sort of kid. Everybody knew her, more or less; a lot of people felt sorry for her, I suppose."

"Why sorry?"

"Mainly because of her father, Job. He belongs to one of those queer sects – the Modern Disciples. I expect you know the sort of thing; thou shalt not do anything at all. Poor kid! She had a pretty tough childhood; she had to come straight to school and go straight home. No after-school activities for her, no games. Even made a fuss because the girls did PE in their knickers. Sarah had no friends. She spent most of her time, when she wasn't at school, working on the farm. No fun for her. The Modern Disciples don't believe in having fun. Job made another fuss when Miss Barker – she was Headteacher – wanted Sarah to play the part of Mary in a nativity play; playacting, the cinema, it was all sin."

"What happened to Mrs Tredugggan?"

"She died – oh, about ten years ago now. I think it was ten years. I never knew her, myself."

"And you know all this about the nativity play. How?"

"Oh, that's one of the legends you hear around here."

Thorn fell silent for a while. "If Treduggan was so strict," he said at last, "how did his daughter manage to meet a man, let alone Lambert, and get herself pregnant?"

"She had a job," Roberts explained. "She worked in the baker's."

I'm surprised she was allowed to," Thorn commented.

"She had spirit."

"She must have had."

"And then, they needed the money."

"Oh!" This seemed an altogether more persuasive argument.

"Well, sir, you've seen the farm: it's like something out of Cold Comfort Farm. Job wouldn't borrow, you see: against his religion again. Usury, that's what he called it. And he needed to put some money into the place to make it half efficient. I reckon if Sarah hadn't gone out and got herself a job, they'd have starved."

"You're satisfied it was Job that killed her?"

"Oh yes, I'm sure of it."

"It still doesn't quite hang together. Granted Treduggan is a religious crank with extreme ideas about purity and sex and everything, and about everything else by the sound of it, it all sounds unbelievable. How could he commit murder and justify it, because his daughter had an affair?"

Roberts shrugged. "Didn't they use to stone women to death in the Bible?"

"For adultery, yes."

"He did it, sir, I'd bet a year's pay on it."

"I want you to go over it all with him again, Sergeant. I want every detail, and I want to be absolutely sure of his motives. I'm not convinced."

"He did it, sir. When he told me, he had that half-crazy look in his eye, as though to say, you can do what you like to me now, I've done what I had to do. If you still aren't convinced, sir, why don't you question him yourself?"

"I can't do that,"

"I don't understand, sir. Why can't you?"

"I just can't. To be truthful, Sergeant, I don't think I can be objective."

Roberts gave him a thoughtful stare. "Very well, sir," he said. "But may I know why?"

"No," said Thorn. Then, recognising Roberts' reaction as one of surprise and dismay that he was not to be trusted with a confidence, "Later," he said. "I'll explain later."

"There is a clear tie-in with the Lambert case," Roberts observed. "You think Treduggan killed Lambert?"

"He was there, he says."

"And if he killed his own daughter, because she had a lover, he could have killed the lover first."

"So, we need a very detailed statement about his movements on Wednesday night."

"And you still want me to do the questioning?"

"Yes, I'll ride shotgun."

It was, Roberts realised, an unorthodox procedure. Thorn was not only his superior in rank and experience, he was also a CID officer, well used to conducting interviews of this nature. Roberts was a policeman of limited experience of serious crime. He had assisted in his day at routine interviews, but he had never been expected to take a leading role, certainly not in such a serious case, which was destined for the Crown Court. It was an awesome responsibility. But Thorn was his superior, and he could not easily dispute his judgement, nor could he disobey his orders.

"Sir," he said after a while, "since this is all rather unorthodox, will you place it on record that it is your idea I should conduct the interview?"

"Yes, yes, of course." Thorn dismissed this request as unimportant, and Roberts heaved a sigh of relief. At least he would be covered.

It seemed to be almost a matter of indifference to Treduggan whether he should have a solicitor. After insisting, Roberts got the name of a local man and rang him. Treduggan was quite willing to talk, in spite of his solicitor's advice to talk to him first. "What for?" he asked, shouting down the phone, handling the unfamiliar instrument like a megaphone. "I did for 'er. I don't want to lie about it, do I?"

The solicitor, Tremain, nevertheless insisted that he should be allowed to talk to his client before the interrogation. Thorn and the Sergeant left the two of them to speak to one another in mutual distrust in the office, and Thorn steeled himself for the coming interview with another large drink. Roberts said nothing but there was a worried look on his face.

"It's all right, Sergeant," said Thorn grimly, "I'm not going to get drunk; I need this."

Tremain shrugged his shoulders dismissively. He too, was unused to this kind of work, and hardly knew his client, who had spent most of his life steering clear of authority and officialdom. "He insists he wants to get it over with," he said, "and he wants to make a statement, a confession. There's not much more I can do."

Despite Treduggan's explicit wishes not to defend himself, it was a difficult interview. Once the twin tapes had been loaded into the machine, Thorn took a seat as far back in the room as he could, behind Roberts, and from where he could watch Treduggan's face.

The Sergeant began by asking about Sarah's death. Treduggan stated in half sentences that he had known about her relationship with the visitor only since Wednesday. Before then, he had guessed there was something going on, because she had been late getting home from work a couple of times. Then she had said she was going to spend an evening with a schoolfriend, the same friend, when asked later, knew nothing about the arrangement, and had not seen her. So, he was already worried about her when, on Wednesday night, he heard her bedroom door open at nearly midnight, two hours after they had both retired. They always went to bed early, he said, because of the early milking.

"I follered 'er," he said.

"On foot?"

"Her bike 'ad a puncture."

"Didn't she hear you behind her?"

"Oh no, she started walking towards town. Nowhere else you can go down that road. I hung back a bit, that's all."

"And did she come into town?"

"No, she turned left, up Purley Head way."

"Was it very dark?"

"It was night time, what do you think?"

"How come you didn't lose her?"

"By the time we were getting close to the town, and there's no proper hedge, so I kept to the grass."

"Then what happened?"

"Well, she took the path up to the point."

"Yes?"

"He was waitin' for 'er, wasn't he?"

"Who?"

"Her fancy man. Don't know his name."

"What did he look like?"

"I didn't get that close. It was dark."

"Where was this?"

"On Purley Head. I told you."

"Exactly where?"

"By the standin' stone."

"And how close were you?"

"Some way."

"Ten yards, twenty, thirty?"

"Nearer thirty, I reckon."

"Could you see what they were doing?"

"They didn't do nothing much."

"They just talked?" Roberts was sceptical.

"Yes, they talked."

"And that's all they did?"

"What are you suggesting, Bill Roberts? Do you think I'd describe what they did if they didn't just talk?"

"Could you hear what they said?"

"No."

"Not at all?"

"Not from where I was. They wasn't shouting or anything."

"Was it – did it look like lovers' talk?"

"Don't know what you mean. They were standinn' close together, and I think the little slut actually kissed un. They was standin' there with their arms wrapped all round each other."

"Then what?"

"What you mean?"

"Well, they didn't stay there all night, did they?"

"No."

"What did you do?"

"I waited till Sarah started back home, then I followed on behind."

"You're sure of that?"

"Course I'm sure! What do you mean?"

"You didn't approach the man?"

"No."

"You just turned away?"

"I followed Sarah home."

"You didn't go up to this man on Purley Head, and speak to him about Sarah?"

"No."

"You didn't want to have a go at him?"

"I were too disgusted with Sarah to think about him much."

"What the Sergeant is saying," Thorn interrupted in an even tone from the back of the room, "is that you were so disgusted, so enraged at this secret meeting, that you attacked the man."

"No, I never."

"You attacked the man," Thorn pursued relentlessly, "you stabbed him to death. And after that you followed your daughter home."

"I never went near un."

"Job," Roberts tried to sound patient and reasonable. "You have already admitted to killing Sarah. Why should you want to lie about killing Lambert?"

"Because I never did it." It was a flat statement.

"You don't really expect us to believe you?"

" I don't much care if you do or not. I didn't do it. There was someone else out there, though."

"Why won't you admit it, Job?"

"I've told you; I didn't do it. It could have been the other bloke."

"What other bloke?"

"I told you, there was someone else up there. I couldn't see un very well, because it was too dark, but he was back towards the coastguard station."

"Tall, short, fat, thin?"

"Couldn't say, I was too busy anyway, watching Sarah and her fancy man. A bloke in a hat."

And neither Roberts nor Thorn could get more out of him on the subject. He went on to describe how he had got home ahead of his daughter by crossing the fields and how he had thought and prayed about what he should do. God told him she had to be punished, like the woman taken in adultery. He had been in anguish for two days and then, worn out through lack of sleep and anxiety, he had gone into Sarah's bedroom early in the morning and he had taxed her with having an affair. She had laughed in his face. Yes, she said, she had been having an affair; the man was a visitor who had been to the islands many times, and he came back year after year. She had met him in the shop first, and then had stepped out to meet him whenever she could. She was completely shameless. He asked her to confess to sinning and to try to atone, but she would have none of it; she would rather die, she said. And so, he had strangled her. He had fathered her, he had the right to end her life.

Thorn stood up and came to stand behind Roberts chair. In a voice which was terrible in its menace and which made Roberts scalp crawl, he said slowly, "And her baby, Mr Treduggan? Did you have the right to kill her unborn baby too?"

Treduggan turned pale and his face suddenly looked gaunt, like a man facing death. "What baby?" he asked.

"Your daughter was pregnant," Thorn was relentless, like an avenging Fury. "She was having Lambert's baby. That's why she went to meet him on Purley Head. You killed two people when you strangled Sarah. And yet you say you didn't kill the child's father!"

But Treduggan said nothing more. The news of his daughter's pregnancy had left him speechless and aghast. Roberts ended the interview formally and returned Treduggan to his cell. He faced Thorn across the desk, still aware of something unfamiliar and a sense of menace in the air.

"Do you think he is lying about Lambert?" he asked.

"He has to be. What kind of religious maniac would punish his own daughter by murdering her, yet not even have a go at the man who had led her astray? He says he couldn't hear what they said, that they didn't do anything, but talk. A lovers' tryst at two in the morning and they only talked? And the outraged parent didn't even get close enough to identify his daughter's lover? No! He did it!"

The doctor called later to explain he would be carrying out his second autopsy the following day. "It's a very bad business, this one," he said.

"It's the connection with Lambert that interests me," said Thorn.

"Lambert? What's the connection?" Cooper was startled.

"Lambert was the father of Sarah's unborn child," explains Thorn.

101

"Lambert! Good God, no!" exclaimed Cooper. "I wish it were that simple."

"What do you mean?" asked Thorn," Lambert wasn't her lover?"

"Lambert wasn't the father." The doctor looked worldly weary. He sat down on the edge of the desk, pushed his spectacles up on his nose, then he ran his hand over his head in a sign of despair. "The baby was Treduggan's. Sarah told me he's been having sex with her ever since his wife died; that's why I was so worried about her, and why I went out to see her this morning. I was going to try to get her to agree to an abortion."

Chapter 7

Cooper's news was a bombshell. The anger which Thorn could still feel, lodged in his chest like an indigestible lump, gave way briefly to an intense disgust, as though he had plunged into some stinking corruption. For a while he floundered, drowning, and he was forced to turn away from the other two men until he felt more in control. He waved an arm weakly and groped in vain for words.

"Are you sure of this?" It was Roberts who spoke first.

"It was the girl herself who told me. She was in a pretty bad state, Sergeant."

"You don't think she was – well, making it up?"

Cooper gave him a straight look, "Which would you think was worse, to admit you were pregnant by a married man, or to admit you had been molested for years by your own father, and that you were carrying his child?"

"But if you're right, Doctor, this statement," he tapped the recording tape on the desk, "this is a pack of lies."

"Again, Sergeant, what do you think is worse for a professed religious bigot, to admit to killing his daughter as a punishment for her sin, or to confess to committing incest?"

"What we need to know," Thorn interrupted, "is whether the girl," - it was somehow slightly more bearable not to use her name - "is whether she did indeed have any contact with the dead man. Was Treduggan inventing the whole thing?"

"Sarah never mentioned another man to me," said the doctor.

"Is there any chance at all that the child might have been Lambert's?"

"She was about eight weeks pregnant."

"And Lambert was in Chichester until three weeks ago." Roberts observed.

"So, Treduggan's story about following his daughter up to Purley Head might be a pack of lies."

"How would he know about Lambert being up there on Wednesday night?"

"He might have picked up some of the gossip. After all, your friend, Ben Jacobs, knew about the body the same morning."

Roberts gave this some thought. "He was pretty accurate about the time, all things considered," he observed. "How would he have known Lambert was up on the Head at one in the morning, when he says he followed Sarah there?"

"There's something distinctly wrong with all this," Thorn said. "We can't believe anything Treduggan says. He's obviously made a false statement, but why would he drag Lambert into it, unless there was some connection?"

"Perhaps there was," said Roberts. "We don't really know much about Lambert's movements."

"Someone must have seen the two of them together at some time," said Cooper. "This is a small place."

"If there really was any connection between them," added Thorn.

"Treduggan says they met at the shop," said Roberts. "Shall I ask a few questions there?"

"Right," said Thorn.

Roberts left with the doctor. Thorn was glad to be on his own for a while until he felt he had mastered his feelings. This was turning out to be a damnable affair. He recalled with bitter irony his thoughts on the helicopter, when he had seen Lambert as the serpent in this paradise, who had poisoned it with his petty crook's venom. Some paradise, he thought to himself. Beneath the calm surface there was a sordid mess which the girl's death had revealed. Thorn was accustomed in his work to dealing with the less palatable elements in an urban society, but he had come here on leave and, like most tourists, he had taken the island and its inhabitants at face value. He had forgotten his habitual guard, his breastplate of cynicism, and had looked at his surroundings, as far as he could, naïvely. He had thought to find a healing property in the romantic scenery and he had been allowing himself the unaccustomed luxury of self-delusion, allowing himself to be an ordinary human being. It had come as a shock to be confronted by some of the more vjle aspects of human nature, even to one so familiar with them.

What he found especially hard to accept was the conflict between his intellectual understanding of his own reaction, and his emotions. Reason told him the deaths of his wife, his daughter, his son-in-law, his grandchild had all, indeed, been an accident in which he could not have acted otherwise. It was the other driver who had been at fault, and he had paid for it with his life. Yet the guilt persisted, the guilt of the survivor. And his intense, unreasoning anger towards Treduggan was, he knew, an extension of that guilt; Treduggan had betrayed and violated Sarah, and then he had killed her deliberately, knowingly. At another time Thorn would have been able to remain detached. He would have seen Treduggan as the criminal or as the suspect, not as an evil and personally repugnant creature, whom he would, given half a chance, attack with his bare hands. It was not only a dangerous complication in the case, but it was debilitating. It was sapping his energy, energy he could ill afford.

He turned his attention to other matters. His abrupt departure for Chichester had forced the postponement of the formal interviews with the Jefferies. He would set about rearranging them. Rather than telephone the Smuggler's he decided to walk. It was a relief to leave the office, where the interview with Treduggan and Cooper's revelation hung on the air like a bad smell. Outside, the busy street at least appeared normal, with nothing to suggest malice. The sun still shone and ordinary people went about their everyday business.

He reached the Smuggler's and went in. It was not very busy; Thorn looked at his watch and realised it was four in the afternoon. He had not given a thought to the time, and he suddenly realised he was hungry; he had not eaten since breakfast. Jefferies was serving at the other end of the bar and Thorn bought his beer and a sandwich from the smiling Jenny. He found a seat at an empty table and ate with pleasure.

"Inspector!" He looked up to find Jefferies standing over him, looking hostile.

"Mr Jefferies?"

"Can we have a word in private?"

"Of course." Thorn got to his feet and Jefferies led the way through the bar into the private apartments. Jenny watched them covertly as they left the functional ugliness of the pub and entered the rich, red womb of the stairwell.

"I'm sorry I had to postpone the interviews with you and Mrs Jefferies," Thorn began. "I expect Sergeant Roberts explained I was called away."

Jefferies merely grunted to show he had heard. They reached the door to the flat. Jefferies went in and held the door for Thorn to follow. Thora Jefferies looked up as they entered and rose from her chair by the fire. Penny, to whom she had evidently been talking, turned and stared.

"Penny," said her father, "this is Inspector Thorn." At the name the girl's face assumed a quite different expression of anger.

"So, you are the man!" She observed.

"I am the man who what?" asked Thorn. "And my rank, by the way, is Superintendent."

"What on earth do you mean by crashing in on my friends and asking questions about me behind my back?"

"Ah!" Light dawned. "You've been talking to your flatmates in Chichester."

"Correction," she said; "they've been talking to me. They rang me yesterday evening to say a policeman had called at the flat asking questions about me."

"Well, that is true," Thorn admitted.

"It's an intrusion on my privacy!" She was clearly not going to be easily appeased.

"You had no right to interview Penelope's friends behind her back," her mother joined in. "Have you any idea of the mischief you might cause?"

"Mischief?" The word seemed grotesque. In the middle of a murder enquiry and with the memory of the Treduggan affair still clogging his perception, Thorn found the idea of mischief bizarre in its inappropriateness. "How can you possibly suggest that a police enquiry could be the cause of mischief, Mrs Jefferies?"

"Reputations are fragile," Mrs Jefferies replied. "The very fact that you have been asking questions about my daughter and her friends in some minds gives rise to unfortunate innuendos."

"Mrs Jefferies," Thorn was trying to be patient, "no innocent person ever suffers from a few simple questions from the police."

"That is pure nonsense!" Thora Jefferies was stung. "There are many people, innocent people, who have been falsely accused or who have been associated with a crime, although they have actually been found innocent in a court of law, people whose lives have been ruined. There is no smoke without fire, people say. You have no right whatsoever to damage my daughter's good name by association."

Thorn attempted to understand and to placate her. "I'm sorry if you have got the wrong impression," he said, "but I think you have this all out of proportion. Your daughter's friends were both very helpful and certainly gave me no cause to think anything but good of her."

"That is hardly the point, Inspector." Thorn suspected the mistake in rank was deliberate this time, but he forbore. "Reputations are very easily soiled and for a young woman her reputation is very important."

"Miss Jefferies," said Thorn, "I don't know what your friends told you, but I merely asked them a few questions I would happily have asked you directly."

"You were asking about my boyfriends."

"Yes, nothing specific, except to ask if you ever met Mr Lambert socially."

"Lambert?" She looked genuinely surprised. "Do you mean the man who was staying here last week?"

"Yes."

"Why ever would I want to meet a man of his age?"

"I didn't say you did, Miss Jefferies. I merely asked."

"Did he come from Chichester, then?"

"You mean you didn't know?"

"No. Why should I?"

"There's no reason you should, I suppose. Have you ever met him?"

"I don't think so. I only know about him because of what my parents have told me. He was staying here when he had an accident and was killed."

"In that case," said Thorn, "I don't think I need to bother you any further. Of course," he added, "I shall still need formal statements from you, Mrs Jefferies, and you, Mr Jefferies."

"Haven't you done enough harm?" Thora Jefferies was still belligerent. It was hostility Thorn had met often in the past, but which he found in all criminals or, at least, potential criminals, alienated from the law by misplaced idealism. He found it frequently in protesters, in those who pretended to be defending their rights, trying to deny the rights of others. It was an attitude which seemed very inappropriate in Thora Jefferies, who gave every appearance of a middle-class lady with great regard for her own standing.

"Perhaps you could both come down to the station tomorrow morning and we can take statements then."

"OK." It was George Jefferies who answered before his wife could speak. Thorn caught the warning glance between them,,but failed to make sense of it. Penny also looked faintly puzzled. She turned her back like a sulky child.

"Say between nine and ten."

"Right."

"Now I'll go and finish my sandwich."

No more was said, and Jefferies accompanied Thorn back to the bar, where he found his place at the table. It was a good thing the pub stayed open all day in the season, he thought. At least he could satisfy his hunger.

As on his previous visit to the Smuggler's Arms, Thorn sensed another mystery. George Jefferies remained an enigmatic figure. His wife was a different kind of puzzle; her manner, her dress, her appearance generally was carefully groomed, respectable, expensive. She resented the merest suggestion of an intrusion into her family affairs, even when it had been in the nature of a simple enquiry into her daughter's life at university in Chichester. She seemed almost paranoid about her daughter's reputation; her reaction had been more in keeping with that of a Victorian Mama than a modern mother. And yet this same woman had accepted a lodger, Lambert, into her home – for the contrast between the business premises and the opulently furnished flat was so marked that one sensed the absolute distinction between the public bar and private home – and she had accepted Lambert, apparently without showing any interest at all in his comings and goings.

He could not face returning immediately to the office. Instead, he turned away from the town and walked steadily in the afternoon sunshine towards Purley Head. He passed half a dozen walkers strolling for pleasure. At the fork in the path he turned left and climbed until he stood once more by the Standing Stone on the summit. There was just a trace of haze blurring the horizon, otherwise it was idyllic. He could hear the restless sound of the sea at the foot of the cliff and, half a mile away across the water, someone was hammering; the musical noise of metal on metal reminded him that work goes on. Above, the air was full of the sound of skylarks, their trailing song falling as they dropped towards the springy turf. He sat down and gazed out at the scene for a while.

Why had Lambert come here at 2 o'clock in the morning? Who had he come to meet? There were three possibilities so far: Clapton, McNab, and Sarah Treduggan. He considered each in turn.

Clapton had lied about making contact with Lambert. They had an independent witness to the fact that the two men had not only met, but also indulged in some kind of fight in Church Street. That was shortly after closing time on Wednesday night. Brenda Lambert had intervened to stop the fight. Could Clapton have arranged to meet Lambert later? If he had, why had Lambert's wife not intervened again? Would she not have argued against it? Or was there more to that encounter than met the eye? On the other hand, if Brenda Lambert had been privy to the arrangements to meet, why had they not met in the caravan? It would surely be unnecessary to walk all the way up here. And if Brenda knew nothing about the rendezvous, how had Lambert and Clapton managed to arrange it without her knowing, presumably after their fight in Church Street?

As for McNab, he remained the joker in the pack. It seemed very reasonable to suppose his presence on the island was far from a coincidence; that both Lambert and his wife had turned up at the same time could be by chance, given that both of them had visited the place frequently in the past. But McNab? That was surely highly improbable. He may well have come here to settle his score with Lambert, and perhaps it had been McNab who sought somewhere isolated with no possibility of anyone seeing him; he was still wanted, and must know he was wanted, for the security van job in Chichester in April. So far it made sense, but why should Lambert have agreed to meet him? Unless he had been coerced into it, it would seem to be an extremely foolish thing to do, to agree to a meeting in an isolated spot like this, in the dead of night, with the man whose brother he had killed, a man who had a criminal record for GBH. And how could McNab, a stranger to the island, within one day of his arrival have set up such a trap that Lambert would fall into?

That left Sarah Treduggan. Unless Roberts came up with something, there was only Job Treduggan's evidence of any connection between Sarah and Lambert. What kind of girl, Thorn wondered, would be capable of having an affair with another man while being forced into an incestuous relationship with her father? The picture drawn for him by Roberts did little to suggest the girl had been a raving nymphomaniac; the doctor's comment that she was "in a terrible state" seemed to contradict that image. Yet a romantic assignation fitted the time and the place better than anything else he had considered so far. But Job Treduggan had been lying. What if the connection had been invented or – and this idea clicked suddenly into place – what if the connection had been essentially innocent, but perceived by Treduggan as a threat in some way? Perhaps his mind was already wavering on the edge of madness, and he had seen his daughter in conversation with Lambert. He saw in Lambert a possible rival, or even someone in whom Sarah might confide her dreadful secret, and, in a panic, he had decided he must get rid of him. He might have arranged a meeting, perhaps in Sarah's name, and gone with the intention of killing Lambert. That would account for his knowing about the time Lambert was here.

Thorn stood up in irritation at the way his mind was wandering into the realm of wild conjecture. The fact was that they did not have enough evidence on which to proceed and to build any hypotheses. This was mere fanciful imagination. There was no forensic team to help. And with that thought he recalled emptying the freezer bags on a tray and examining the contents. There had been nothing but cigarette ends, small stones and two crisp packets. Since he was close to the Standing Stone, he took another look at the area. This time he looked a little further from the base of the stone, checking in cracks and crevices where the wind might have been at work. Ten minutes bent double produced a muddy piece of cardboard which had been a box containing a 35 mm film, yet more cigarette stubs and a small coin, a two-penny piece. Thorn picked everything up, wrapped it in a clean tissue and turned back towards the town once more.

Roberts had been thorough. He had questioned Mrs Davies, the owner of the baker's shop, about any customers who had taken a special interest in Sarah. Mrs Davies had been upset at the news of Sarah's death and very shocked. "She was such a lovely young slip of a girl," she observed. "In spite of that dreadful father of hers. You'd think to hear the way they talk that some people had never known what it's like to be young. That awful religious bunch he mixes with; according to them, it's a sin to open your eyes in the morning or to wash your face in case some man or other sees you and thinks you'm good-looking. What happened to her, my lover?"

"We're not sure how it happened," Roberts prevaricated. "We'd best leave that side of it to the coroner."

"Coroner! You mean there's going to be an inquest, then?"

"Yes, it's routine in the case of a sudden death like this."

"And you don't know how she came to die?"

"Not really. Look, Mrs Davies, this hasn't got anything to do with Sarah's death, but it's more in connection with other enquiries. We'd have been asking Sarah herself, if she'd still been alive."

"And what is it you'm be wanting to know then?"

"We think Sarah may have met somebody, a man, maybe more than once or twice."

"And how do you think I would know about things like that?"

"The man in question was a visitor, a man called Matthew Lambert. We have reason to believe he came into the shop a few times and got to know Sarah here."

"Goodness, gracious me! We get thousands of visitors in the shop every week, Sergeant, you know that."

"Yes, I know that, Mrs Davies, but this man was a bit special."

"Special? In what way?"

"I think Sarah met him outside the shop as well."

"A boyfriend, you mean?" Mrs Davies' round face was all concern. The shiny, red forehead puckered in a frown. "I don't recollect Sarah ever spending any time talking to youngsters, or talking about a young man who set his sights on her, for that matter."

"Lambert wasn't exactly a young man, Mrs Davies."

"Here, what are you suggesting? You suggesting young Sarah was carrying on with an older man?"

"Not carrying on, no, meeting him, perhaps." Roberts took out of his pocket a copy of the photograph of Matthew Lambert. Mrs Davies squinted at it.

"I've seen this one before," she said slowly. "He's been in here several times. But he's old enough to be Sarah's father!"

"Do you think Sarah might have been seeing him outside working hours? Did she ever talk to you about him?"

"Not in so many words, no," said Mrs Davies, "but, come to think of it, he did seem to come in either just when Sarah was off to her lunch break, or just on closing time."

"But she never mentioned him by name, Matthew Lambert?"

Again, Mrs Davies frowned, thinking back. "No, I don't think so."

"Can you think back to last Wednesday? Did Lambert come into the shop then?"

"I remember last Wednesday. Sarah was in a funny old state, not her cheerful self at all. I asked her if something was worrying her, but whatever it was, she wasn't telling me. I was getting quite worried about her. Anyway, she was like that all day. And your friend here," she waved the photograph about, "he came in just on closing time. I was busy serving at the other end of the shop, but Sarah spoke to him. Come to think of it, it seemed to be a serious sort of conversation."

"Do you know if he was waiting for her when you closed?"

"I didn't see him. And Sarah didn't dare linger about or her father would be after me. He's done that before now, you know; came storming in here one morning because Sarah was half-an-hour late one night. She had a puncture that time."

"So, you don't know what she talked about with Lambert?"

"No. Is it important, then?"

"Could be, very."

"Well, then," she bent forward confidentially, "don't tell her as I told you, but Joyce Luckett was in here at the time, and she was waiting for Sarah to serve her. Well, you know what a long nose she has. I expect she was craning her neck like a hunting dog, trying to hear what was being said."

"Thank you, Mrs Davies. That's a great help."

"That's all right, my lover. How is Tina? I haven't seen her for two or three days."

"She's fine." And Roberts left the baker's to make his way to a small house in Church Street to talk to Joyce Luckett.

Mrs Luckett was one of those busybodies who love to hear talk of others, but who have a paranoid dread of any scandal about themselves. The sight of Roberts in uniform on her doorstep roused apprehension and resentment: what would the neighbours think when they saw a policeman at her door? Her heart was pounding in her thin rib cage as she opened the door, having first peered around the lace curtains.

"What in heaven's name do you want here, Sergeant?" she asked nervously.

"Just a word, Mrs Luckett."

"What about?"

"Can I come in?"

She hesitated briefly, then stood aside to let him in, looking quickly up and down the street before she closed the door. Roberts' big frame filled the tiny hall. Mrs Luckett reached around him to open the door to the parlour, used on the rarest of occasions. Everything shone. An old harmonium stood in the corner with a Methodist hymnbook on top. The light was dim behind thick curtains.

There was barely room to sit down except at a table, covered by a thick, red cloth.

"Mrs Luckett," Roberts began, "I believe you were in Mrs Davies' shop last Wednesday afternoon."

"I expect so; I go in there most days. I do like fresh bread, you know, Sergeant. You can get cheaper bread at the Co-op, I know, but it's that sliced stuff. I don't know why Mrs Davies charges quite so much for hers, but..."

"Yes," Roberts cut her off, "well, if you can remember back then, you had to wait to be served."

Mrs Luckett sniffed. "That's not unusual, either. It's all the visitors, you know. And she could easily take on some extra help in the summer. It's scandalous the way we locals, who've lived here all our lives, have to wait just to buy a loaf of bread or a saffron bun."

"Do you remember queueing up last Wednesday?"

"Last Wednesday? What's so special about then? Oh, that was the day before they found that dead man at Purley Head, wasn't it?"   "

"That's right." Once more Roberts took the photograph from his pocket. "Do you recognise this man?"

"That's the man in the shop!" Mrs Luckett exclaimed with the triumphant air of one who has just struck gold. "He was in Mrs Davies' shop talking to Sarah Treduggan. I thought to myself there's something going on there. You'd have thought she'd known him for years, the way she was talking to him."

"Did you hear anything she said?"

"What do you take me for? I'm not an old tittle-tattle, you know. I don't go listing to other people's conversations!"

"No, of course not," said Roberts soothingly, "it's just that you were standing close to them, so you might have overheard what they said."

"What's he done, then?" She narrowed her eyes, delighted with anticipation of learning new secrets.

"He's dead," said Roberts.

"Dead! You don't mean he's..."

"Yes, he's the man on Purley Head."

"And to think I was standing this closed to him!"

"Yes," Roberts kept his patience. "So, please, did you hear what Lambert and Sarah Treduggan talked about?"

"Why don't you ask Sarah? I mean, they were whispering together, so maybe she'd rather keep it to herself."

"Mrs Luckett," Roberts said, "I can't ask Sarah at the moment. She's... indisposed."

"Oh, I'm sorry to hear that," said the woman, "I thought she'd been looking a bit peaky these last few days. Nothing serious, I hope?"

"Please tell me what you heard last Wednesday."

"I didn't hear anything much." She was mildly affronted by Roberts' insistence. "They were whispering, and the man – this man – he seemed to be trying to calm her down. Sarah kept looking around as though other people might overhear. It sounded as if they were making some sort of arrangement to meet later."

"You don't recall exactly what they said?"

"Not exactly. I couldn't hear what they said at all except when he went out of the shop."

"So, what did he say then?"

"He said something that sounded like 'stone, 1 o'clock'."

"'Stone 1 o'clock'. You're sure?"

"That's what it sounded like. It didn't make sense to me."

"Was there anyone else in the queue who might have heard this?"

"The place was packed. If Sarah hadn't finished her conversation there and then, I would have walked out, but then I was the next in line."

"Who else was in the shop at the time? Do you remember?"

"There were two or three visitors, that stuck up Mrs Jefferies from the Smuggler's, old Mrs Poulter, Joe Blackie and that young Julie Kernow."

"Think back a bit," said Roberts. "Did one of the visitors have red hair?"

"Now you come to mention it," said Mrs Luckett, "there was one man who had red hair and a beard as well. He was standing behind me. Why? Do you know who he is?"

"Maybe."

"The funny thing was, that when this man," again the emphatic wave of Lambert's picture, "when this man left, the red-headed man seemed to be hiding from him. He dodged behind the big stand they've got loaded with tins of biscuits and things. And he didn't wait to be served, either."

"You mean he left?"

"As soon as the first one stepped outside, the red-headed one left as well. Almost as if he was following."

Roberts stood up. "Well, thank you for your help," he said, and turned for the door.

"What's all this about, Sergeant?"

"It's just routine, Mrs Luckett." And she had to be content with that.

Thorn, listening to all this, was again impressed by Roberts' good sense. "McNab," he mused, "red hair and a new beard? Could be."

"And he overheard Lambert arranging to meet young Sarah at the Standing Stone at one o'clock. It's a ready-made opportunity to tackle Lambert on his own before or after he met Sarah."

"A bit risky, though, with a witness on the spot."

"Maybe it was just an opportunity. If he could get Lambert on his own, before or after Sarah arrived...Well done, Sergeant. It's another piece in the puzzle."

"What we want now is for McNab to turn up."

It had been a grim, tiring kind of day. Thorn sat in an armchair in the Roberts' sitting room, aware of the covert observation of Tina's eyes over her knitting. She was practised enough in her role of a policeman's wife not to ask questions, but her concern, though not expressed in words, was clear to Thorn. He was trying to be honest with himself about his ability to cope with this enquiry. He was emotionally involved, and in normal circumstances would have told any subordinate in the same position to give up the investigation. Unfortunately, the circumstances were against him, and his hesitation was brought to an abrupt end when Roberts turned on the News at Ten. The main item was the discovery of a bomb at the security conference. It was immediately obvious that there was absolutely no hope now of his being replaced by an investigating officer from the mainland.

Thorn hardly answered when both the Roberts began an interested discussion of the news. He was almost indifferent to the indignation and dismay which they exhibited at the intrusion of international terrorism into their peaceful corner of rural England. He was thinking only that he was now trapped until the murder of Matthew Lambert had been resolved. In the circumstances, he pondered, it might be best to speak to Doctor Cooper about his own mental condition. At least, then he would have made a formal note of the facts, just in case his behaviour, God forbid, should become irrational.

"Would you like a milky drink, Superintendent?" asked Tina, putting away her knitting.

The phone rang as Thorn smiled yes. Roberts handed him the receiver. It was Clegg, calling from Chichester. "McNab is back," he said, "at least we're pretty sure it's him."

"What's happened?"

"A man answering McNab's description did Clough over tonight. Clough's in hospital. Couple of broken ribs, badly cut face – a razor job – concussion."

"Clough! Why should McNab have a go at Clough?"

"Good question. That's one of the things I'll be asking him as soon as we've got him. Maybe he blames both Clough and Lambert for his brother's death. They were both in the van, when the van drove into his car."

"What chance of catching him this time?" Thorn frowned into the receiver.

"He's in the city somewhere. We got road blocks up. According to our witness, McNab has a beard now, by the way."

"Get him," Thorn said. "I want a word with that bastard."

"I'll let you know the moment we get him."

"Thanks."

"Might have been better if you'd stayed on for a couple more days."

"No, things have taken another turn here, too."

"Okay. Stand by for an early call."

Thorn replaced the receiver and passed the information to Roberts.

"A complete nutter, is he?" the Sergeant commented.

"Who knows? Let's hope they catch him soon."

Sleep was slow to come and, when it did, was full of unpleasant dreams and floating visions in which the girl's face, staring at him in the tawdry mirror, filled him with horror as he confused her with his daughter. He knew it was not Alice lying there, yet his feelings were strong, and he woke up in the dark, choked with emotion, and sat up, his heart pounding. The house was silent, but the sound of the sea called him to the window, and he leaned on the sill and stared at its restless darkness. He stood there for an hour until he felt numb with fatigue. He climbed back into bed and slept.

Chapter 8

Tina Roberts took one look at Thorn at breakfast and said nothing. His face showed signs of wear. He had a headache and was grateful not to have to make conversation. Roberts followed his wife's example and, as soon as he had finished eating, he left the table to make his way into the office.

Thorn joined him there shortly afterwards. The two men worked silently at their notes until the Jefferies arrived to make their statements. There was no reason to keep them apart, although Thorn began with George Jefferies, and then, to the annoyance of the pair of them, took a separate statement from his wife.

They told him nothing new. Lambert had turned up unexpectedly on June 21 looking for accommodation. George Jefferies had been in the bar at the time and had called his wife. After a brief conversation she had agreed to take Lambert as a guest, paying bed-and-breakfast rates of £140 per week. He had agreed as soon as he had seen the room and he had paid three weeks in advance.

"Did he pay cash?" Thorn asked.

"Yes." Mrs Jefferies looked mildly defiant, as though challenging him. He wondered if she thought twenty pounds per night was expensive and was on the defensive. No, she was not the kind to feel guilty about charging the going rate.

"Exactly how did he pay, Mrs Jefferies? With large denomination notes?"

"Tens and twenties, I think."

"So, he handed over £420 in cash?"

"Yes."

"Did he have any other money in his wallet?"

"I don't know." Again, the impatient tone. "I didn't pry. All I know is, he gave me the right money."

"And you gave him a receipt?"

A pause, she looked uncomfortable. "I suppose so," she said. She glanced at her husband. His stare gave nothing away. "I don't remember giving him a receipt there and then. Perhaps I didn't have a receipt book to hand."

"No doubt you'll have the carbon copy, if you wrote one later," suggested Thorn.

"What is this?" George Jefferies interrupted, "You trying to catch us cheating the taxman or something?"

Thorn gave him a cold look. "That isn't what I had in mind," he said. "But Lambert failed to draw any money from his bank account before he set out for the Islands. I'm curious to know how he came by more than £400 in cash. There was no receipt in his wallet when we found it, but there was some other money."

The rest of the interview revealed nothing of any interest. Both the Jefferies stuck to their account of the events of Wednesday evening and night. Lambert had returned to the Smuggler's before midnight and seemed to have gone out again about 1 o'clock in the morning. Now she had given the matter some thought, Thora Jefferies was quite sure they had locked up and retired to their flat just before one that night – they had not been too busy for once. And she was also quite sure she had heard someone moving about on the stairs just after that. She had assumed it was Lambert. He hadn't ever brought anyone back to his room.

"What about the burglar alarm?" Bill Roberts' intervened. "Wasn't that set?"

"That's set from inside the bar," said George Jefferies. "The private accommodation is outside the alarm area."

Thorn sat and looked at his notes. "Had you met Lambert before?" he asked.

There was an involuntary turn of the head from the woman to look quickly at her husband. He looked away from her as if deliberately ignoring her. Thorn was puzzled. It was an innocent question.

"What do you mean?" she asked, as though buying time.

"Lambert had visited Scilly several times before." Thorn explained. "I believe he usually stayed at one of the hotels, but I wondered if he had dropped in at the Smuggler's."

Thora Jefferies fumbled in her handbag and took out a small handkerchief. Her hand showed the slightest tremor. "He may have been there," she said, "but I don't remember it. We get a lot of visitors, you know."

Thorn turned to George Jefferies. "Did you ever see him before?" He asked.

"I don't remember him."

"Well, if either of you do remember anything else, anything you think might be of help, let us know."

"Is that it?" George asked, "Can we go?"

Thorn nodded. "Yes. We'll get the statements written up and ask you to read them through and sign them."

The Jefferies left. The two policemen looked at one another, sharing the same doubts. Thorn, beginning to feel very tired as the investigation continued without becoming much clearer, was growing steadily more aware of

125

unanswered questions that seemed to be increasing daily. Where had Lambert got his money? Why had McNab returned to Chichester and attacked Clough so savagely that he was now in hospital in intensive care? Above all, had Lambert gone to Purley Head at one in the morning to meet Sarah Treduggan? What had been his relationship with Sarah? If they were lovers, had Lambert known of Job Treduggan's activities? That seemed unlikely, for he would surely have done something about it. Or would he, Thorn asked himself? Perhaps Lambert was the most despicable of men, who had merely used Sarah as a sexual object, and who had no other feelings for her. Yet, if that were true, why was he willing to meet her at the Standing Stone in the middle of the night?

"It seems to me, sir," said Roberts, interrupting his thoughts, "that the deeper we dig, the less we uncover. We still don't really know much about Lambert, do we?"

"Where would you get hold of £500 or more without going to the bank or drawing your salary?" Thorn wondered.

"Wish I knew the answer to that, sir. I could do with that sort of money myself."

"You could sell something," mused Thorn, "but what could you sell that's worth that kind of money?"

"A car?"

"That's possible."

"Maybe someone owed him the money and coughed up just before Lambert left Chichester."

Thorn picked up the telephone and called Chichester. Clegg was not in the office, and Thorn left a message for him to call back. The sergeant who took the call had no news of the injured man. Thorn put down the phone with a frown of frustration.

"Sergeant," he said, "drive up to the caravan site and find Clapton and Mrs Lambert. It's time we asked them a few more questions."

He was in luck; Roberts found the couple at the caravan and within half-an-hour they were back in the police station. Mrs Lambert looked apprehensive, Clapton was again on his guard.

"You stated that you did not speak to Matthew Lambert when you saw him waiting for you outside the Pirate last Wednesday evening."

"That's right," Clapton agreed.

"We have a witness who states that she saw you, both of you, in Church Street at about 11 o'clock that evening in conversation with Mr Lambert." At this the two looked at one another, but said nothing.

"Do you still maintain you didn't speak?"

"Why does your so-called witness think it was us? At that time of night the Pirate was just beginning to empty. It could have been anybody she saw."

"I don't think so, Mr Clapton. She also formally identified Lambert from his photograph."

It was Brenda Lambert who broke in: "Tell him, Peter!" Clapton frowned, gathering his thoughts. Thorn waited.

"All right," said Clapton, "so, Matthew did speak to us."

"What about?"

"The usual. He said he just wanted to talk to Brenda. I told him to sod off. Remember the court injunction, I told him; we'd have the law on him."

"But he didn't go?"

"No. He just said he wanted to talk to Brenda, not to me."

"So?"

"I warned him again, but he wouldn't back off, he just got more and more uptight and aggressive. In the end I went to push him away, but he took a swing at me. We ended up having a bit of a bundle."

"How did it finish?"

"I screamed at them to stop," said Brenda. "They didn't at first, then they stopped thumping one another and looked at me."

"What did you say exactly?" asked Thorn.

"I told Matt that if he really cared for me, he'd want what was best for me."

"And that made him stop?"

"I don't know if that was the reason. He said,' I don't love you, you bitch! I never did. But I'll get even with you one way or another.' Then Peter sort of swung him round and gave him a push, and he stumbled away. He didn't follow us any further."

"And why didn't you tell us all this when you made your first statement?" Thorn asked.

"You wouldn't have believed it," said Clapton.

"I might have been more prepared to believe you were telling the truth then, I'm less inclined to now, since you have obviously been lying so far."

"This is the truth."

"I want you to think very carefully, Mr Clapton, before you answer the next question. Did you make any arrangement with Matthew Lambert to meet him later that evening?"

"No." The answer was immediate, with just the right touch of indignation. "We had a bit of a fight, Matt shouted at Brenda, I pushed him away, and we watched him stumble away towards the town for a bit, before we headed back to the caravan."

"Neither of you saw him again?"

"No, I told you."

"So, describe how you spent the next two or three hours."

"We've already told you."

"So, tell us again."

"What for?"

"You've lied to us once already, Mr Clapton."

"You can't blame him, Superintendent, can you?" Brenda Lambert interrupted. "Knowing what you know now, you were bound to suspect Peter of having something to do with Matt's death. He didn't go out at night. We spent the night in the caravan."

"And you went straight to sleep?"

"No, of course not. We were both upset after the fight."

"So, what time did you go to bed?"

"We sat up with a drink for an hour or so, I suppose."

"How long before you went to sleep?"

"I don't know." She was searching her memory. "Maybe half-an-hour after we got to bed."

"So, Mr Clapton could have got up and slipped out after you were asleep."

"No. I'm a light sleeper. And I went to sleep with Peter's arms round me. He'd have woken me if he moved."

Thorn was silent for a moment, then, "Do you know if Mr Lambert had any private resources?" He asked.

"What do you mean?" Brenda Lambert looked perplexed by the question.

"What I say, Mrs Lambert: did he have any sources of income apart from his job as a security guard?"

"No, not as far as I know," she said, her forehead creased.

"Was he short of money? Well off?"

"I don't know," she said. "He wasn't paying any alimony, so he had only himself to keep. I don't know what he had."

"But as far as you know, he didn't have any other source of income?"

"No."

"What's all this about?" asked Clapton.

"You'd known Matthew Lambert for fifteen years, you said?"

"Yes."

"How would you describe him?"

"What do you mean?"

"Generous? Kind? Thoughtful? Intelligent? Stupid? Selfish?"

"You already know what I think of him, Superintendent."

"I know that you discovered he was – er – unkind to his wife."

"Unkind!" Clapton was on his feet. "He was bloody vicious."

"Yet up to then, Mr Clapton, you had remained friends, good friends, it would appear, all through your time in the Marines together."

"That was different."

"Perhaps," Thorn picked up a paper knife and toyed with it. "You must have liked him then."

Clapton was at a loss for words, seeing his past relationship with the dead man all at once in a new light. "He was a different bloke then," he said finally, his voice quiet as he remembered.

"Tell me about it."

"I've told you once. We were both tearaways to begin with. We weren't all that old, remember. You see, that's one of the things the services do for you. They give you a ready-made set of rules – Queens Regulations. You know where you stand. If you break the rules, you know you're taking a chance. You don't worry about what's right or wrong, only what you can reasonably get away with."

"What about women, Mr Clapton? Was he what you might call a womaniser?"

"He was – well, normal. You know what it's like in the forces, I expect."

"Tell me."

"There's nothing much to tell. When you've been at sea for a few weeks at a time, well, you go for a run ashore, spend an hour or two in a pub, pick up a girl, a scrubber, maybe. Nothing serious."

"So, Lambert was good company for a run ashore?"

"He was okay."

"One of the boys, you'd say?"

"Not the way I'd put it."

"So, how would you put it?"

"I don't know. We were oppos."

"Oppos?"

"Good mates." Clapton was silent a moment, then, almost reluctantly, he added, "I suppose he did have his good side."

"In what way?"

"One of the things you come to take for granted is that your life can depend on your oppo doing his stuff."

Thorn, not fully understanding, kept quiet.

"I mean, like when we were doing our diving course. You have to work in pairs, you see, for safety's sake. If one of you gets into difficulties, it's your oppo who has to come to sort you out. You could always depend on Matt. Any of the blokes would work with him, though he didn't really have any close friends. He never let anyone down once he'd committed himself. Yes, I suppose he was good in that way."

"Not completely selfish, then?" Thorn prompted.

"No, I suppose not." Clapton thought back. "And he could even be quite soft sometimes."

"Soft?" It sounded an odd word, applied to an ex-marine commando.

"He was a pushover for animals. He once nearly beat up one chap in Italy because he was being cruel to a donkey."

Thorn made an impatient gesture; kindness to animals, worthy though it was, was not somehow very relevant to his enquiries.

"He was a bit of a sucker for kids, too," said Clapton. "Early on we were out East, and somehow or other we got ourselves shanghaied by the Chaplain. He took us to an orphanage. Anyway, to cut a long story short, Matt ended up sponsoring one of the kids, a girl it was, a bright young thing she was and all. He paid five pounds a week towards her education for the next ten years! Last I heard, she had got herself a job in a bank in Hong Kong. Amazing, really. five pounds a week for ten years!"

By the look on Brenda Lambert's face, this came as news to her. Clapton caught sight of her expression. "Didn't you know?" He asked.

"No."

"Well, you know he was a sucker for kids?"

"Well," a slight pause, almost embarrassed, then, "yes, I realised he liked them."

"Yet you never had a child?" Thorn prompted.

"I told you," said Brenda Lambert, angrily defensive, "I can't have children after what Matt did to me."

"When did this particular assault take place, Mrs Lambert?"

"The year after we got married."

Thorn frowned, looking down at his desk-top. "But if your husband was as keen on children, and you were married for the whole year…"

"I don't see why I have to answer such personal questions," Brenda Lambert looked red in the face now, a mixture of embarrassment and anger.

"I'm sorry I I have to ask them," said Thorn. "Remember, I only have your word for it that it was your husband's assault on you which affected you in this way."

"I think that's enough," said Clapton, rising to Brenda's defence once more. "Don't you think it's enough

133

for us to have to accept we can't have children, without you actually suggesting we might be lying? What would we do that for?" He glared defiantly at the policeman.

"Very well," Thorn concluded the interview and the couple left. But he was still left with the feeling that he had only part of the story. Witnesses who forgot to mention things that had happened were generally trustworthy; those who deliberately concealed evidence were much more suspect in everything they said. And there was an obvious conflict here; the wife who claimed her dead husband had abused her, and evidence that he must have wanted children. They must have been in their early thirties when they married and would surely have thought of starting a family quite quickly. It was yet another small enigma.

The phone rang. Roberts picked it up, and almost immediately passed it over to Thorn. It was Clegg.

"We've got McNab," he announced with satisfaction.

"Well done, Inspector."

"I'll be starting the interview pretty soon. We want to know why he attacked Clough. We've already charged him with GBH. There shouldn't be much trouble making it stick. We have a witness who saw the end of the assault. But we'll want to find out as much as we can about the attempted robbery, too. I imagine we'll want him in police custody for quite a while before we hand him over on remand."

"Thank you for letting me know," said Thorn. "Can you leave any questions about his activities over here?"

"Leave them? Don't you want him questioned? I thought he was a suspect in your murder case."

"He is, but I think I'd like to come and do the questioning myself, if you don't mind."

"As you like. Whatever the outcome, it looks as though Mr McNab will be inside for a long stretch this time."

"I'll be there tomorrow," Thorn concluded. "Keep him safe and warm for me."

"See you then."

This time Thorn arranged a flight from the islands in a fixed wing aircraft which took him as far as Exeter, and thence on to Gatwick. With a car waiting at Gatwick, he could be Chichester in a few hours. He explained to Roberts what he was doing, and told him to make a thorough search of Sarah Treduggan's bedroom. He also told the sergeant to read through all the letters in the box he had found at Lambert's lodgings, then, together, they put the finishing touches to the report of the enquiry to date before Thorn rang the Deputy Chief Constable.

Even with the second death on the islands, the enquiry was treated politely rather than urgently. The security conference was becoming a nightmare. Explosives had been found within ten miles of the conference centre, but the terrorists who had planted them there were still at large. The news had leaked, and the media were in hot pursuit, yelping like a pack of hounds at the heels of the hard-pressed police, and making their work even more difficult. A run-of-the-mill murder enquiry in a normally law-abiding part of the region was, Thorn recognised, attracting no attention whatsoever from the national press, and had so far had only the smallest mention, even in the local papers. He sympathised with his mainland colleagues, was grateful for his own

135

comparatively anonymous status, but was also frustrated further by the lack of any kind of assistance.

Job Treduggan, now formally charged with his daughter's murder, would have to wait until his trial. The preliminary hearing was set for two days' time. Thorn saw no purpose in opposing bail. The thought of keeping the man in police custody, virtually in the same building, where Thorn himself was living for the time being, made his flesh creep. The alternative would be to transfer him on remand, probably for several months, to a mainland prison. He was unlikely to make a run for it. Better that he should be staying on St Mary's, where he could attend to his animals as long as he could. Thorn spent some time discussing these proposals with Treduggan's solicitor, with the DCC, and with Doctor Cooper. The doctor was of the opinion that Treduggan, though he must be unbalanced, in order to have committed the murder, was not likely to take his own life, nor that of any other person.

"He may be able to plead diminished responsibility in the event," said Cooper, "but I think he doesn't believe he has done anything wrong. On the contrary, he actually thinks he was doing God's will."

Thorn shook his head.

"Superintendent," said Cooper, "this business is very distasteful, I know, but it seems to get under your skin. Is there any special reason?"

Thorn gave him the bare facts of his recent experiences. With the dry precision of an experienced witness, he described the expedition with his wife, his daughter, his son-in-law and his grandchild. He gave an objective account of the accident. He listed the dead. Cooper listened without comment to the end.

"I see," he said at last. "Can I just say, your feelings will catch up with you eventually, you know. You are aware of the differences between an accident, however awful, like the one you describe, and a deliberate act, like Job's. Your mind is probably telling you already that you are not to blame. The guilt will go in time, or most of it will. It's part of the grieving process. And one of the things you find most disgusting is that Job Treduggan feels no guilt, when he was not just the innocent instrument, but the originator of his daughter's death.

Thorn nodded. "At least you have some idea of how I feel."

"Is there no chance you could hand over to another colleague?"

"No," Thorn shook his head and turned to look at the sea.

"Do you think you can cope?"

There was a long pause. Thorn looked at the scene outside: the boats made their leisurely way across the harbour, gulls soared and swooped for scraps of food, their pristine white feathers cutting sharply across the pure blue of the sky. Beyond the water, the red-brown-stained rocks at the foot of the cliff changed to grey as his eyes climbed to the summit and the thin, green line of grass. It was, thought Thorn, timeless. It was much the same a hundred years ago. It would be much the same in another hundred years. Other people would be manning the boats. Other eyes would be watching. What he did, what Cooper did, whatever Treduggan's fate, this scene would not be affected by it. It was all irrelevant. And he was suddenly overtaken by the chilling thought, that what he saw was only beautiful because he was looking at it: beauty was a human reaction, not an intrinsic quality. For the boatmen, the harbour was not a pretty place to look at, but somewhere to make a living. And now, for himself, too, this island had become not a beautiful retreat from the world, but merely a curious environment in which to carry out his function as a policeman.

"I'll survive," he said in the tired voice of a man who has given up the luxury of feeling.

Later that evening, as he packed a few things in a bag for his trip, there was another call from Clegg. Clough, the man who had been sitting with Lambert when he drove into the ambush, and who had been savagely attacked by McNab, had died without regaining consciousness.

—

Chapter 9

He was glad to be heading away from the islands for a while. The weather was now settled and hot. The flight to Gatwick, with the sunlit fields spread below him, should have given him a feeling of tranquillity, even of beauty, but the anger, disgust, self-criticism and anxiety about his ability to pursue this case to a conclusion left him profoundly depressed. The two weeks he had spent attempting to recuperate from his personal tragedy had done him no good. Previously, he had at least appreciated that his own trauma was indeed personal, that the rest of the world continued legitimately and cheerfully as usual, while he was weighed down by grief and injustice and a sense of a life – of lives – which would be for ever incomplete. Ultimately, he knew in his heart, he would recover to lead something approaching a normal life, although the sense of loss would never completely disappear. But this latest quest in the sordid story had turned the whole world into a mass of corruption. He had been surviving, perhaps recovering, because he believed there was still such a thing as peace. Now he was beginning to think he had glimpsed it in the islands: it was a long time since he had discarded the illusion of innocence and replaced it with the concept of goodness, which sometimes held sway and reduced vice to a petty matter. He was now in danger of losing that belief for good. Goodness was an illusion, swimming on the surface of corruption, like the gently-rolling beauty of a sea of oil that flops lazily on a beach, killing all life.

Clegg met him at the police station. They did not talk much, except to exchange factual information. McNab was now in custody and had not as yet been charged with Clough's murder. He was showing the usual reaction to arrest: a total lack of cooperation, a call for his lawyer, a refusal to answer questions. It would not be easy. Thorn readily agreed to leave the questions he wanted to ask until the following day. The change of approach could be a valuable way of shocking the prisoner into a statement.

Back in his hotel room that evening, Thorn read through all the notes relating to the attempted robbery. He could make no sense of McNab's vicious attack on Clough. That he should want to get even with Lambert by knifing him and throwing the body over the cliff, imagining it would fall into the sea, that was an understandable act of savagery. He had overheard Sarah Treduggan arranging the meeting at the Standing Stone at 1 o'clock. Even if he had not known where the stone was, he had only to follow his victim from the Smuggler's Arms. What happened next was open to conjecture. It seemed probable that Lambert had met Sarah, otherwise she would have witnessed the murder and would surely have raised the alarm. Perhaps Job Treduggan really had seen "another bloke" on Purley Head and the "other bloke" had been McNab. But why had Lambert met Sarah in the first place? Why had he not accompanied her home? Unless McNab had been close enough to the two lovers to overhear their conversation, there was no one who could tell him what had been said.

Thorn, desperate for a quiet mind, bought a bottle of Scotch from the bar. He was not given to drinking alone, but his personal and professional feelings had become confused. He was at his wits end. His intellect, until dulled by the whisky, told him he needed more time for his grief to run its course, but he had never felt such despair. Eventually, fatigue and alcohol rendered him unconscious. He slept like one dead.

He woke with an appalling headache, still befuddled with drink. It was 2:30 am. He sat up with a groan and undressed with difficulty, every move painful. He hated himself. Naked, he padded into his bathroom, drank two tumblers full of water, and took a shower. He still felt dreadful. At least he was too preoccupied with his physical state to worry about anything else. The room swam, and he felt nauseous. He lay down hesitantly, not sure if he would be sick. He began to shiver, although the room had felt too hot earlier. He dragged the covers over him, closed his eyes, and thought only of the pain in his head.

When he woke again, daylight was trying to penetrate the curtains. The bedside lamp was still on. He sat up and pain lanced through his head again. It was 8 o'clock. It was not going to be a good day.

In the dining room a kindly waitress brought him aspirin. He took several cups of coffee and slices of toast. He felt terrible. He walked to the police station and his brain slowly began to work again. Why, he wondered, feeling as he did, did he carry on with his job? He could quite easily ring Clegg and say he was ill: indeed, he could probably obtain official certification from any doctor or psychiatrist to excuse him from working. So, why didn't he? What was it that compelled him to go on punishing himself like this? However drugged his sleep had been, it had left him feeling physically ill, not refreshed. As was often the case when his body was aching with weariness, his brain continued relentlessly to exhaust him further. He suddenly realised that his work was an addiction. It was more of an addiction than alcohol could be, but an addiction, nevertheless. He did not do it out of a sense of conviction, it was not some burning sense of justice, it was not even for personal glory, nor was it because there was a satisfaction like that of completing a crossword puzzle.

141

Quite simply, he continued as a detective because – well, because it was what he did.

"My God!" Clegg exclaimed. "You look bloody awful. What happened?"

"Nothing. I'll be okay."

Clegg let the matter go. He had plenty to concern him already. McNab was still being unhelpful. As an erstwhile villain, that was hardly surprising, even though he had already been told there was an eyewitness to his attack on the dead man. He knew he had no chance of an acquittal, but he maintained the usual stance, letting the police make all the running. Why should he help?

The appearance of a new interrogating officer, Thorn, caused McNab no more than a slight flicker of interest. Across the table he saw a worn, shabby man, eyes sunken and red rimmed. There was a droop to his mouth, as though the world was sour as a cut lemon, and his shoulders slumped as though in despair of ever attaining any of the good things in life. He looked like a man on the verge of retirement, but one who had never achieved anything in a lifetime of work. Yet when he spoke at last, it was with an authority at odds with his appearance.

"My name is Thorn," he said. "Detective Superintendent Thorn. I want to know why you visited St Marys last week."

McNab was disconcerted for the first time. "St Marys?" he repeated.

"We have several witnesses who saw you there."

"Aye. Why shouldn't I go there?"

"That isn't the question. I want to know why you did and what exactly you did while you were there."

"And why should you want to know that?"

"McNab, you're not exactly a stranger to police procedures, nor to the law. At the moment, you're probably about to be charged with the murder of a security guard here in Chichester. You could make things a little easier for yourself, if you told us of your meeting with Matthew Lambert last Wednesday evening."

"I don't see what you're driving at."

"The evidence is stacked against you in the Clough case. I can't see how you can hope to avoid conviction. You will be in for life this time, McNab. Admissions of other crimes, even equally serious ones, might help; denying them or trying to conceal them certainly won't."

"I don't know what it is you're trying to pin on me this time." Behind the red beard McNab looked almost smug. It was as though he was contemptuous, challenging Thorn to provide a shred of evidence. It was like a game of poker, and Thorn seemed to perceive, incredulously, a kind of malicious pleasure on the part of McNab, as though he was deliberately playing with him.

"Very well," said Thorn, the pain in his head intensifying at each word he uttered, "I want to know exactly what you saw on Purley Head last Wednesday night, when you went there to meet Lambert. I want to know what you overheard of his conversation with the girl, Sarah Treduggan, who else you saw there that evening, and what you did with the knife you used to stab him to death before you threw him over the cliff."

McNab stood up, sending his chair clattering to the floor. The amusement had disappeared from his face to be replaced by shock. "Dead?" he exclaimed. "Lambert's dead, ye say?"

It was Thorn's turn to be disconcerted. "You should know!" he said.

"Ye canna pin that on me. I didna kill Lambert. Why should I?" McNab was leaning on the table, his beard thrust out menacingly, challenging the policeman.

"As an actor," Thorn replied dryly, "you'd make a good bus conductor, McNab. I understand you were very fond of your late brother?"

"Now what are ye on about?"

"It was Matthew Lambert who drove the van into your brother's stolen car, wasn't it? The man you expected to help you hijack his van not only double-crossed you, he killed your brother. I'd say that gave you a pretty good motive to follow him up to Purley Head last Wednesday, wait until he'd had his meeting with his girlfriend, then stab him to death."

McNab said nothing but stared back at Thorn intently, trying to gauge whether what he had heard was a bluff. He looked wary, suspicious. He stood up straight, his eyes still on Thorn, and one hand went to his beard which he stroked thoughtfully.

"You're wrong," he said. It was a statement of fact, not an attempt to convince, nor even an emotional denial.

"McNab," Thorn continued with manifestly patient forbearance, "you were seen and identified on St Mary's. You had every opportunity and the strongest of motives to kill Lambert. There can be no other reason for your visit to the island."

"No, I had no cause to kill him. It wasna him driving the van that killed my brother."

"He was the driver assigned that day. He and Clough both made statements to that effect."

" Maybe they had their reasons, but it wasna Lambert driving all the same."

Clegg, sitting across the room, caught Thorn's eye. There was a moment's silence during which McNab retrieved his chair. He had regained his composure; he had the advantage of them both.

"I need a fag," he said.

Clegg lifted his eyebrows and indicated with his head to Thorn to step outside the interview room. Thorn recorded the interruption, and adjourned to follow Clegg. They left McNab to the supervision of a uniformed constable.

"I owe you one," said Clegg as they got to his office.

"You do?"

"Your loss is my gain. He's as good as admitted Clough was driving the van which killed his brother. We can nail him now for murder, or at least for manslaughter. We've got witnesses and now we have a good motive."

"I suspect you're right," Thorn said. "I thought I had it sewn up. McNab followed Lambert to the islands to duff him up, or even to kill him. So I thought. But if Lambert wasn't the driver, why would McNab want to see him at all? Why didn't he go straight for Clough?"

"Leave him to us now," said Clegg. "We'll get it out of him. You look like death."

Thorn agreed. He left the station and found a dark, cool café where he sat and drank several more cups of coffee. It was not very busy there. It was the kind of establishment where a middle-aged man in a business suit attracted no attention. He looked like someone waiting for an appointment, no doubt. Thorn sat, drank, avoided looking at bright lights, thought methodically. He was inclined to believe McNab's assertion that Lambert had not been the driver of the security van on the day of the fatal attack. But that implied that Clough had been driving and had smashed into the hold-up car. The implications of this surely were that Lambert, maybe, had intended to drive, and would have stopped. Why had he not done the driving? If he had been the inside man, surely he would have insisted. Unless, that is, Clough had realised what was afoot, and had insisted on driving, intending, maybe, threatening Lambert with disclosure if he objected. Perhaps Clough had overheard Lambert confirm the route to be taken. Things began to drop into place. Clough, as far as Thorn remembered from the brief meeting he had had on his first visit to Chichester, seemed a decent enough chap. Perhaps he had told Lambert he would keep his secret as long as he behaved himself in future. Or perhaps he had insisted they should both state Lambert was the driver. He may have been trying to keep himself out of trouble afterwards, threatening to spill the beans about the planned hold-up, if Lambert said that Clough was the driver. They would probably never know the truth.

Leaving all that to one side, there still remained the problem of explaining McNab's visit to the islands to see Lambert. There was some hope that Clegg would uncover the reason, but if, as he said, Lambert had not been the driver, McNab would have no reason for wanting him dead. And if that were so, McNab could be eliminated from the list of suspects in the Lambert case. There were rather a lot of ifs. For the moment, however, Thorn was inclined to strike McNab's name from his list. Once Clegg had completed his examination, he might have more definite ideas one way or the other.

Just before lunch he returned to Clegg's office. His head felt a little better, though he yearned to go to bed in the hope the world would go away for a while and he might feel alive, positive and fit. Not much chance of that, he thought to himself, accepting instead Clegg's suggestion of a pub lunch. He confined himself to Perrier water. It brought an amused glance from his companion but no comment.

Clegg was pleased at the way his case against McNab was at last shaping up. He had now been formally charged.

"Have you got any more men to help you yet?" he asked Thorn.

"No. You've heard of the security scare at the conference?" Clegg nodded. "I don't think a case of murder rates highly, compared with threats to our beloved leaders."

"No wonder you're looking knackered. Are there any lines we could help you with? There seemed to be several leading back to Chichester."

Thorn reflected for a minute. "If you keep me informed on the McNab angle, I'm going to discount him for the moment. I still don't know enough about Lambert himself. You're bound to have to look into Lambert yourself, if only to sort out the truth of the hijack. The more you can tell me about him, the better. I've got two other suspects that I need to find out about. One is a man called Job Treduggan."

"You're not serious!" Clegg's eyes lit up with amusement. "No one has a name like that." But the amusement died as rapidly as it had been sparked as Clegg recognised the intensity of Thorn's stare.

"He has already admitted to one murder."

Clegg stared back as the implication sank in. "Lambert wasn't the first?"

"Oh yes, Lambert was the first." In brittle, controlled sentences Thorn brought Clegg up-to-date with affairs on St Marys.

"There's more to it, isn't there?" prompted Clegg.

"More to what?" Thorn prevaricated.

"I've seen men, good men like you, when a case has got to them. Usually it's because there's a personal connection. The last time you were here you were under stress. You said you'd tell me about it in your own time. Looking at you, I'd say you need to talk. It is this case, isn't it?"

At first Thorn said nothing, but he stood up and led the way to the door. On the opposite side of the street there was a park. Clegg followed him. They walked past benches where solitary office workers broke pieces from their sandwiches to feed birds at their feet. Down the side of the shallow lake there were ducks. The two men stopped and observed them for a while.

Thorn recounted how he had come face-to-face with the body of Sarah Treduggan, and with her father. He explained his own, unprofessional rage, still unresolved, and he did his best to give an objective account of his reasons. His description of his own accident, in which his family had been eliminated at a stroke, was made dryly. He understood why he felt like this, he said, but it made it impossible for him to be detached, especially when trying to deal with Treduggan.

"Christ!" Clegg blasphemed softly. "You shouldn't be on this case, man. Apart from the impossibility of being objective – and that would be hard enough for anyone – it's tearing you apart. You should be on leave. You need counselling or something, not more stress."

"There isn't anyone else available."

"Balls!"

Thorn turned and saunters slowly along the path. Clegg followed. "Why don't you pull out?" he persisted. "It's not your manor, not even your force. You'd have the backing of the Federation, and of your doctor."

"I know. The fact is I don't want – no, I can't leave it now. I was thinking to myself the other day, the only thing I have left that makes sense to me now, is the job. It doesn't make me happy, but it does, somehow, give me some sort of raison d'être. If I gave up this case in the middle... No, well, I think I might actually fall apart. Does that sound complicated, stupid?"

"No. I understand what you're saying. Once you're in this job, you're trapped. My wife walked out on me a couple of years ago. Can't really blame her. No woman should have this kind of work as a rival. I was devastated – still am, in my heart of hearts – and now, well, I *am* the job. But how much more can you take? You really do look bloody awful, you know."

"I'll survive." It was said without enthusiasm, as though survival was not, in any case, of any great consequence. Nor was it. All that Thorn could do was to continue.

"Well, we can probably help you with Lambert's background," Clegg said. "You said you had a couple of suspects to his murder?"

"Treduggan." Thorn frowned. "He swears he didn't know anything about the relationship between Lambert and his daughter. He could be lying in his teeth. The trouble is that I just can't weigh up his evidence, nor him properly; I'm too personally involved. I simply can't tell if he's lying or not. I might just as well be trying to take evidence from a Trobriand Islander. I just have to listen to the opinion of Sergeant Roberts. He has lived on the island for seven years, and there's the local GP, who seems very sensible, more so than I am. Yet the main suspect is Lambert's ex-oppo, from his days as a marine, a man called Peter Clapton. He's Lambert's ex-wife's lover. I need to know more about him, too. I think I'll try to dig into his background while I'm on the mainland."

"No Mr X, then?"

"There's always the chance of a Mr X, I suppose, but it must have been pretty crowded up on Purley Head at 1 o'clock in the morning last Wednesday. We know for sure Lambert was there, so was Sarah Treduggan. Job Treduggan was not far off, watching them, then there was possibly McNab, although he denies it, and Job Treduggan talked about 'another bloke'. If it wasn't Treduggan or McNab, Clapton might well have been there – he hasn't got an alibi except the word of his mistress – but to add in yet another unknown person seems a bit excessive. It doesn't seem all that likely that one of the locals would hold that much of a grudge against him, except for Treduggan, of course."

"Sounds like Treduggan or Clapton, then."

"Yes."

Clegg agreed to do a thorough check into Lambert's background in Chichester. It would give Thorn the opportunity to look more closely at Clapton, about whom he knew little. In fact, he thought to himself with surprise, all he knew was that Peter Clapton had joined the Marines fifteen years ago. He had also stated in his interview with Thorn that he had been brought up in care. At Clegg's suggestion, he decided to leave further interrogation of McNab to his colleague. He wanted to establish as clearly as possible what had taken the Scotsman to the islands to see Lambert, if it had not been revenge, and he was especially anxious to have an accurate account of how he had spent that fateful Wednesday. Clegg promised to do his best.

Back in Clegg's office, Thorn made a couple of phone calls and discovered very easily that Clapton's former CO, a Major Stanhope, was in Deal, and would be prepared to talk to him. Within an hour he had packed and was on a train, heading east. He found a small, comfortable hotel, ate a light supper, and crawled into bed with immense relief.

Major Stanhope sat at his desk and contemplated Thorn. He was, the policeman supposed, in his 30s, extremely smart in a uniform which was cut to perfection. He was clean shaven, his hair cut short, and he had a well-scrubbed, healthy air. Blue eyes stared across the desk from a tanned face that, nevertheless, bore no noticeable lines. He looked as fit as a first class athlete. He probably was, Thorn realised, remembering that commando officers had to do exactly the same gruelling, physical training as their men. He smiled at Thorn with the practised smile one sees at cocktail parties. There was no warmth in it, and the blue eyes were appraising.

"How can I help you, Superintendent?" He asked, sitting bolt upright on his chair. His large, square hands, fingers intertwined, rested on the blotter in front of him.

Thorn explained briefly his involvement in the murder enquiry. Lambert's name brought a raising of the eyebrows, as did the subsequent mention of Clapton, otherwise Stanhope listened intently and politely but did not interrupt.

"Both these men left the service some time ago," Stanhope commented as Thorn stopped.

"I know," said Thorn. "What I was hoping for was an insight into their characters and, in the case of Clapton, a little information about his background."

Stanhope remained impassive. "I'm not sure I can be of any real help," he said. "You must understand that I know these men in their capacity as marines. I'd like to think, within the service, I could predict fairly accurately how any man would behave, but how such a man would behave in the looser structure of civilian life – well, that is not so easy to forecast."

"That is not what I'm asking." Thorn was patient. This man was intelligent, guarded; he would not readily give away any information, even about men who had left his command some time ago. Within this guardedness Thorn sensed there was still a deep loyalty. "I believe," he said, "both Lambert and Clapton were good marines. Certainly, Clapton gave me to believe they worked well together. He also said that Lambert had been 'a good oppo' and that anyone would trust themselves to him."

"That's probably true," Stanhope confirmed. "I took the precaution of looking out both men's records, and, when I glanced at them, I remembered they had both done extremely well in all aspects of their training."

"Were they particular friends?"

"I believe they were."

"Clapton also told me that his friend sponsored a Chinese orphan for several years."

"Yes, that is correct. It was shortly after I'd taken command. We were in Singapore at the time. It was the Chaplain's idea. He took some of the men out to a local orphanage and, when they got back, he suggested they might like to contribute something towards their welfare. I think it was Lambert who suggested making it more, a sponsorship deal. Two or three of the company undertook to do something; just a pound or two a week. Lambert stipulated a fiver, I think, and he kept it up as long as he was in the service. By then, the girl would have been getting on for twenty, I suppose."

"Did he ever meet her again?"

"Shouldn't think so. We left Singapore a few months later, and as far as I know, Lambert never went back. I doubt if the girl would have been able to afford a trip to the UK. I seem to recall she was getting a job in Hong Kong."

"That's what Clapton told me." So far, Thorn realised, he had learned absolutely nothing. "What about Clapton?" he asked. "I understand he was brought up in a children's home himself."

Stanhope opened a file in front of him. "That is so," he said, looking at the first page. "He was in a home in Sussex until he was sixteen. He did rather well at school in the circumstances. Went to the local grammar school and got himself six O-levels. Always wanted to join the Marines. As soon as he was old enough, he joined."

"What did he do until then?"

"Apparently he got himself a job with a local builder. He gave his employer's name as a referee when he joined us."

Reluctantly Stanhope gave Thorn the name and address of the builder who had employed Clapton, and the name of the children's home where he had spent some eight years of his childhood. There was nothing else of any interest to discuss. At Thorn's request, Stanhope sketched out from the files the careers of both men in the Marines. There were one or two minor disciplinary offences; nothing extraordinary; there were several complimentary records showing courses of training completed, and completed well. Both men had been, if not model marines, then at least highly satisfactory ones, members of a professional, disciplined and skilled force.

It was still only lunchtime. Thorn returned to his hotel and rang Clegg to tell him he would return to Chichester in the morning. Meanwhile, he had a quick lunch at a pub, and found himself a garage where he hired a car. Avoiding, where he could, the heavier coastal traffic, he drove in the afternoon sunshine, arriving at about 4 o'clock in the afternoon at the small town where Peter Clapton had spent the years in care. Thorn drove up the gravel driveway to the slightly shabby, Georgian house. The front door was open. He went in. The inner door, also open, led to a hall, full of easy chairs and low tables. It was deserted. Thorn found a bell push by the inner door, and he pressed it.

After a few minutes a plump, middle-aged woman entered the hall from the interior of the house. She smiled.

"Good afternoon," said Thorn. "I wonder if I might have a word with you or whoever is in charge?"

"That's me, my dear. At least it is this afternoon until my husband gets back. What can I do for you?"

Thorn introduced himself. He showed his warrant card. The woman looked briefly worried.

"It's all right," Thorn reassured her, "I just want to find out a few details from you or your records, Mrs...?"

"Buckle. You'd better come in, Superintendent. You won't mind if I phone someone to check your identity, will you estimate"

"Please do. Can I suggest you ring Chief Inspector Clegg in Chichester or Inspector Richards in York? I won't give you the numbers: it would be better if you got them yourself from enquiries."

Five minutes later, his identity established, Thorn was sitting in the comfortably furnished office. Mrs Buckle left the door open; the school bus would be arriving at any time, she said, and the children would be clamouring for drinks. Meanwhile, she put a kettle on to make a pot of tea in the kitchen next door. This was not, Thorn realised, the most convenient time to arrive.

It took a long time to get the information he was looking for. The Buckles (Tom Buckle arrived a quarter of an hour after the bus had delivered a dozen assorted, noisy children at the door of the home) were pleasant and hospitable, obviously well-suited to the job they did. The children were happy, affectionate, demanding. Unfortunately, the Buckles could tell Thorn nothing much about Peter Clapton. They had only been at the home themselves for six years. The records carried only the barest details. The former house parents, a Mr and Mrs Latchford, retired when the Buckles took over. Since then, Mr Latchford had died, and his widow now lived in a small bungalow, 3 miles away. Mr Buckle phoned her: she was at home and would happily talk to the Superintendent. He thanked them and left.

Mrs Latchford was small, bent, wiry and alert. She asked to see Thorn's warrant card before unchaining the door. He went in, the small sitting room was tidy and crowded. There were photographs everywhere of children. There were also pictures of adults, couples, families. This time he was not only given a cup of tea but was made to sit in a comfortable chair by the fire and was submitted to an interrogation: where had he come from, why, what had he thought of the home, had he seen any of the children, did they look happy, how long was he spending here. He had hardly made a polite reference to the photographs surrounding him, and facing him on the mantelpiece, before she was off again on a long description of her time as house mother and the children she remembered. The photographs were nearly all of children or former children who had been in the care of her and her husband. She was

155

clearly proud of them, and many of them still kept in close touch, frequently bringing their own children to see her.

"We couldn't have any children of our own, you see," she confided, "but we have had a huge family, all the same. We were blessed, really. We loved them all, you see. We had to be firm, of course, but that's part of being a parent, don't you agree? Do you have children?" The question was posed with smiling enthusiasm.

"No."

"You don't know what you are missing. When you have a family, especially one as big as ours…" She stopped, seeing the look on Thorn's face. "You must forgive me, Superintendent, if I talk so much. I suppose you're busy, like all young people these days."

At another time Thorn would have been amused at the phrase. By now, however, he was beginning to feel impatient. It had been a long day, and he had spent it trying in vain to get a picture of Peter Clapton who, so far, appeared to have been an unremarkable young man, and whose past had little bearing on the events of the last week. However, he smiled politely and came to the point.

"Peter Clapton!" The old lady looked thoughtful, as though searching through her memory. "I've not heard from him or about him for years. The last I heard, he had joined the Navy."

"The Marines," Thorn corrected her gently. "That was about fifteen or sixteen years ago."

" Yes, I suppose it must have been."

"I know most of what he has been up to since then," said Thorn, perhaps unwisely, realising almost as soon as he has said it, that Mrs Latchford would expect a blow by blow account of Clapton's life over the past fifteen years. "I'm simply trying to fill in the background.

Since you brought him up, you're clearly the best person to tell me about him as a child."

"Peter was one of our real success stories," Mrs Latchford replied. The smile of recollecting pleasure came over her face as she spoke. "He'd had a very difficult time, you know, and he was quite a little rebel at first. He tried so hard to be tough and to fight us both. He fought everyone at first. But it was a natural way for a young boy to defend himself against the publicity and the bad reputation."

"Bad reputation? How old was he when he came into care?"

"Peter? Let me see; he'd be seven or eight, I suppose."

"And you say he already had a bad reputation? Publicity, you say, at the age of seven?"

"Oh, no, Superintendent; you don't understand me. It wasn't so much Peter who had the reputation. It was – well, it was the family: more exactly, it was his father."

"His father? Was he well-known in these parts?"

"Not specially." She recognised the bewilderment on Thorn's face. "I'm sorry, I'm not being very clear, am I? I expect everyone to know about my children and their histories, just because they were part of our family, you see. No, poor little Peter, he came to us with one of the worst backgrounds we'd ever come across. We'd not have been particularly surprised if he'd simply been neglected by parents that spent all their time fighting, or because the father was a drunk or something, or even if the mother had just run off. The truth in Peter's case was much harder to come to terms with, both for him, as a child, and for us, trying to help him."

157

"What was the problem?" Thorn prompted her. "Why did he come into care?"

"Peter's father killed his mother, murdered her with a knife. Can you imagine that? It was an unhappy marriage altogether, it emerged. The husband tended to use violence towards his wife; at the trial it all came out, the arguments, neighbours giving evidence of noisy arguments, and the sound of breaking glass and china. Poor Mrs Clapton used to hide indoors for weeks on end until black eyes looked normal again after one of their fights. And that poor little boy in the middle of it all, hating it, unable to stop it, not understanding why. Then one evening the husband came home late from work – he was a farm labourer; they didn't have much money, of course, and that was part of the trouble – and he found that his wife had organised a new life for herself and Peter: she'd fixed up a cleaning job in a big house the other end of the county, and she was foolish enough to tell him she was leaving the next morning, and taking her son with her. It was a fatal mistake, telling him. He went berserk. Peter witnessed the whole thing. He sat in one corner of the big, horsehair sofa and watched his father's rage. He must have been scared out of his wits. And then he saw his own father stab his mother to death." The old lady's face was, thought Thorn, listening with fascinated horror, like that of some ancient storyteller. Wrapped in her memories of bygone days, she told the story as though reciting a narrative learned by heart, but with a kind of artless skill, like a professional actor.

"It took him a long time to learn to trust anyone after that," she said. "Poor Peter! Yet he grew into a really loving, intelligent boy. He went on to the grammar school and did very well. But when he was old enough, he wanted to get away from this place. He always said he'd like to join the Navy. That's why I thought he had done, I suppose he wanted to make a fresh start. Everybody had accepted him for what he was. Mind you, they still remembered the business, and the trial. Well, you do, don't you?"

One thing, Thorn reflected as he sipped a late night drink in the bar of the small hotel in town, that always seemed to be the case in a murder enquiry, was that the more he dug into the past of those involved, the more certain he was to expose half buried history of early violence and crime. He wondered whether such digging was always helpful. He was well aware that there could be a parallel here between Peter Clapton's involvement in the protection of Brenda Lambert from her violent husband, and Lambert's untimely death by stabbing, and the violence and murder committed by Clapton's father all those years ago. Had Lambert's confrontation in Church Street at 11 o'clock last Wednesday been the trigger which had released the pent-up hatred and violence of more than twenty years, and caused him to hate his erstwhile friend, and to follow him in the early hours of the morning up to Purley Head? Had he avenged the mistreatment of Brenda Lambert, and possibly, the callous affair with another woman, Sarah Treduggan? Meanwhile, Lambert had been loudly claiming he needed his wife. All that was clear was that the circumstances of Lambert's death were now even less clear.

Thorn drained his glass. He was halfway to the payphone, about to phone his wife, as was his habit when away from home for the night, on an enquiry, when the reality of his own loss stopped him in his tracks. It was as though a hand clutched at his heart, and he had to lean against the wall of the dining room corridor for a moment, before he made his way to the small bedroom. In spite of his emotions and confusion, the physical sense of shock and despair, and the mental tumult occasioned by the events of the day, within a matter of minutes he fell into a deep and dreamless sleep.

Before he left the little town, where Clapton had spent his formative years, and had attended the school, Thorn paid a visit to the offices of the local newspaper. The editor was only too willing to help him find the editions which had recorded the arrest and trial of William Clapton for the murder of his wife. An hour later, carrying an envelope containing photocopies of the relevant columns, Thorn left to drive back to Chichester.

Chapter 10

Clegg and his men had been busy. Questioning of McNab had been slow, and he had not admitted very much which would be immediately useful in court. Nevertheless, from remarks, comments, allusions, inconsistencies, Clegg had come to the conclusion that McNab had pursued Lambert to St Marys with every intention of killing him in revenge for the death of his young brother. It was only when he had confronted Lambert on the island that the truth had emerged, and somehow McNab had been convinced that it was Clough who had driven the security van on that fateful day. According to McNab, he had left the island that same afternoon, several hours before Lambert's death. Clegg had phoned Penzance immediately and, at about the time that Thorn had been booking into his hotel the previous evening, Clegg had heard from Penzance that a man answering McNab's description had been seen boarding a London train on Wednesday evening.

It looked as though McNab could be crossed off the list of suspects. His connection with Lambert may well have been as imagined, a conspiracy to stage the hold-up of the wages van. Perhaps Clegg would be able in due course to discover why Lambert had not driven after all; the most likely explanation was that Clough had got wind of the plot and had frustrated it. The only question that remained was why Lambert had allowed him to do so, and then had maintained the deception in his statement, himself taking the blame for the death of McNab Junior. But even that could be imagined without too much difficulty; a matter of blackmail on Clough's part. "You say you were driving and I won't say anything about your involvement in the plan." With no police record, perhaps

Lambert had been forced into the affair against his better judgement in any case. Whatever the ins and outs of that business, they now had little relevance to the events leading to Lambert's murder. The answer to that mystery still lay in the islands.

Clegg had also carried out his promise to investigate in more detail Lambert's background, especially his childhood. Thorn was very impressed by the speed with which Clegg's men had worked. They had not had time to produce a properly written or typed report, but the facts as far as they had them, were all in Clegg's hands in note form. Clegg had devoted a lot of man hours to the investigation and Thorn recognised the work of a thoroughly professional department in the speed and efficiency. He was grateful for the help.

Matthew Lambert had been born some forty-one years ago in Chichester to a Harold and Jean Lambert. They had run a public house, apparently successfully, the Wellington Arms, as tenants for some five or six years. At the end of that time they had bought a free house in a run-down district of the city. It was tired-looking when they took it on, but they had turned it into at least a financially successful establishment. They had, over the course of the years, introduced live music and entertainment, which had pulled in the punters. The police had kept it under observation, because there was little doubt that it was the centre of a lot of doubtful activity. While they had never managed to find anything other than soft drugs, peddled on the premises of the Red Diamond, they had their very precise suspicions about some of the female clients.

It was in this rough and doubtful environment that the young Matthew Lambert had grown up. Unlike his friend, Clapton, he had never shown great promise at school, the local secondary modern, but nor had he been particularly noted for criminal or antisocial behaviour. He left school at fifteen and found various jobs, mainly on building sites. At eighteen he had enlisted in a fit of boredom. His father, who, like many men of his calling, drank more than was good for him, had probably been kept in check by his wife, a strong woman; Clegg's information suggested it had been Jean Lambert who had been the motivating force which made the backstreet pub into a successful business. The licence was in her name. She was still alive, in a small house on the Essex coast somewhere, but her husband had died five years ago.

Now that McNab's movements on the day of the murder had been established, there was nothing to keep Thorn in Chichester. As he had so often done in the past, he had been following a lead which had ended in a blind alley. It was all part of the job. Sometimes it was entirely by elimination that one arrived at the solution to a problem. With McNab eliminated from his list, he could narrow his enquiry to two, more obvious suspects. Much though his personal antagonism turned him against Job Treduggan, he was not convinced that he was capable of the murder of Lambert just because he had admitted to the death of his daughter. Why would he admit to one murder, and not the other? Clapton was a more likely bet, especially bearing in mind his early history. Both Clapton and Treduggan were still on the island, and that is where he should now be himself. He rang Sergeant Roberts.

"We've had a break-in," Roberts reported. He sounded anxious.

"What happened?"

"We were both out yesterday evening. Someone forced the lock on our back door."

"Anything taken?"

"Nothing personal," said Roberts. "Whoever it was has an interest in this case. Once he'd got into the cottage, he broke into the office by the inside door. He smashed the computer, and he tore down all the pictures and notes from the wall."

"Did he destroy any evidence?"

"All the computer files were backed up on a separate drive, and he couldn't get into the filing cabinet. I've had to order a replacement computer, and the office is in a mess, but no, he can't have taken anything important. We can't go on like this, sir, we need help."

"I know, Sergeant. I'm used to having a forensic team on hand. We haven't even had time to search Sarah Ttreduggan's room. Any idea who the burglar was?"

"Not as yet. The back of the cottage faces the harbour, of course, and it's deserted at that time in the evening. I dare say I shall be able to find whoever it was, but I need time and, begging your pardon, like, I'm too busy following your enquiries, sir."

It was a shock, but also suggested one or other of the lines of enquiry must be leading somewhere. There was no real, physical evidence for the intruder to steal. Written notes and reports were all locked in the filing cabinet or in the computer. The only samples they had collected were a couple of plastic bags full of cigarette ends.

As he drove a hire car westward for hours, and watched the sun-baked countryside slip by the window, he conjured up images of the people involved in the case. He tried not to think logically about them, merely to picture them and to listen without judgement to the memory of what they had told him. Sometimes, he knew, recording interviews and expressions, the angle at which someone sat on his chair or held his head, the physical appearance of the scene, the tone of voice of a witness, these could all suddenly result in a new viewpoint, a new idea, a key. The truth must lie somewhere in the facts he already had, but his recollection brought no revelations.

He was in time to catch the last helicopter flight to St Mary's. The sun was setting, low and red; it was as though some maniacal artist was trying to paint the whole sky. As they approached the island, the western cliffs showed red as if on fire, while the east was in deep shade. For a moment Thorn felt immensely uneasy at the sheer scale of the view: it was like someone walking over his grave, as he saw cold, deep blue shadow and an impenetrable seascape at the foot of the cliffs below him, and an infernal conflagration of the dying sun on the other side of the islands. Once more he was aware that a romantic observer would have seen wild beauty where he saw savage, menacing and unfeeling nature. He stepped off the aircraft onto the concrete apron with a sudden sense of inevitability, as though he were an instrument of an impersonal fate...

Roberts took his small suitcase. "Welcome back, sir. How did you get on? Anything useful?"

"Yes and no, Sergeant. I'll fill you in when we get back. Any further developments here?"

"'Fraid not, sir, but at least we have a new computer!"

Inside the Roberts' cottage there was an enticing smell of cooking. "I thought you'd want a meal after a day's travelling," said Tina, welcoming him back.

As they sat down to eat, Thorn sensed something out of the ordinary in the air. Tina, bright, busy, cheerful but only on the surface. For once her conversation was polite rather than animated. The meal was wonderful, Thorn admitted, savouring the subtle flavours of fresh vegetables, meat, herbs, served in sauces as fresh and distinctive as a great wine. When Tina went to collect the coffee, Thorn turned to Roberts. "None of my business," he said, "but is anything the matter?"

"In what way?"

"Tina doesn't seem quite herself. Was she upset by the break-in?"

Tina reappeared at this moment. She poured coffee. "I'm sorry," she said.

"What for?" Thorn asked, surprised.

"You're right, I'm not myself at the moment. It's not the burglary, though that was unpleasant, the thought of someone breaking into our home like that. No, it's Tom."

"Tom?" The name meant nothing to him.

"Our son," Roberts explained.

"I'm sorry." Thorn was no wiser.

"Children are always a worry, aren't they?" Tina said.

"What's the problem?" asked Thorn. "Problems at college?"

"No." It was Bill's turn. "The fact is, he's written to say he's moving in with his girlfriend."

"I'm being silly, I expect," Tina said." It's his life, I know, but he's so young, eighteen."

"It might be worse, if he'd got himself married," Thorn pointed out.

"I know. All the same, it goes against the grain." "Lots of youngsters move in together these days. I think a lot of them have their doubts about marriage. You can't altogether blame them, when you consider one in three marriages end in divorce. It all seems so casual."

"Do you know this girl?"

"Oh yes," Tina said quickly. "We met her when we went to see Tom, and she's been down here on a visit, too."

"She seemed like a very nice girl," put in Bill. "Intelligent, good-humoured, and she was obviously fond of Tom."

"You've probably got nothing to worry about," said Thorn

"I know," Tina gave a little smile. "I suppose I'm just reluctant to see my little boy turn into a man."

As he undressed and got into bed, Thorn found himself thinking of the Roberts' small problem. In the few days he'd spent as their guest he had come to like them very much. There was a lot of affection between them. He did not doubt their children, brought up in such a home, would make out all right. He remembered Bill Roberts' reasons for not going for promotion: the two of them liked it here on the island, and they liked the people. They would not want to abandon their home in pursuit of some short-term career gain. And, while for him the job was what defined him as a person, for the Roberts it was their home, their family, their way of life on the island.

There seemed to be a recurring theme to his life and to the investigation of the past week: parents and children. The Roberts had presented him with one more variation on the theme with their concerns for the future of their son. He thought now of the other people he had been dealing with. Clapton, whose father had killed his mother, Joe Treduggan, who had killed his daughter. Brenda Lambert wanted children but could not have them, prevented from so doing by the violence of her dead husband. Yet Matthew Lambert had himself adopted a girl of another race, and maintained her for ten years. On the edge of sleep now, his brain still toyed with the same ideas: he thought of Thora Jefferies and her indignation at what she saw as a threat to her daughter's good name. And in the centre of the investigation was himself, still sore from grieving over his daughter and his grandchild, as well as his wife. Now Roberts, and more especially Tina Roberts, worried in their turn for their children.

Something in all this was nagging at his consciousness, preventing sleep. He sat up and put on the light, and took out a notebook. He was not sure what it was in all this idle speculation which was tugging at his sleeve, asking for recognition. Maybe he was simply reading too much into the whole affair. All suspects and victims had parents or children, after all, that was the nature of things. Perhaps the truth was so simple that he, in his depressed state, was seeing connections and comparisons which were not valid. Having lost his daughter, he was oversensitive to the relationships between other parents and their children. Even so, two glaring facts gave him pause: the fact that Peter Clapton, as a child, had witnessed his own father kill his mother, and the fact that Joe Treduggan had confessed to killing his own daughter. He tried to redress the balance by looking again at other parent-children relationships. Leaving aside the Roberts, who were not properly connected with the investigation, he looked at each of the main protagonists. First there was Lambert himself. There was nothing out of the ordinary about his childhood, it would seem. Brought up in a pub in a rather seedy area, there was nothing to suggest he had been maltreated, nor that his relationship with his parents was miserable or unhappy. His subsequent record as a young man in the marines did not suggest he was an extraordinary personality, although, on the good side, he had paid for the upkeep of the Chinese girl. Thorn did not know whether such an act suggested an exceptional fondness for children. If it did, then there remained this curious question of why the Lamberts had not started a family immediately, unless the answer was purely a matter of chance, a piece of bad luck

In Clapton's case, there could well be a psychological hang-up to his wanting children, yet Brenda Lambert, unable to conceive, said they wanted a child. More exactly, Thorn recalled, she had said she would have liked children by Clapton; he had not discussed the matter. Clapton himself might not want children. Logically, though, he might be more likely to be wary of marriage rather than of children.

That brought him to Job Treduggan and his daughter. From what he had seen of the farmer, Thorn found it impossible to take his measure. He knew he would never be able to understand his thought processes. Indeed, he did not want to, even if that could help him understand the events leading to his murdering Sarah. What concerned Thorn more closely was the connection between Sarah and Lambert. Perhaps the mysterious letters would help there. There was a big age difference. How had they come to know one another? Lambert may well have seen Sarah in the shop, but how had he managed to meet her outside, and why, and with what intent? Had they been lovers? Now they were both dead it seemed unlikely that the truth of their relationship would ever be known, yet Thorn felt it was important, if only to explain a little further how Lambert ticked. The letters would surely help.

And that was all, except, as an afterthought, for the Jefferies and their daughter, Penny. Strange coincidence that she should be a student in Chichester and that her mother had let a room to Lambert from the same town, but there had apparently been no connection between Penny Jefferies and Matt Lambert. Thorn considered yet again the overprotective attitude of Thora Jefferies and of the echoing anger from Penny that her flatmates had been questioned without her knowledge. The threat to her "reputation" struck a strange, outmoded note.

No, there was nothing in all these speculations. To pursue them much further would not, surely, help. Thorn switched off the light. He was overtired. Still he could not sleep. The image of Thora Jefferies came into his head. He found her unappealing in the extreme, haughty, yet somehow lacking in genuine taste. The clothes she wore, the artificial pearls and too large fashion jewellery, more suitable for a teenager, the furniture she was surrounded by, the decoration of the flat, all spoke of money spent without real taste. He wondered why she had been prepared to accept Lambert as a paying guest. And that thought led to another small but unresolved mystery: where had Matthew Lambert obtained the cash to pay for his lodging, when he had not drawn the cash or written a cheque, according to the bank account? That, decided Thorn, as sleep finally crept up on him, was the mystery he should try to resolve first, rather than all these hypothetical ideas about family relationships.

After breakfast Thorn and the Sergeant spent two hours tidying paperwork. In spite of so much travelling, Thorn realised, very little of substance had surfaced. The vague ideas which had come to him during the night moved him to decide his first task must be to establish the source of Lambert's income. He had paid the Jefferies for his room in cash, yet he had drawn none from the bank. He had also spent two weeks as a tourist, buying all his meals and by all accounts drinking quite a lot. Perhaps, as he had suggested jokingly to Clegg, he had indeed won the money on the horses, but, if not, it was a factual problem not open to woolly speculation. Like a gardener who spends all winter browsing through catalogues, Thorn was becoming tired of theory and wanted to do something more definite, and practical. He would have to talk yet again to Thora Jefferies.

Before he could begin on this task, however, the phone rang, and he saw from the look on Roberts' face that the news was serious.

"That was Doctor Cooper," Roberts said as he replaced the receiver. "Job Treduggan is in a bad way. He says he'll have to have him admitted to hospital."

"What's he done?"

"No, he's not physically ill. That's the problem. The doc says he needs to get him into the mental hospital on the mainland. He says Job's behaviour is stranger than ever, and he shouldn't be left alone."

"Blast!"

"I think I'd better get down to the farm again and organise someone to look after the livestock, sir."

"Yes, yes, Sergeant, of course. I'd better have a word with Cooper."

"He said he'd call in to see you as soon as he's organised things."

"How long will that be, does he know?"

"He said he is arranging for Sister Brand to fly over with Job and they'll be picked up at the heliport. Once he's done all that, he said he'll come over here."

Left on his own in the small office, Thorn was unable to settle to any serious work. Instead, he stared out of the window at the constantly moving scene in the harbour. Then he went back into the house where Tina willingly made him coffee.

"Why don't you pay your son a visit?" he suggested without preliminaries.

"No, he wouldn't thank me for it. He would see it as interference. I have to accept he isn't a little boy any more. To tell you the truth, Superintendent, I know in my heart of hearts this is a crucial time. A false move now and I could alienate Tom for ever. He'd say I don't trust him or his judgement and he'd be right. He's a sensible young man really, and we've done our best to bring him up. Now it's my turn to take a back seat and let him go. They say it's the hardest thing of all for parents to do."

Thorn nodded. "Perhaps you're right," he said.

"Oh yes, I am. All the same, being right and acting on it isn't the same as not worrying. But then, that's what having children is all about, isn't it? Worrying. They say you never stop, however old they are. But I wouldn't have it any other way."

Thorn returned to his desk but was still unsettled. He did not have very long to wait until Cooper arrived.

"I was wrong," the doctor admitted almost as soon as he got in the door. "I thought old Job would be better occupied on the farm rather than sitting on his old backside in a cell somewhere, getting more and more suicidal. I've been calling on him, you know, twice a day. I realised he wasn't entirely normal, of course – whatever 'normal' means. I'd have given him antidepressants, only his blasted religion means he takes no medication, because he thinks of them as drugs."

Thorn raised an incredulous eyebrow.

"Yes, I know, you'd think taking prescribed drugs a pretty minor business compared with killing his daughter, wouldn't you? Anyway, this morning I realised he wasn't safe. He seems to have sunk into a kind of deep despair now, the kind of despair and depression you can only really treat with drugs. I found him sitting in the gloomy sitting room, and he'd been there all night. He had not eaten. He hadn't even fed the animals or done the milking. It was almost a catatonic state. I had to send him off."

"I need to know more about Treduggan and his daughter." Thorn said.

"I thought it was all pretty straightforward as far as you were concerned," the doctor queried. "It's a clear-cut business, isn't it? He's admitted to the murder."

"It's not just Sarah's death I'm concerned with," said Thorn. "It's the connection, if there is one, with Lambert."

"Lambert? How does he come into it? I know you think he was Sarah's lover, the father of her unborn child. He wasn't. She told me so herself. At least, she told me Job had been having regular intercourse with her for years. She was quite sure it was his child. I tried to establish that it could be some other man's child, but she told me vehemently that was impossible. There wasn't anyone else, she said."

"Why didn't you make her move out?" Thorn's anger made his voice brittle.

Cooper met his eyes steadily. "Superintendent, don't for one moment imagine that I was not as shocked as you are at this affair. Perhaps I am, if anything, more shocked. I've known both Job and his daughter for years. He was always a sour skinflint, even before his wife died. Sarah was a quiet little thing, but she had spirit and she had a few brains, too. Ask old Miss Barker, the old schoolteacher. I reckon Job's farm would have collapsed years ago if Sarah hadn't worked like a slave, and I don't think it was just for independence that she got herself a job in the bakery. In some ways it was the making of her. It got her out of the house.

"And don't run away with the idea that I had the least suspicion of what was going on until Sarah told me. I'd never have known if she hadn't got pregnant. Of course, I tried to get her to move out. She was very mixed up herself, you know. She hated him for what he did, but she felt responsible, too."

"She felt responsible?"

"I believe it's not unusual in such cases. Rape victims are often not prepared to believe they are no more than innocent victims themselves."

Thorn frowned at the desk in front of him. "I still want to know where Lambert fits in with all this."

"I really can't help you there. Are you quite sure there is a link?"

"Oh yes, there's a connection all right. We have independent evidence that Sarah arranged to meet Lambert on Purley Head that night, and we have Job Treduggan's statement that he followed her to the meeting."

Cooper looked thoughtful. "I wonder," he said. Thorn looked at him sharply but said nothing. He waited. "Something Sarah said," Cooper went on after a while, "when she came for an examination, I had the devil's own job getting out of her why she had come. She was, well, fearful, I suspect. I was very surprised when she eventually said in a tiny voice that she thought she might be pregnant. I just stared at her, I'm afraid, to begin with. Then I recovered my composure, and I asked her the usual questions. I gave her a quick examination. When I confirmed the pregnancy, she was very upset. I asked her who the father was and if he knew. She said no, he didn't know. Would he stand by her, I asked. At that point she really broke down. She was at her wits end. Poor kid! That was when she told me about Job. Apparently, it first happened about a year after her mother died, and she'd been suffering all this abuse for years. Somehow, in the course of this near-hysterical account of her father's incest, she sobbed something about a friend advising her to see me. I didn't ask what friend. I suppose it could have been Lambert. I must say, it seems unlikely though."

So, Thorn said to himself, let's suppose it was Lambert who had advised Sarah to see the doctor. That meant he was privy to her secret and to Job's, maybe. If Job knew that he knew… But he had followed his daughter to Purley Head and witnessed her meeting with Lambert. If he had overheard their conversation, he would know his secret was out. What if he had attacked Lambert there and then to keep his secret hidden? If Sarah had seen that attack, she might have still been too frightened, or too guilty about her involvement, to do anything other than run back to the farm and cower in fear there. It might have happened that way. Judging by his one and only meeting with Job Treduggan, however, and by Cooper's description of the deterioration in Job's condition, further questioning would probably be inconclusive, and it would certainly be impracticable for the time being. When the doctor left, Thorn was not slow to follow him out into the street. Once more he was aware of the cheerful bustle as holiday-makers and locals went about their business. It contrasted with his own sombre thoughts. When this was all over, he reflected, perhaps it would be wise to move on rather than attempt to continue his broken holiday here. He could not in all honesty imagine himself taking a holiday anywhere in his present state of mind. Enforced idleness was not likely to be a cure for his depression. It might be better to get back to work in his own office, with people he knew, working to a routine which would keep him totally occupied, giving him little time to think about his own problems. His own team would be easier to manage than this cock-eyed, understaffed, amateur show. And he felt a deep sense of unfairness as he was looking at families happily wandering down the main street of the small town, the men in shorts and tee-shirts, the women in summer tops or cotton dresses, children heading eagerly for the beach or for the promised boat trips, eating ice creams, laughing, while he only wanted to escape.

He reached the Smuggler's Arms and rang the bell of the private entrance. Penelope Jefferies opened the door. She looked vaguely cross. When Thorn said that he would like to speak to her mother, she hesitated for a moment, then reluctantly stood aside for him to enter. She led the way up the red throat of the staircase, opened the door to the sitting room, and announced him. Thora Jefferies was alone. She turned irritably from the window and asked him directly rather than politely what he wanted this time. Penelope, who had followed him in, walked sulkily over to a chair and sat down, her arms straight along the armrests, crossed her jean-encased legs, and stared at him.

"May I sit down?" Thorn asked.

Thora Jefferies waved towards the sofa. He could not look at both women at the same time. He was too old a hand at interviewing techniques to be disconcerted by the tactic, but he took note of it.

Thora Jefferies had clearly not intended to make anything easy for him. She waited for Thorn to speak. Thorn thought she looked older, a little drawn. Her eyes were still hostile, but there were deeper lines under them and they seemed to lack lustre. The two women avoided each other's eyes, perhaps, he surmised, he had interrupted a family quarrel.

"I hope I've not interrupted anything," he lied. He hoped he might provoke further, possibly revealing hostility. "The fact is, Mrs Jefferies, we're still very puzzled about Matthew Lambert's money."

"His money? What do you mean?"

"You will remember, I'm sure, that you told us he paid you in cash for three weeks' lodging in advance." Thora Jefferies nodded. "You probably also remember I told you he hadn't drawn any money from his bank account, not even his wages."

"I don't know what it is you're expecting me to say."

"I'm not expecting you to say anything, Mrs Jefferies, I'm just hoping you might be able to help."

"I've told you all I know, Inspector."

"Superintendent."

"I don't understand how you think I can help you with information about his money or bank account."

"Did Mr Lambert receive any letters while he was here?"

"No." She was mildly disconcerted by the question.

"You maintain you never even chatted casually to him at breakfast?"

"Why should I?"

"Forgive me, but I would have thought it was normal to pass the time of day with your guests, at least, it's what most landladies seem to do."

"Really? I don't know why you should think that, but, even if you're right, then I must be different."

"Mrs Jefferies, are you really trying to tell me you didn't even suggest places to visit or which islands to visit by boat?"

"Why would I? He knew the islands well enough already, I believe."

"And how did you know that?"

"I'm not sure. Perhaps Mr Lambert told me when he arrived."

"Did he also tell you he had always stayed in hotels here?"

"No."

"Well, he did. So, he must have known about booking and whether it was necessary. And, if he was in the habit of staying in hotels, why didn't he book in here just for a couple of nights until there was a vacancy in a hotel? Instead he paid for three whole weeks."

"I don't know, Inspector – Superintendent. What I know is what I've already told you."

"But I can't check out anything you have told me, Mrs Jefferies. I only have your word for all of this. You have admitted you didn't put the money through the books."

"I don't see why you are making such a fuss about a minor affair."

"Nor do I understand why you are being so obstructive."

"I don't know anything."

Stalemate, said Thorn to himself. He was sure she was holding something back, but what it was he had not the faintest idea.

"You must see the problem, Mrs Jefferies. According to our information, Lambert left his job in Chichester without even drawing his wages from the bank. He had not drawn cash. He paid his fare to the islands, arrived here and paid you, bought meals for two weeks, drank every evening in here or in the Pirate, he even did the occasional bit of shopping, including a sweatshirt that cost him upwards of twenty pounds, and he did it all without drawing any money. How?"

"I don't know."

"If he didn't have any source of income here on the islands, then he must have had several hundreds of pounds in cash when he arrived. Almost the first thing he did when he got here was to pay you. Surely you must have seen his open wallet when he took out the money."

"I suppose so." She was still wary.

"And you still say you didn't even see him peel notes off? £500 makes a pretty thick wad."

But he got no reply. Penelope Jefferies whom Thorn observed from the corner of his eye, was clearly interested in her mother's replies, and as sceptical about them as Thorn himself. She was watching Thorn with narrowed eyes, lips pinched tightly together in speculation.

"Tell me," he said, casually to Pemelppe, "am I mistaken, or did I interrupt a family dispute?"

"It's none of your business, Superintendent." The girl was frosty. "But if you must know, yes, my mother was trying to interfere with my career." Thora made no comment.

"I thought you were a student."

"I am. For some reason my mother, who doesn't know anything about these things, has always opposed my choice of college."

"You mean she didn't want you to go to Chichester?"

"She has always said it was a mistake, a bad choice. She wanted me to try for Exeter or Southampton."

"Why?" Still Thora was silent, though clearly angry, and she left the room..

"Oh," Penelope explained, "Exeter because it's closer and easier to come home in the vacs, that sort of thing."

"Well, I suppose I can understand that. Southampton?"

"She says someone once told her it was a good place to train as a teacher; it's rubbish. Chichester's very good and established, and a friend of mine recommended it. But I get the same old disapproval every time I come home. I really don't know why she bothers; she doesn't know anything about it. But she has a bee in her bonnet, as they say. Well, goodbye, Superintendent."

It was all very strange, Thorn told himself, as he headed back towards lunch.

Chapter 11

Sarah Treduggan's funeral was held in the morning. The service took place in the Methodist Chapel.

"I thought the Treduggans belonged to the Modern Disciples," Thorn was puzzled.

"Job did – does. I don't know about Sarah. Things are different here, sir, as you can see. She'll be buried in the churchyard of the parish church – that's C of E – but the Minister here will conduct the committal."

Job did not attend, although arrangements would have been made, if he were fit enough. There were only a dozen mourners. It was almost as though this young life had no significance. Thorn felt the bitterness well up in his throat.

After the interment he introduced himself to the Minister. No, Sarah was indeed a Methodist, he was told: it had caused difficulties for her at first, when she had told her father she was going to switch from the Modern Disciples to Methodism.

"When was that?"

"Oh, let me see – she would have been thirteen or fourteen, I suppose. Make no mistake, Sarah was a plucky little girl in spite of her morose and strong-willed father . Perhaps that's where she got it from.

"They are fundamentalists, very strict. Almost everything is seen as a sin. It's a very cold and depressing sect and, I have to say it, it's a distorted view of the world. The God they seem to believe in is more the God of wrath and judgement than the God of love. Even so, it took a great deal of courage for Sarah to opt out."

Wrath and judgement, thought Thorn, as he closed the churchyard gate, was that what drove Job to kill Lambert as well as Sarah? But wrath about what?

Roberts drove to the Treduggan farm. At last they could make a thorough search, though Thorn did not expect to find anything significant or relevant to his enquiry. He unlocked the door and the two men stooped to enter the gloomy little hall. Thorn turned to the sitting room, leaving Roberts to climb the stairs to the bedrooms. He heard the Sergeant's heavy tread on the thick, wooden planks which formed both floor and ceiling. He looked round the dark sitting room. It was full of furniture, mostly antique and heavy. There were no books except for a large Bible. Against one wall there was a rolltop desk, unlocked, with cheap, lined writing paper and envelopes. There were also a couple of ledgers: he glanced at them; farm accounts, neatly written with backward-sloping handwriting, a little childish maybe, – Sarah's? Apart from the ledgers the desk contained a few typewritten papers which appeared to be mailshots, not yet discarded in case there was a real bargain among them. There were no personal letters, although there were bills, mostly receipted. Job Treduggan's cheque-book was there, together with a paying in book: he had paid in very little except for a small monthly cheque from the island dairy, presumably for his milk. The last payment from the cheque-book was dated two weeks earlier and made out to the town supermarket for groceries in the amount of £34. Looking back, Thorn found similar payments every two weeks or so – very little, he thought, though, maybe the kitchen garden plus milk, eggs, home-made cheese, could provide quite a lot of food for the two inhabitants without their having to buy. Thorn began to get the impression that the Treduggans, Job especially, lived a very frugal and lonely life. The total absence of any personal correspondence suggested acute isolation. At least Sarah had ridden her bicycle into the little town every morning and mixed with housewives and visitors. She had also had a cheerful companion in the shop, Mrs Davies, who seemed genuinely fond of her. But Job, since the death of his wife, seemed to have had nothing but a ramshackle farm to run, the animals to look after, and occasional meetings of the Modern Disciples, purveyors, it appeared, of doom and gloom. It was, perhaps, the pernicious effect of deep loneliness which had driven him to his abominable crime.

"I think these might be of interest," Roberts said, his wide shoulders filling the doorframe. He held a small bundle of letters in one hand. "They're from Lambert to Sarah. They were hidden under the mattress."

Thorn felt a mixture of distaste and excitement as he took the proffered letters. He still felt uncomfortable when he had to examine evidence of this sort. Love letters were intensely private things. By sharing the reading with Roberts, he felt obscurely that he was not so guilty; it was as though Roberts' part in the process made the reading less personal.

The letters were kept in order. The first was dated little more than a year ago, the remaining three letters at intervals, the most recent, June 15, six days before Lambert's arrival in St Marys.

"My dear Sarah," the first letter began, "it was nice to meet you. I've been visiting the islands for years and I think they are a great place for a holiday. Great scenery, lots of wildlife, good pubs. You couldn't ask for more. But I was a bit lonely this time, you know. I explained about my wife. In a way it's just as well we don't have any kids, I suppose, but in other ways I always missed not having any. I told you about Lee Kwang; she is about your age

183

now, but I've never seen her since the first time I met her in the orphanage, and it's not the same, getting letters from her from time to time. Anyway, she'll be too busy now, I expect, now she's got her new life in Hong Kong.

"So, in a way, meeting you was like finding a replacement for Lee Kwang. Except, you're not Chinese, and I won't be paying for your education or anything. I know the situation with your father isn't easy, and he wouldn't understand. He would probably think there was something dirty going on. Imagine, a man, old enough to be your father, who likes a drink, making friends with his daughter! Just friends. I don't suppose many people would believe it, come to think."

At this stage Thorn was quite sceptical, seeing this extraordinary letter as little more than the first step in an experienced conman's seduction of a naïve girl. He felt faintly sick.

Rather to his surprise, however, the correspondence continued in the same vein. The third letter was different in tone, clearly a direct response to something Sarah had written to him. Thorn was surprised by a kind of paternal tenderness in Lambert's tone.

"Got your letter this morning," he read. "You sound very fed up, though, reading between the lines, I don't really believe it's because of the farm and its troubles. You say you are worried about your Dad, but you say you wish you could go away and leave him. When you say you hate him at times, I suppose most kids feel that way sometimes about their parents. I know I did about mine. They ran a pub, - well a club it was actually, and they didn't really have time for me. Anyway, I wouldn't want to sort of entice you away from your own Dad. I don't understand exactly why you say he disgusts you. That sounds a bit strong. You do sound in quite a state though. I wish I could get over to the islands to see you, but I don't think I can take any leave until the summer. I'll get over there then, but I expect it will all have blown over by then. Probably winter blues."

The rest of the letter was given over to chitchat about his job and the weather and a few remarks about the wild birds he had seen in the park.

They opened the last letter, written a week before Lambert's visit.

"Whatever it is that is going on, it must be bad if you can't say in a letter. I can see you're very upset by it, and I'm very worried. I'm going to try to get my holiday brought forward a couple of weeks, so I can see you maybe as soon as next week. I will call into the shop, as soon as I can. I know you won't be able to get away to talk to me without your Dad knowing, but we'll think of something. And if it really is that bad that you want to leave the farm for good, well, I think I can help. I've had a sort of windfall. You say whatever it is that's bothering you is a kind of family secret. It sounds very mysterious. Perhaps it won't seem so bad when you've had the chance to talk about it with me. Things don't usually seem so bad when you talk about them."

It was beginning to look as if they'd misjudged Lambert. Strange though the idea seemed, perhaps his relationship with the dead girl really had been paternal rather than amorous or even romantic. Thorn now believed that Sarah Treduggan had turned to the older man as someone who she could confide in, and Lambert's letters hinted very strongly that she was going to tell him about the incest. What would be his reaction? Had Job Treduggan followed his daughter and overheard their conversation? Had he then killed Lambert in order to keep the secret and, worse, killed his daughter because she had witnessed the murder?

"What do you think he means in this bit?" Roberts pointed out the passage in which Lambert suggested he might help financially if Sarah needed to escape.

Thorn reread the letter. What did Lambert mean by a windfall? Where did his money come from? A win on the horses seemed all at once more possible, unless..

"Could he be blackmailing someone?" Roberts suggested.

"I suppose it's possible." Thorn remembered his earlier ideas about Lambert and Clough.

Fate took a hand in the investigation. In his need to find out Lambert's potential blackmail victim, Thorn decided to visit Brenda Lambert. It crossed his mind that if Lambert was in possession of facts he could use for blackmail, he may well have been using the process for his own advantage, not waiting to demand money only to give it to the girl. It would explain how he had managed to survive for two full weeks without drawing any money from his bank account, and how he had managed to pay Thora Jefferies for the room. Thorn hated loose ends. If he could discover the victim of Lambert's supposed or even proposed blackmail, and if Lambert had indeed already extracted money, it would clear up that unexplained matter.

A secondary thought came unbidden. He tried to suppress it, but Roberts voiced it independently.

"Seems to me, sir," Roberts said, "Lambert may have had something on Clapton, not on one of the locals."

"Exactly what I was thinking," Thorn agreed, "He may have known about Clapton's father. But I have my doubts about Clapton's desire to keep that totally secret. It wouldn't surely be that damaging if it got out."

The two men made their way back to the caravan site that afternoon. They drew a blank. At the office they learned the couple had gone out that morning to visit one of the out-islands. They would not be back until late afternoon. The two men retraced their steps down to the quay. The boats would not be back for another hour at least from the various islands. Roberts addressed himself to a man wearing the traditional clothes of the Cornish fisherman, boots, navy blue trousers, blue smock, peaked cap, and he tried without much success or hope to find out if a couple answering the description of Clapton and Mrs Lambert had boarded a boat that morning and, if so, where to. He learned that they had been seen, but they had been unable to board the boat because there had been an accident.

"Tide was a bit low this morning," the old man explained, "the passengers had to climb down a lot of the steps. They were wet and slippy, like. The woman must have lost her footing, she fell sideways and dropped right over the side. She ended up proper awkward."

Thorn asked, "What happened to her?"

"Young Graham took her up to the clinic when they'd managed to carry her to his car."

"And how is she now, do you know?"

"Seems the doctor says she'll be all right. Badly bruised. Lucky she didn't break nothing."

Thorn and the Sergeant made their way back to the clinic. The receptionist confirmed what they had been told on the quay, that Brenda Lambert, though badly bruised, had no broken bones. There had been internal bruising as well and Doctor Cooper had decided to keep her in the clinic under observation for a couple of days. He had tried to contact Superintendent Thorn but had not been able to get through. The receptionist did not know what it was about. He was out on his afternoon calls now and had said that he would call in at the police station at the end of his rounds. No, she did not know where Mr Clapton had gone, but he had left the clinic after seeing the doctor. He had obviously been very upset, she said; when Doctor Cooper had seen Clapton after examining Mrs Lambert, voices had been raised in the consulting room. Accidents at the quay were remarkably rare in fact, but it was understandable that he should be angry that it had happened. Anyway, Clapton had "stormed out" of the clinic.

The two men went back to the police station and waited. Cooper arrived at teatime and came straight to the point.

"Have you heard about the incident at the quay this morning?" he asked.

"Yes, Brenda Lambert. She fell down the steps onto the side of one of the boats."

"That's right. No great harm done, I think, though I'm keeping her in for observation for a bit."

"So, what is there to be excited about?" Roberts asked.

"It's not Mrs Lambert I'm concerned about particularly. As I said, I'm sure she'll be OK. It's more Clapton's reaction to something I said afterwards. He was naturally enough concerned about her after the accident. I told him she was badly bruised and shocked, of course, and that there was some internal bruising. She landed quite awkwardly, you know, and she was very lucky she didn't break a thigh or even her pelvis, let alone her spleen. Anyway, I examined her very carefully and I was able to reassure Mr Clapton – or so I thought. I told him she was badly bruised but otherwise all right. He told me she'd been attacked two years ago and had been severely injured in the abdomen, so he was especially worried. I told him I'd seen no evidence of such damage and that Mrs Lambert was, apart from today's bad bruising, perfectly healthy. Then he said she was no longer capable of having children. Now, I not only examined her very carefully, but I had x-rays taken as well and Brenda Lambert is perfectly normal, quite capable of conceiving and carrying a child. But when I told him so, at first he simply didn't believe me, then he became abusive, telling me I was a country quack who didn't know what I was talking about, and he got very angry indeed and stormed out of the clinic. I left orders he wasn't to be allowed to visit unless I was there, and I tried to contact you."

"Well, well, well," Thorn exchanged glances with Roberts. "So, why all the subterfuge? Why would Brenda Lambert tell her husband he had prevented her from ever having children?"

"Perhaps," Roberts suggested, "she didn't." And, as Thorn and Cooper waited for an explanation, "Perhaps she told him right from the start she couldn't have children. Well, it begins to look as if Lambert would have liked children, doesn't it? What if she didn't want them? Easy enough to start taking the pill without telling her husband. All she'd have to do was tell him she couldn't conceive."

"And she told Clapton a different lie, blamed it on Lambert to get his sympathy. Could be, I suppose: we'd better ask her."

"Can you leave it until tomorrow?" Cooper requested. "I'd really rather she got a good night's sleep tonight. It's not a matter of life or death, of course, but unless it is vitally important to your enquiry, –"

Thorn agreed to wait. Nevertheless, he wanted to speak to Peter Clapton again as soon as possible. Apart from the most recent revelation, which might rattle the man and shake his faith in his mistress' credibility, Thorn wanted to worry out of the ex-marine whether or not Lambert had been blackmailing him. If he had, then new perspectives opened up: for the blackmailer to succeed, there had to have been contact between Lambert and Clapton, contact which once more contradicted statements made by both Clapton himself and by Brenda Lambert. Thorn began to feel that searching for the truth in all this was like grasping an eel. He asked when were visiting hours at the clinic and was told they were officially between six and eight in the evening, although the rules were not strictly enforced. Better then to try to intercept Clapton at the clinic at six, if he called. It was always possible he would be too annoyed at Brenda Lambert's deception, but that was less likely. With the doctor's help he arranged for the receptionist to telephone, should Clapton turn up in the evening.

While he waited for Clapton to put in an appearance Thorn took Lambert's wallet out of its labelled, plastic bag and looked again at its contents. They told him nothing he didn't already know, but he found a receipt for the sweatshirt he had bought. To kill time he walked the short distance up the street and found the small shop whose name was printed on the till check. It was just round the corner from the Smuggler's Arms and Lambert must have passed it virtually every time he left the pub. Thorn went in. A short, dark-haired woman greeted him. He presented her with the small piece of paper. She frowned as she tried to remember the sale. She looked at the price, £29, and the date. At first hesitantly, then with more confidence she recalled the sale had been for a sweatshirt. She described it. It matched Thorn's recollection of the smart garment which he had seen, soiled and bloodstained, on Lambert's body. Out of habit Thorn asked more questions: did she remember the customer? Was there anything unusual about him? But he was surprised by the answers. Lambert had asked to examine the sweatshirt and had decided to have it, but he had opened his wallet and there had been no money in it. Telling the assistant to keep it for him, he had left the shop, turned left, towards the Smuggler's Arms. He came back within five minutes with cash. When he had paid, the assistant had noticed he had two £20 notes and one tenner in his wallet, as though he had cashed a cheque at the bank. But the bank was in the opposite direction. He must, therefore, have returned to the pub and collected the money from his room.

It did not make sense. Lambert, Thorn knew, had not drawn any money from the bank. He had, indeed, relied on the proceeds of blackmail. Surely he would have kept the money in his wallet. Why on earth would he have obtained money and then left it in his room at the pub to go out and visit the shop, which was just round the corner?

He thanked the woman and left the shop to walk as far as the sea wall where he sat on a bench and looked at the boats without really seeing them. It was another of those little anomalies which Thorn could not accept. If there was something unusual or atypical to be discovered, it was, in nine cases out of ten, significant. It was often the resolution of apparently insignificant anomalies which led to important changes of perspective and understanding. So, if it was improbable that Lambert had left his money in his room, and at the same time, it was known that he didn't draw the money from his account, it was possible that he simply had gone to his source of money to get the £50 that morning. But telling the shop assistant to wait while he obtained cash suggested total confidence on

Lambert's part that his victim would cough up immediately as, indeed, he had. Then the obvious struck him: of course, Lambert knew he could get the money immediately, if the meeting had already been arranged and he was already on the way to meet his victim, Clapton, maybe. No, that was not quite right either: Lambert had just appeared from the direction of the Smuggler's Arms, and had returned there. Stop, Thorn told himself: had the shopkeeper actually stated Lambert had come from the direction of the Smuggler's Arms, or just that he had returned there to get the money? He couldn't remember. He went back and asked. No, she had not said where the customer had come from to enter the shop. She did not remember seeing him turn into the doorway. She was clearly intrigued by Thorn's interest in such an insignificant detail, but she did not ask why. Her black eyes glittered with interest, and with suppressed curiosity as the policeman left again.

So, Lambert already had an appointment to meet his victim, Clapton, and was on his way there when he noticed the sweatshirt in the shop window. He knew he would have the cash to pay for it in just a few minutes, and chose not to pay by cheque or credit card. It still seemed a little odd to Thorn, unless Lambert got a special kick out of using his victim in this way, like a savings bank, contemptuously. The incident was probably insignificant, except that it might pinpoint a date on which the victim had handed over money. And it began to look as though blackmail might well be an important, if not the most important, motivating element in the murder of Matthew Lambert.

Peter Clapton turned up at the clinic that evening and was, once more, angry and abusive when he was denied immediate access to Brenda Lambert. Thorn managed to manoeuvre him into Cooper's consulting room, where he was told in no uncertain terms that he would not be allowed to visit, if he intended only to distress the patient. He dismissed the idea as nonsense, and tried to insist he should be allowed to see her. Thorn said he had reason to suspect the patient would be upset, and said Clapton would be allowed into the ward only if he, Thorn, went with him. Predictably, this provoked another storm of abuse over intrusion into privacy, until Thorn pointed out very quietly that Clapton was not next of kin to Brenda Lambert, and had no legal right to see her at all. Clapton reacted with a look of pure hatred which gave way to the realisation of his status, or lack of it, and his anger turned to misery. Backed into a corner, he finally agreed terms, and Thorn followed him into the small ward.

Brenda Lambert lay flat in the white bed. The severe bruising she had suffered from the fall was probably painful, and prevented her from sitting up. But her face was strained and anxious. When Clapton entered the room, Thorn saw the woman's eyes move from side to side, searching Clapton's face, trying to assess his mood. Her expression was intensely grave and troubled, utterly unsure of her lover's feelings.

"Hello," she said, almost in a whisper. And she glanced at Thorn, who had followed Clapton. Then the same worried look returned to her lover's face.

"Hello," said Clapton. He stopped a yard from the bed, returning her stare. Neither of them spoke again for perhaps a minute, each merely scrutinising the other's face. Silently, Brenda Lambert began to cry. She made no sound, but tears ran down her pale face. Clapton moved forward to her side.

"Don't," he said, and took her head in his hands, and kissed her gently.

"I'm sorry," she whispered. He made comforting noises. Thorn, watching, made no sound. He waited.

"Why?" Clapton asked. "Why did you lie?"

"It's a long story," Brenda Lambert said.

"Don't you want kids?"

At first there was no response. Instead, the tears began again, this time not silent, but, because the sobbing was obviously painful, she managed to control it. "Not now," she said. "I'll explain. I promise, but not now." After a while she regained her composure, and wiped her face. Thorn recognised the despair and fear in it, even now that Clapton was back. "I didn't want to lose you," she said after a while. "I'm going to, though, aren't I?"

"No. Why do you say that?"

"I know what children mean to you. I know you want them. I – I just can't."

"Don't upset yourself," Clapton interrupted. "Just get well. We'll talk about it then.

"You'll come back?" She could not believe it.

"Yes, of course I will."

Again, she gave him a long, questioning look, not believing him.

Thorn had seen enough for the present. He turned and left the room to wait for Clapton outside in the corridor. Brenda Lambert was in no fit state to answer his questions at the moment, and in any case, it was Clapton he really wanted to talk to. Brenda Lambert was truly jinxed. Her first marriage had ended in violence, and her husband had been murdered. Her relationship with Clapton, endangered by her pretence that she could not have a child, was likely, it seemed, to return to a close understanding, judging by the scene he had just witnessed.

But any happiness she found would almost certainly be short-lived, if his suspicions were justified. It now seemed Lambert had been blackmailing his former "oppo", perhaps because he had discovered the secret of Clapton's father. Clapton, already his enemy because of his treatment of Brenda, must now have become enraged that he was subject to extortion. The quarrel in the street last Wednesday evening was the final straw which led him to slip out of the caravan and...

But how had Clapton known where to find Lambert at 1 o'clock in the morning? What exactly had been said in the course of the scuffle, witnessed by Brenda Lambert? Had a rendezvous been arranged? If so, the woman must have known of it. Thorn pounded the window sill with his fist in frustration. He was no nearer the truth than he had ever been.

Chapter 12

Thorn intercepted Clapton as he left the clinic. It was not the best place to interview him, and he merely asked him to call at the police station the following morning at 10.30, allowing enough time to speak to Brenda Lambert first. He suspected that Brenda would be unaware of any blackmail threats from her husband, but he considered it a possibility which he had to allow for. Without asking her directly, Thorn hoped he would at least get some intimation of her knowledge or ignorance. He suspected, in fact, that the attempted blackmail of Clapton might well have involved keeping the truth about his parentage from Brenda. It would be an important interview and it would therefore be desirable to have Roberts in attendance. As for Brenda Lambert's behaviour and her now clear deception of both her husband and her lover, that was probably a minor matter, though Thorn was puzzled by it. It seemed to him unnatural for a woman to choose not to have children, unless there was some real danger, either to her own health or that the child might carry a hereditary disease or defect. It was not an area he wanted to explore, but he felt he had to.

He took his time returning to the police station, strolling by the harbour wall. The tide was nearly at the flood, lapping lazily on the sand below him. The water was dotted with pleasure craft of different shapes and sizes. He noticed a new arrival, a sleek yacht, white and gleaming. She was at anchor, her bows still pointing towards the open sea as the last of the tide took her. At the stern a young man in jeans and sweater, was clambering into an inflatable dinghy to paddle ashore. As Thorn headed towards the Pirate, where he thought he would buy himself a drink and give the Roberts a little longer on their own, before disturbing them, he observed idly that the dinghy was converging on the same point of the harbour and would probably come ashore close to the pub.

The Pirate was busy and noisy. He chose the public bar rather than the snug and, although the noise level dropped perceptibly as the predominantly local customers took stock of him, he was glad not to associate with visitors. One or two of the customers nodded or greeted him briefly as he went to the bar. By the time he got there the conversations were back to their normal level.

"What'll it be then, Superintendent?" Ben Jacobs asked with a welcoming smile.

Thorn ordered a pint.

"Good to see you," said Ben as he took the money. "How's it going, then? Making progress?"

"So so."

"You'll sort it out, I reckon. We was saying, "– he nodded vaguely at the row of men standing at the bar, all seriously studying the drinks before them, or engaged in conversation – "it's been a shockin' month or two, what with that fellow being knifed up on Purley Head, then Sarah Treduggan and old Job. The sooner you get that all sorted, the better."

Next to him two men were deep in discussion of the problem of youngsters on the islands finding houses to live in. He was left to drink in peace. He took a swig of his beer and, as he put it down, glanced across the bar beyond the busy figure of Ben Jacobs, and into the snug. Waiting to be served was a smiling, self-confident young man. Penelope Jefferies pressed close to him, one hand through his arm, proprietorially. The sweater he wore marked him as the same man who had just left his boat in the harbour.

"Ben," Thorn asked the publican the next time he came to his end of the bar, "that young chap with Penny Jefferies, do you know him?"

Ben cast a look back into the snug. "Never set eyes on him before," he said. "I do hear as he's got his boat in the harbour, though. Why?"

"Just idle curiosity," said Thorn. "What about the girl, does she often come in here? Seems a bit rummy when she lives in the other pub."

Ben laughed, "Show she's got better taste than her parents," he said. "No, she's only been old enough to come in here for the past year. She is away upcountry most of the time, like, so I can't say as I've seen a lot of her. Once or twice, maybe."

Thorn continued to watch the young couple from behind his tankard. They appeared to be well acquainted, two friends, perhaps lovers, glad to see one another again after a separation. They were too far off for Thorn to overhear any of their conversations, but it looked to be light-hearted in tone. They laughed quite a lot, with much eye contact. They were clearly very comfortable with one another. Thorn finished his drink and left.

He asked Bill Roberts if he recognised either the boat, which he pointed out, or knew of Penelope Jefferies' boyfriend, whom he described. Neither Bill nor Tina recognised the description.

"Whoever he is, he's probably just a visitor," said Roberts.

"I get the impression she knows him well."

"Well, she's been living away from home for the past year. I expect she's made a few friends on the mainland in that time."

"I didn't know you were interested in such things, Superintendent," Tina was teasing him. "I thought it was women who took an interest in girls' boyfriends."

Thorn laughed. "You're right," he said, "it's not really any of my business. It's just that the Jefferies interest me as a family."

"There's nothing very interesting about the Jefferies," protested Tina. "They lead a very quiet life here. I suppose they're very busy in the season, though the Smuggler's isn't all that popular with the islanders. I don't know how they spend their time in the winter, though. They don't mix much, never have."

"You must feel pretty cut off in the winter. I suppose it is a different place then."

Tina reflected before she answered. "Well, we are cut off, especially when the weather is bad," she admitted, "but at the same time, all the residents on the island feel closer together."

"I understand a lot of island communities are like that. You have to depend on one another, I suppose, when things go wrong, or the boat can't get across and make its usual deliveries."

Tina nodded. "That sort of thing," she said. "And we do get some spectacular winter storms, you know. Atlantic gales. We really are cut off then. It's because we're not just cut off from the mainland, but we are actually surrounded by the storm. The lifeboat has more than enough work to do then."

"But it doesn't get you down to be so isolated?"

"Oh, that's when the islands come to life. You may not believe it, but we're always so busy we hardly find time to do everything. You see, there's the choir, the amateur dramatics, the dances, the whist drives, the bridge evenings, there's something on every week, usually two or three things in a week. It gets especially busy round Christmas and again at Mayday and Easter."

"Never a dull moment," commented Thorn, amused.

"It's not to everybody's taste."

But, thought Thorn, it was not a bad way of life, if you could rein in your ambitions, as Bill Roberts had. Or you could simply be content to cultivate your own garden or, in the case of the Roberts, your allotment, ignoring the rest of the world.

"You say the Jefferies don't join in much," he prompted.

"No, not really. I can't think of any social group or club they belong to, can you, Bill?"

"No, not now you mention it."

"What about Penelope? Did she join in?"

"Well, she's never been here much of the time," Bill explained. "She was off at her boarding school during term time, you see. In the holidays she was here, of course. She's got her own boat, a dinghy, does a bit of sailing, or did, anyway. But she couldn't join in all that much; I mean, amateur dramatics or singing, that sort of thing, you've got to be practising, haven't you?"

"Maybe she made up for it at school," Thorn said.

"If you ask me," said Tina darkly, "she can't have had much of a life of it at all. Her parents were tied up at the pub and hardly ever leave the islands. I don't remember the last time George Jefferies left the island even for a day, and his wife seems to pop over to Penzance for a day's shopping once in a blue moon."

"I see why you say it's a dull life for them," said Thorn. "Maybe they're just not very sociable."

"Yes," Bill said, "but why choose to keep a pub in that case?"

It seemed a valid question. Ever since he had first met the Jefferies and visited their home, Thorn had felt there was something odd about them, their lifestyle, their attitude. The lack of cooperation, not to say obfuscation with which Thora Jefferies in particular had met his questions, the oversensitive reaction to his questioning of Penelope's flatmates, the attempt to conceal a minor piece of tax evasion, and the lack of interest on their part in a paying guest, all sounded false notes. Tomorrow, he decided, he would get Bill Roberts to probe a little into the Jefferies' background. It might have little relevance to the circumstances surrounding Lambert's death, but for the time being, the enquiries were almost at a standstill. His interviews with Lambert's widow and with Peter Clapton might lead to some clarification of the issues, but he felt instinctively there was something still to be uncovered which would make sense of the whole business.

He went to bed early. Before turning in, he stood at the window for a few minutes and, since it was a warm night, he opened it and leaned out. Below him the sea made little clucking and gurgling noises as the wavelets lapped against the beach. The workaday boats which had carried the visitors to the out islands hung at the end of their mooring ropes, moving only slightly as the tide ebbed. On the headland to the right leading lights gleamed clearly. At regular intervals the beam of the Bishop Rock Lighthouse swept round the sky.

The lifeboat, too big to be kept in the boathouse, which had been built sixty years earlier to accommodate her brave predecessor, swung at her moorings on the other side of the harbour. Between the pleasure boats and the lifeboat Thorn could see a couple of dozen small craft, cabin cruisers, large sailing dinghies, half a dozen larger sailing boats, including the newcomer, its white hull gleaming as she rolled gently on the tide, reflecting the lights along the wharf. As he watched, he saw activity in the cockpit as first one, then a second figure emerged from the cabin. The two climbed into the inflatable, and paddled ashore. Before she stepped out onto the slipway, Penelope Jefferies gave the young man a warm embrace and kissed him goodnight. She walked joyously up the slip, turned to wave happily, then was swallowed in the darkness between two houses. The yachtsman pushed the dingy away from the slipway, and paddled back to his boat. Thorn undressed and got into bed with a thoughtful frown.

"The Jefferies?" The Sergeant was baffled. "Yes, sir, I suppose I can make a few enquiries about them, if you want, but surely you don't think they're involved in this in any way?"

"Just do it," said Thorn. "I have absolutely no reason to make these enquiries, except instinct, Sergeant. There's something wrong and I can smell it, but there is no logical reasoning involved. I have been making investigations of one sort or another for years, and you'll just have to trust my instincts. But be discreet: the Jefferies are more than a little sensitive about their privacy. That's why I'm curious. You could make a start checking their application – the original one – for a liquor licence. Seeing where they came from. Dig a little. And try to find out a bit about the young chap on the white boat, the one that Penelope Jefferies went out with last night."

It was time for Thorn himself to return to Mrs Lambert in the clinic. She looked older, more vulnerable. His first reaction surprised him; he felt sorry for her.

202

"Hello, Mrs Lambert, how are you feeling?"

"Very sore," she smiled but her eyes remained wary and hard.

"I'd like to ask just a few more questions, if you feel up to it." She nodded, and Thorn pulled out a chair. "I realise this is very painful for you to talk about, but I must get the records straight." Again, she nodded but her eyes avoided his, and her expression was that of someone who knew she was trapped. "Now," he went on gently, "the first thing I must ask is a personal one. You told me, when you made your first statement, that you were unable to have children because your husband had assaulted you." She nodded. "That is not true, is it?"

"No." She uttered the word with the utmost reluctance, like a small child, guilty at having been caught out in a lie.

"Why did you tell me, then?"

She looked from side to side. Her lips opened and closed as she sought the right words, and she was agitated. "It's so – so complicated," she said at last.

"Try to explain."

"I don't know if you can understand," she said, "but I just can't bear the thought of having a child."

"Mrs Lambert," Thorn attempted to be encouraging, "I may be a policeman, but I'm also a human being. I imagine that there must be quite a lot of women who are afraid of having a child."

"No, I'm not afraid; not in the usual sense, anyway. I know people say it's painful and all that, it's not that."

"Then what is the problem?"

Again the pause as Brenda Lambert groped for the right words. "It's – well, you could say it's because I'm afraid of the responsibility."

Thorn was really puzzled. "But you've been a married woman. You've run a house. You had a job. You're right, I don't understand."

"If you have a child," said Brenda, "you have to love it, devote yourself to looking after it, caring for it."

"Yes?"

"What if I couldn't keep it up? What if it was one of those babies that cried and cried night after night and day after day? What if I lost my patience after a while?"

"You think you would?"

"I don't know!" She was not just uncertain, she was upset by her own uncertainty.

"But why should you? Don't you think you are as capable as the next woman? And you would have had the support of your husband."

"It's too much of a risk."

Thorn, baffled, began to feel stirrings of impatience. He tried to stifle them. "Did you tell your husband you couldn't have children?" He asked bluntly.

"Yes."

"What was his reaction?"

"He was – disappointed. He wanted me to have some tests."

"But you refused?"

"I had to. Otherwise he would have found out."

"What was his reaction?"

"He got very angry."

"Is that when he started hitting you?"

She nodded.

"If you'd told him the truth, don't you think he would have understood?"

"It would have made things worse!"

"How could it? How could things possibly have been worse than to have your husband so angry with you that he hit you? More than once, I imagine." She nodded miserably at the memory.

"It destroyed the marriage," she said.

"Are you saying the failure of your marriage was not down to your husband at all but to you?"

"Yes – no – I don't know. Matt was so keen to have children."

"I can understand that, Mrs Lambert. Couldn't you have looked for help? Asked your doctor? Don't you think your fear might have been – still is unfounded?"

"You make it sound as though it's all in my mind," she cried.

"Isn't it?"

"No. I've still got the scars to prove it." And, before his startled gaze, she moved painfully in the bed to pull her nightdress up beneath her breasts to leave a bare strip of flesh between nightgown and sheet. She pointed to a wide, white scar which ran round the side of her body on a level with the bottom rib as far as her spine. Uncomprehending, Thorn stared at the scar, then at her face.

"My mother did that to me when I was seven," she said. "She also broke my right leg, three ribs, and one arm. I lost four teeth on one occasion, and hair torn out at the roots. I got over the broken bones, but the worst damage is in here," she pointed to her head. "No one can mend that.

And she said she still loved me, and that she always would. I believe her." She pulled the nightdress down again. "You see, Superintendent, some people simply aren't psychologically capable of caring for children, even when they love them. I – well, I can't risk it."

Thorn was silent for a while. The woman on the bed, now her secret was out, still looked sad, but the fear of discovery had gone. She looked stronger.

"How much of this have you told Mr Clapton?" he asked.

"He only knows I don't want children. He doesn't know why, and I don't want him told."

"Don't you think he'd understand?"

"You didn't, did you?"

"But in view of Mr Clapton's own childhood experiences –"

"I don't understand." She looked genuinely puzzled. Thorn's experiment in fishing had caught nothing, it had merely drowned the worm.

"He was in a children's home, too."

Still the puzzled look.

"It's none of my business, Mrs Lambert, but I think you are wrong, if you think that way. In my experience violence isn't automatically inherited. And not to have children when you can –"

But it really wasn't his business, he reminded himself. He stood up. He had found out what he came for, that Brenda Lambert did not know about Peter Clapton's childhood, or at least, that his father had murdered his mother.

"Thank you for putting the record straight," he said. "Concentrate on getting better. Goodbye."

Yet another instance of parent-children relationships which bedevilled this case. Thorn thought about it as he strode back to the police station. Was there such a thing as a normal, loving, and straightforward family to be found on this island?

He had barely had time to exchange a word with the Sergeant, before Peter Clapton arrived.

"Mr Clapton, before I ask you any questions, is there anything you feel you should add to your statement?"

Clapton frowned. "No. What else is there?"

"When Matthew Lambert left Chichester to come here on holiday, he had just been paid."

"Yes?"

"His pay, including his holiday pay, was credited directly to his bank account."

Clapton maintained his look of total bafflement.

"We know for a fact that he did not draw any money from that account, up to the date he died," Thorn continued. "Despite that fact, he paid in cash for three weeks' bed-and-breakfast accommodation at the Smuggler's Arms, he paid for all his meals in cash, went drinking most evenings. Ever since I discovered all this, I've been puzzled as to how he found the money."

Clapton's expression did not change. If anything, he looked even more perplexed by this line of questioning. Was he such a good actor, Thorn wondered.

"In the course of our investigation," he ploughed on, "we have come across evidence which suggests Matthew Lambert might have had some kind of hold over someone else on the island. We have strong reason to believe he used that information to extort money."

There was now a flicker of understanding, but Thorn could see no trace of fear in Clapton's expression, rather it was interest and curiosity. Either the man was indeed a very good actor, who had perhaps rehearsed this conversation in his mind, just in case, or he was learning something entirely new.

"I must ask you again, Mr Clapton," Thorn insisted, "have you anything further to add to your statement which could be relevant to our enquiries?"

"I don't think so," said Clapton, as though reviewing carefully all he knew. "I don't know what you're trying to get me to say."

"I want you to think very hard before you answer the next question," said Thorn. "You knew Lambert for many years. You were close friends. You shared the same mess deck, no doubt. In the course of your friendship was there any information about yourself which Lambert discovered, or which you gave him in confidence, which he might conceivably have held over you?"

"Are you seriously suggesting," Clapton asked, "that Matt Lambert might have been blackmailing me?" He looked amazed at the idea.

"Not suggesting, asking."

"Superintendent, I don't honestly believe Matt Lambert was a blackmailer anyway. He certainly didn't try to blackmail me. And, in answer to your question, no, there's nothing in my past he could have used that way."

Thorn shifted in his chair, and reached across the desk to draw the thin file in front of him. "While I was on the mainland, I had occasion to visit your ex CO in Deal. I also went on to see a very old friend of yours, Mrs Latchford."

Peter Clapton sat up at this news. "You went to see Mrs Latchford?" he repeated, surprised, and then a tad indignant. "Why did you have to drag her into it?"

Thorn opened the file. The photocopies of the reports of the Clapton murder trial stared up at him and at Peter Clapton. He looked at them, not at first understanding their significance, then light dawned slowly. "And you think," he said, "that Matt Lambert knew about my father and used the information as ammunition? You think he was blackmailing me?"

"Was he?"

"No, of course not. Look at the date on these old reports. It all happened when I was nine years old. Do you really think it still bothers me? That's nearly 30 years ago!"

"Mrs Lambert still doesn't know anything about it."

"What? Have you been up at the clinic asking her questions, upsetting her again? Hasn't she had enough? It's bad enough you should accuse me of murder."

"You are not accused of murder, Mr Clapton."

"As good as. You're saying Matt was blackmailing me and that gives me a motive for killing him."

"You had just had a quarrel with him earlier that evening, when you say he tried to pester Mrs Lambert. You also thought he was responsible for making her infertile. If he was also threatening to tell her about your father, you may possibly have seen that as a very real threat to your future relationship."

Clapton stared at him with a mixture of incredulity and contempt. "You must have a very twisted mind," he said. "No wonder the police have such a lousy reputation."

"To your knowledge," Thorn went on doggedly, "does Brenda Lambert know about your father's trial?"

"No. But nor did Matt. I never mentioned it. By the time we knew each other it was already history, and unimportant."

"Matthew Lambert was not attempting to blackmail you?"

"No."

"You still maintain you did not see him again after you left him in Church Street?"

"No."

"Thank you, Mr Clapton. You can go."

Clapton made no immediate move. "That's it?" he asked

"Yes." That's it."

"No apologies?"

"Mr Clapton, I am doing my duty, no more, no less. A man has come to a very violent end, an unnatural end, and my job is to find out how. In the process other people are likely to be hurt, offended, insulted, more especially so if they conceal or try to conceal the truth."

"You still don't believe me?"

"What I personally believe or do not believe has no importance. What matters is evidence. I have no evidence to suggest you are lying on this occasion, even if you have done so in the past. You are free to go. I suggest you do so, and that you spend your energies more positively. Go and see Mrs Lambert, man. She needs you."

Clapton got up, perplexed by Thorn's response, and left quickly.

"In spite of that," Thorn observed to Roberts, "I believe him this time. I don't think he was the victim of blackmail, always supposing there was one."

"You don't think," suggested the Sergeant, "Lambert got money from McNab for favours received?"

"Not all that likely, Sergeant. Not if McNab came over here in the first instance to do him in."

"No, I suppose not."

"How have you been getting on with your researches?"

"Ah, now, that has been quite interesting so far. George Jefferies moved here from Brighton where he ran a pub for two years before that. That was his first pub, it seems. He and Thora Jefferies managed it for one of the bigger breweries, who trained their own managers. I rang the brewery and they said they'd ring back when they'd looked up their records. I also rang to see if George or Thora Jefferies have form. That was more interesting."

"Oh?" Thorn's ears picked up. "I gather from your expression the answer is yes."

"Yes and no, sir. George Jefferies used to be a copper. He worked in the Met. Did five years with them apparently. But the interesting thing is, he left under a bit of a cloud. There were incidents in which he was implicated, being a shade heavy-handed with suspects. Nothing definite, but he left, and his records say he was 'unsuitable material for a police officer'."

"Do they indeed? And when did all this take place?"

"He left the Met in fifty-five – twenty-five years ago."

"What happened to him after that?"

"All they've got on the computer is that he took a job with a big security firm. Not a very important position. It had its head office in London, but they could be sent anywhere in the country. I haven't had time to contact them yet to find out how long he worked with them or where, and when he eventually got into the licensed trade."

"Maybe we're clutching at straws. The fact that George Jefferies was once a policeman who tended to go in for a bit too much rough stuff twenty-five years ago doesn't seem much of a link with the murder."

"You're probably right, sir."

"What about Penelope Jefferies' boyfriend?"

"That was a bit easier. I had a quick word with the harbourmaster. The boat is registered in Southampton to a Mr Paul Stringer." Roberts smiled, as one privy to a secret.

"So, what's so significant about Mr Stringer"

"Son of Bertrand Stringer –"

"You mean the Undersecretary of State at the Treasury, whizz-kid extraordinary? That Bertrand Stringer?"

"The very same. Penny Jefferies seems to have landed herself quite a catch. Not short of a bob or two, I imagine, and young Paul should go far."

"Yes indeed. I suppose they met at university?"

"Sorry, sir, didn't have time to find out. You said to be discreet."

"Well done, Sergeant."

At least, thought Thorn, this was an entertaining development. It could not possibly have any bearing on the case in question. He left Roberts in the office to await his phone call and took himself off to walk and think. He needed to clear his head.

The tide was at the full again. There were fewer boats at the moorings. The large launches full of trippers were scattered about the off-islands by now, their passengers hiking over the treeless slopes of the smaller islands, or perhaps perching on cliff tops, dazzled by the sun dancing on the waves below, some of them, no doubt, looking over the Abbey Gardens on Tresco. Chloe was at anchor, deserted. The dinghy was out of sight. Thorn walked briskly away from the town, heading towards the Treduggan farm. He consciously altered direction when he realised what he was doing. After half an hour's walking he arrived at the cliffs again, beyond the golf course. He found a deserted spot, sat down and thought. Something was nagging at him. He reviewed all the events and evidence to date for the umpteenth time. All the important evidence was circumstantial. Oh, for some really solid, forensic evidence, he thought. Even the murder weapon had not been found. And by now it would be too late to search any premises for blood stains or bloodstained clothing. The time for that would have been within a few hours of the murder, but, even then, there was a strict limit to the amount of searching that could have been done by himself and Sergeant Roberts only. He was very conscious that this investigation was a long, long way from the methodical, professional and painstaking enquiry he would normally have organised in his own station.

He remembered with a curse the box of letters he had brought back from Chichester and which he had not read through. They were from the Chinese girl, Lee Kwang, and unlikely to reveal anything of importance, but he had found them and should read them. He had glanced at two of them. They were quite mundane, letters from a small girl to her foreign patron. He would make himself read the rest.

When he had completed his mental review, he came once more to the same conclusions: three people had definitely been on Purley Head at the time of the murder, Lambert himself, Sarah Treduggan and Job. Job had a motive to kill Lambert and it was quite possible Sarah had witnessed him doing so. That did not square with Job's statement, but just because he admitted to the murder of his daughter, he did not necessarily have to be telling the truth about Lambert. If he decided to wrap up the enquiry with the suggested solution, that Job Treduggan was a double murderer, Thorn felt sure no one would seriously challenge it, but he felt in his gut it was not so, and Job's reference to "another bloke" on Purley Head should be substantiated. But who was he? Frustrating as his enquiries were still proving, Thorn knew he had to find out for his own satisfaction.

Chapter 13

That evening brought a change in the weather. From the west clouds gradually shaded the sky until it took on a sombre appearance. The sun set behind the cloud and a moist wind began to rise; it would soon bring rain, and would soon blow itself out, said the locals, as they gathered in the pub for the evening. By morning their predictions had been proved accurate, and the sun rose in a clear sky again. Visitors looked anxiously from the windows of the boarding houses and hotels and caravans, smiled happily at the prospect of another day on the beach or rambling round the off islands. The gusty rain had swept the street clean and the more percipient of the tourists remarked that the grass was a little greener.

Very few people knew that the summer storm, short though it was, had played like a mischievous prankster in the harbour. Paul Stringer, who was no greenhorn, had anchored the Chloe adequately in the centre of the harbour, unaware that the fine sand in which his anchor had fetched up, provided unsatisfactory purchase. At about three in the morning, as the rain lashed down and the tidy yacht danced to the rhythm of the choppy waves, the incoming tide joined forces with the wind and pushed the boat, slowly at first and then with gathering speed, towards a jagged little reef. Caught on a lee shore, while sleeping healthily in his bunk, the young man was woken by his fall to the deck as the Chloe heeled over. There was no real danger, but Paul Stringer was to be found at 8 o'clock in the morning ruefully making arrangements for the hole in Chloe's side to be repaired. He was not going to be able to sail away for a week or two, that was clear.

Thorn had observed the position of the Chloe when he made his now customary visual check on the harbour before going downstairs to breakfast. The hole was in the starboard side, and therefore hidden from his sight, but the boat was quite obviously, even to a landsman like Thorn, lying at an unusual angle, and one of the working boats, which carried goods between the islands, was alongside. There was much puffing out of cheeks, and puffing on pipes, and scratching of heads, and not a little laughter. The young man's insurance would provide a little income for the boatyard in Porthvean. Glad of an excuse to behave for once like an ordinary tourist, Thorn joined the onlookers at the harbour wall.

The main quay was thronged with visitors, awaiting the inter-island excursions. In the circumstances it was sensible of the young yachtsman to paddle his dinghy ashore close to where Thorn stood. On the sand, Penny Jefferies waited. As the dinghy grounded, she helped her friend haul it up above the high-water mark. He had a couple of canvas grips and a duffel bag. Penny took the bag and slung it over her shoulder.

"Are you sure your parents won't mind?" Paul Stringer asked.

"Of course not. If it makes you feel any better, you can always offer to pay, but I shall be very annoyed if they let you. We do take in visitors in the season occasionally."

Thorn turned back towards the office. The diversion was over. In front of him, the young couple made their way towards the Smuggler's Arms. They were still within earshot when Thora Jefferies, shopping basket on her arm, smart as ever in a long coat and a mannish trilby, met them apparently by chance.

"Mummy," Penny cried, "meet Paul. He's a friend of mine, and he's been shipwrecked. I said we'd put him up for a while."

Thorn feigned a sudden interest in the contents of a dusty shop window. Covertly he watched the reflection in the glass. Thora Jefferies was taken aback by her daughter's assumption, but was unprepared to be rude to her friend and refuse. She asked politely how Paul came to be shipwrecked. Was Penelope being funny, she asked. When Paul explained, she said of course he could stay at the Smuggler's. She asked how he came to know her daughter. He explained they had met through the activities of their respective university sailing clubs. No, he was not at Chichester, but Southampton University.

"I'm afraid I have a little shopping to do," Thora apologised. "Penelope will show you where to put your things. I shall be back shortly." To her daughter she added, "You'd better explain to your father that you've seen me."

They went their separate ways, and Thorn returned to the police station. He picked up Sergeant Roberts' report on his investigations to date into George Jefferies. Now that he knew Jefferies had been a policeman, who had left the Metropolitan Police under a cloud, he began to understand better the publican's uncooperative attitude. Many ex-coppers he had come across, who had left with a sense of grievance, maintained this stance afterwards. They were often cynical, knowing something of the processes of the law from their experience in the police, but were frequently not at all convinced that it had any moral justification. Like weary journalists after a lifetime watching the behaviour of politicians, they interpreted all the events as outward manifestations of personal moves towards acquiring power, status and self-aggrandizement. George Jefferies might well see Thorn's enquiries into the death of Lambert in such a light. And Thorn sensed the publican felt little curiosity, and no regret about the sudden death of a man he had only known as a temporary guest.

All the same, having made some effort to discover Jefferies' history, it seemed pointless not to finish the job and fill in the missing years between Jefferies' joining the security outfit, and his taking over the management of his first pub in Leicester. There would be little point in phoning the security firm. If they were worthy of the description, they would be unlikely to release personal details, even at such an interval, over the phone. If necessary, he could make a formal request for assistance to the Met to make enquiries on his behalf. Meanwhile, the brewery, which had promised Roberts to return his call and describe his training, could be hurried up a little. Thorn picked up the phone and called the number given in the report.

At first he met with prevarication, but he persevered until he was speaking to the Head of Personnel, a man whose voice was irritating and self-satisfied as well as offhand.

"You said you would ring us back with information," said Thorn. "We're still waiting."

"Oh, but your man only rang yesterday, Superintendent. We are very busy at this time of the year, as you can imagine."

"Really?" Thorn was mildly sarcastic.

"It's the summer, Superintendent. Business is at its peak, you know, and it's when all our employees want to take their holiday."

"My heart bleeds," said Thorn. "I want a simple piece of information. George and Thora Jefferies were trained by you and appointed as managers to their first pub in Leicester. You must have taken up references. I need to know where they were immediately before they joined you, and what they were doing."

"Unfortunately," the suave voice began, "my secretary is on holiday at the moment, and the temp is not too familiar with the files."

"Let me just remind you," interrupted Thorn, "this is a murder enquiry. I'm sure in the circumstances you wouldn't mind walking across the room as far as the filing cabinet, looking up Jefferies, reading me the appropriate information. I'll hold the line. It shouldn't take more than sixty seconds." He amused himself by picturing the annoyance on the man's face as he heard the phone clatter onto a desk. He watched the second hand of the wall clock, and grinned as it swept round three times. More noises, then he heard the heavy breathing of a fat man for whom moving round the room was an exertion.

"I have the files here," the voice sounded sulky, like that of a schoolboy who had been forced to do his homework in spite of attempting to dodge it. Thorn did not reply.

"Are you still there?"

"Yes, I'm still here."

"George Jefferies applied for training in March of that year," said the voice. "At the time he was employed by a security firm as a doorman in a club in Chichester. He was planning to marry at the time, at the end of March, according to his letter of application. I imagine he was aiming to get married at the end of the tax year to get the maximum tax rebate."

"You say he was working in Chichester at the time?"

"The address is a private house in Chichester. The security firm was a London firm, I see. It must be one of those big organisations that hire out bouncers. They're much more common these days."

"And his fiancée," Thorn insisted, "did she come from Chichester, too?"

"I – don't know – oh, yes, here we are. They both had to attend the preliminary interview, of course, because our husband and wife teams must both be suitable material. I see we wrote separately to Mrs Jefferies, or rather to a Miss Wright."

"Address?"

There was the impatient sound of someone taking in his breath. "347, Jubilee Street,"

"Good. Now, will you please photocopy the information and send it to me at this address?"

"Very well, Superintendent. I hope that is all."

"It will do for the moment," said Thorn, and he replaced the receiver just as Sergeant Roberts entered the office.

"You look pleased, sir," Roberts observed. "Good news?"

"Bingo!" Thorn said. "One coincidence too many, Sergeant! That was the brewery. George Jefferies and his wife hail from Chichester."

Roberts did not comment immediately. He frowned and walked over to the window, where he stared pensively at the harbour scene.

"What's troubling you?" Thorn asked.

"Well, sir, to quote your own words back at you, when we discovered Jefferies had been in the force twenty-five years ago, you said it was a bit too much like clutching at straws to make a link. The fact that he also lived in Chichester all that time ago… Well, it looks to me just a bit like another straw."

"Point taken. All the same, it's worth looking into. Look, I've jotted down the address Thora Jefferies gave as her home address in those days. Can you phone Chichester and ask Inspector Clegg if it means anything, and if Thora Wright, as she then was, had a record of any kind? I'm going back to the Smuggler's for a quick word."

As he closed the door behind him, Roberts was already dialling. Of course, Thorn told himself, he was adding two and two together to make five. He was well aware that coincidences could happen, and did, but the way in which so many threads seemed to lead back to Chichester would raise questions in the most reasonable of minds, surely. Except for Sarah Treduggan, all the main participants in this tragedy, the victim himself, as well as Brenda Lambert and Peter Clapton, the McNab brothers, one of whom had visited the islands, were all connected with Chichester. The entire Jefferies family also had connections with the town. There had to be a reason. There must be.

He opened the door and walked into the bar. There were no customers to be seen, but George Jefferies and his wife were both behind the bar, engaged in an animated discussion, and so preoccupied they failed to notice him. He watched and listened from just inside the door.

"You stupid, bloody cow!" George shouted. "The last thing we need is a paying guest poking about at a time like this."

"He's not a paying guest. He's Penny's guest."

"Then let him take a room at the Trelawney Hotel, or the Atlantic, for God's sake. He's not poor, I imagine."

"No, he's not poor: he is the son of Bertram Stringer, the Minister."

"Oh my God! It gets worse! If he's staying, he's bound to attract attention. "

"I don't see why. It would look far more suspicious if I told Penny he wasn't welcome."

Thora suddenly realised someone had come in. She looked at Thorn. "What now?" she asked.

"I just wanted to ask you one question," he said, as he took a few steps towards them. "What was your maiden name?"

"Why do you want to know?" It was a strange, defensive response.

"Just to complete our records."

"If you must know, it was Wright," she said, but she seemed reluctant to admit it.

Thorn thanked her, ignoring the glare she gave him. George Jefferies had turned away and was busy sorting glasses. Nearer the bar, Thorn saw he had several small scratches on his face. Thora, he wondered? But he was thinking about what he just overheard. Why should George Jefferies be so concerned at the arrival of Paul Stringer? What did he mean, when he talked of his "poking about"? The Jefferies, it was now very clear, were hiding something. His instincts told him what they were hiding must have a connection with Lambert – after all, Thora Jefferies had agreed, uncharacteristically and far too quickly, to let him stay. There was still some question about how he had paid, and there had been no receipt given him. These small anomalies, added to the information he had now received, meant that he needed answers to more questions. Thora's evident reluctance to tell him her maiden name might indicate a shady past of some kind, but perhaps Clegg's enquiries would give him an idea.

A sudden thought struck him: was George or Thora Jefferies the blackmail victim, and not Clapton? It would explain why Thora Jefferies had not been able to produce a receipt. It would explain also how Lambert had been able to return from the shop to the pub to collect the £50. It would also explain why he had chosen to stay at the Smuggler's Arms rather than a better-appointed hotel. Yes, it all began to hang together. And, if the Jefferies were Lambert's blackmail victims, it gave one or other of them the motive to kill him. They could have followed him that night, when they heard him leave the pub, in the hope they could get him alone, away from his room. Their alibis, after all, could not be corroborated. But why had Lambert written about a "windfall"?

Back at the police station he asked Roberts, "Did you get onto Inspector Clegg?"

Roberts nodded. "Yes. He's got his Sergeant digging up the old records to trace Thora Wright, and he is also contacting a former Station Sergeant who retired a few years ago. He says he has a flypaper mind, and if Miss Thora Wright ever stepped out of line into the nick, he's sure to remember her."

"That's something."

"But there's more."

Thorn waited with a quizzical expression.

"The address, Jubilee Street,"

"What about it?"

"They knocked it down fifteen years ago, and redeveloped the whole area. Until they did, it used to be a major red light district. It sounds as though Miss Wright came from a none too salubrious background."

"Well, we mustn't read too much into that. You can't blame her for having parents who lived in a dubious neighbourhood. It might explain why she has set out to furnish her home wth what she obviously thinks is good taste, but which looks like a brothel. Come to think of it, it might also begin to explain this curious obsession with reputation. The way she and her daughter react to police questions is odd, isn't it? It cuts a lot deeper than it does with that pathetic little woman in Church Street. What's her name? The one who told you she'd seen McNab in the bakery."

"Mrs Luckett."

"Yes, Luckett, that's the woman. You said she was scared someone might have seen you going into her house."

"But she's not that worried, really."

"Exactly. Who is that worried?"

"No one normally, I suppose."

"So, what are they hiding? And are they hiding it from their own daughter?"

While he waited for the call from Inspector Clegg, Thorn took the stack of letters from the box he had brought back from Chichester and, with cups of tea to sustain him, began reading them. Miss Lee wrote very little as a child, but the letters were longer as he worked his way through them. They were generally dull, reflecting the restricted life of an orphan. They mentioned mostly the home and the sisters who ran it. There was not much love shown, and Thorn found himself contrasting this orphanage with the children's home he had visited in Sussex. It took a considerable effort of will to continue the reading methodically. Lee Kwang was obviously an excellent pupil. She listed all her marks, year after year. Thorn's flagging interest revived as he neared the end of the correspondence. At the age of seventeen Miss Lee had entered university and three years later she had graduated in Maths and Business Studies with a first class degree. She was now twenty-two and working in the Investment Section of the Bank of Hong Kong.

Thorn's patience was rewarded when he came to the last letter. In it the young woman said that she had been able to save money from her salary and to invest it very successfully. She had repeatedly expressed her gratitude to "Uncle Matthew" for having given her the opportunity of a good education. Now, she said, it was pay-back time. She was depositing money in a Swiss account for him. He would need the code to access the account, so she would telephone him as soon as he sent her a time and a telephone number.

This, then, would explain the windfall. Theories of blackmail could be discarded.

"We're back with Clapton, then," Roberts said with a sigh of resignation.

"Not quite. We can't be sure Lambert actually got the money. The only people that could confirm that, one way or the other, are the Swiss bankers, and they won't tell anybody, except Lee Kwang herself. I'll get onto the Met and see if they'll contact the Hong Kong police to trace her."

It was Clegg, calling again from Chichester, who made Thorn wonder if he had found an answer to the second question, what were the Jefferies hiding. Thora Wright not only lived in a red light district, but she had a couple of convictions for soliciting. The retired Sergeant remembered her as a good-looking girl with a cynical attitude. More interestingly, he remembered George Jefferies. He too, had been noteworthy because he did his job as doorkeeper efficiently and with excessive enthusiasm, "a man who enjoyed a bit of a punch-up", the former Station Sergeant described him.

"I can understand the brewery accepting George as a trainee-manager," commented Thorn, but Thora..."

"I'll bet they never knew she'd been on the game," said Clegg. "As far as they were concerned, George would be the licensee, and Thora would simply be his wife and assistant. Sounds pretty chauvinist by today's standards, I suppose."

"I expect you're right," Thorn agreed. "And as soon as they were accepted and trained, they moved to Leicester and wiped the slate clean. They aren't exactly the most open-hearted and welcoming couple you could ever meet, but they seem to have stuck together. Must have been something there, I suppose. By the time they came to move to Scilly, they were able to shuffle off their past like a snakeskin.

"Well, you can't hold that against them, can you?"

"No. And I suppose they have a daughter, Penelope, and they do everything they can to give her a good start, private schools, university. And then she chooses Chichester to train, and Thora panics. After eighteen years, I wouldn't have thought there'd be much chance a student would discover her mother's origins in an area of the city which had already been knocked down and rebuilt."

"You can still understand how she might get worried. It's her daughter she thinks she's protecting, remember."

"Yes." Thorn recalled the protests about threatened reputations.. "But it's all circumstantial."

"Why the doubts?"

Thorn frowned. "A lot depends on whether Lambert was a blackmailer, or whether his protegee had provided him with money. Clapton still had a good motive; he is very protective of Brenda Lambert. Meanwhile, we have no physical or forensic evidence. This all seems to make sense, and it may yet be true that Lambert was blackmailing the pair of them, and threatening to tell Penelope Jefferies, who has been brought up with ideas about social advancement. Perhaps Lambert threatened to tell her that her mother had earned her living in the oldest profession. To tell you the truth, I'm not sure the girl would have believed it."

"But her mother wouldn't want to risk it, surely."

"No, probably not. And Thora seems truly impressed that her daughter has a friend who is the son of a cabinet minister."

"Did she know about him at the time of the blackmail?"

"No, but the principle's the same, isn't it?"

"So," said Clegg, "what's your problem? Why the doubts?"

"We're talking about murder here," said Thorn. "Do you really believe someone would kill in the circumstances?"

"Well, someone has killed," Clegg replied pointedly.

Thorn was still not convinced. "All right," he argued, "let's agree that Lambert stumbled on the Jefferies' secret –"

"That would be easy enough," Clegg interrupted him. "He grew up in the back streets and his own parents kept a house of, let's say dubious repute in a street next to Thora Wright's 'office'. She may even have used their so-called club to meet her clients. Years later, when Matthew Lambert was making one of his visits to the islands, he recognises Thora Wright as was, checks her out, and realises he has a potential blackmail victim."

"Sounds plausible."

"I wonder why he didn't try it on earlier."

"Maybe he did."

"I thought that he needed the money in a hurry."

"He did, Sarah Treduggan was getting desperate."

"So, he takes himself off to the Admiral Benbow.."

"Smuggler's Arms," Thorn corrected him.

"– Smuggler's Arms, where he doesn't even have to pay any board, but can collect money whenever he asks for it."

"At which point," Thorn continued the narrative, "George suddenly says enough is enough slips out of the pub and kills him."

"Maybe he asked for too much."

"It still doesn't quite sound right."

"How will you find out?"

"I have no idea," said Thorn. "This whole business is very frustrating because we have nothing but circumstantial evidence to go on."

"Well, let me know what happens. I mean, it's beginning to feel I'm involved in this case still."

"Couldn't have got this far without you", said Thorn. He replaced the receiver just as Sergeant Roberts, seated at the new computer, swore suddenly, then apologised. "I've cut my hand," he said. "Can you pass me the first aid box, sir? I don't want to get blood everywhere."

"How can you cut yourself with a computer?"

"There was a small piece of glass caught in the keyboard," Roberts explained, taking the box from Thorn. Holding a tissue to the wound, he groped in the box and retrieved a pair of tweezers with which he pulled the offending shard from the wound and covered it with a plaster."When the new computer arrived, I hung on to the old keyboard," he explained, peering at the tiny glass fragment."I thought I'd cleaned up after the break-in. I even hoovered up all the glass, or I thought I had. This bit was wedged."

"It's from the monitor, you're saying?"

"I think so, yes."

"Let's hope our burglar cut himself, then."

"I reckon it could be quite dangerous, smashing a monitor, come to think about it," Roberts said."Aren't the screens pressurised or something? They'd go off with a bang, wouldn't they?"

"I think not," said Thorn, "but they're probably full of some kind of gas, helium maybe, or should that be argon? I don't know much about cathode ray tubes, I'm afraid."

"Still," Roberts said,"whoever smashed the computer may have cut himself like me with any luck."

"George Jefferies," Thorn observed, musingly,"has some cuts to his face. Could it be? I thought maybe Thora had done it – they seemed to be having a serious disagreement."

It was reason enough for another visit to the Smuggler's. The two policemen found the place almost empty again, except for George and Thora Jefferies, their daughter and Paul Stringer. There was a certain tension evident in the way that George Jefferies busied himself at the end of the bar opposite the others. Thora was doing her best to be smilingly polite to the young man. Penny was clinging to his arm.

Thorn spoke to George, who turned with a scowl. "Mr Jefferies," he said,"how did you come to cut your face like that?"

"What's it got to do with you?" he replied.

Thora answered Thorn's question. "I knocked a wine glass off the shelf," she said quickly. "My husband was bending down at the time and the bits flew in his face."

"Very nasty," Thorn remarked."He was lucky none of the glass went in his eyes."

"I was very worried," she said, and Thorn thought, if that had been what happened, George's reaction would have been fury.

"Was there anyone in the bar at the time?" he asked.

"No, it was when we were clearing up."

It was a good story, impossible to prove or disprove, but, if Thora was making it up, she was very quick-thinking.

"I don't know what you want this time." Thora changed the subject, "but, as you can see, we were having a private conversation. Can't whatever it is wait?"

But Thorn's attention had been caught by something he saw to her right. Penny Jefferies' hand was on Paul's shoulder. She was simply but elegantly dressed in a silk shirt and a fine cashmere sweater. On her arm she wore a green bracelet which might have been jade. The colour reminded him of something.

"Forgive me," he said, "but your bracelet reminds me of one I've seen elsewhere. May I have a closer look?"

Both women were mildly bemused, but Penny slipped the bracelet off her wrist and handed it to him. She watched while he examined it. It was not a solid circlet of jade – if, indeed, it really was jade rather than a good imitation. It consisted of five parallel rows of carved beads, flat on the underside, where they were stuck somehow to a backing strap. After looking at it very closely, he handed it back and said, "Remarkable! It's just like the one I have seen .If you can spare a few minutes, can you please pop into the office so I can make a proper comparison?"

"What are you talking about?" Thora was suspicious. "Are you suggesting the bracelet was stolen?"

"No, nothing like that," said Thorn, and, leaving Sergeant Roberts as puzzled as the others, he left them to their family discussion and led the way back.

"What was that all about?" Roberts asked, once they were out in the street.

"I believe we may have our very first, solid evidence, Sergeant."

In the office Thorn retrieved one of the small, plastic bags containing evidence. He opened it.

"This," he said, pushing a small, green piece of plastic to one side, using a paperknife, is part of Penny Jefferies' bracelet. There's one piece missing. This is it. You'll see it fits perfectly."

"Penny Jefferies?" You're not suggesting she's mixed up in the murder, surely?"

"Not if she really did arrive the following day, but we need to look into it."

They did not have to wait long. Penny's curiosity was roused. Possibly her boyfriend was intrigued. Whatever the reason, the young couple arrived within the hour. Penny slipped off the bracelet and passed it over, looking in vain for the matching one.

"When," Thorn asked, "were you last up on Purley Head?"

"Purley Head?"

"Yes, near the Standing Stone."

"Years ago."

"Years?"

"I can't remember when, but it was literally years ago. I spent most of my time here sailing or on the beach."

"Can you explain, then, how a broken piece from your bracelet came to be found near the Standing Stone?"

Penny frowned. "Ah, I understand," she said. "It's not my bracelet, Superintendent. It belongs to my mother. I borrowed it. I often borrow her things, and I've always liked this bracelet."

"Did you know it was damaged?"

"I hadn't noticed, no." She examined it and found the small space where the missing piece belonged. "I'll take it and get it repaired," she said.

"I'm afraid we have to hang on to it for the moment as evidence."

"Evidence?" It was Paul Stringer who intervened.

"This is your mother's bracelet, you say?" Thorn ignored the young man.

"Yes." The two youngsters looked at one another, troubled.

"We'll come back to the pub with you." Thorn did not want Thora Jefferies to have advance warning.

The two Jefferies were both in the bar. It was Jenny's day off. When Penny tried to speak to her mother,

Thorn put up a hand, like a traffic policeman, and said, "Mrs Jefferies, something has come up. I'd like you and Mr Jefferies to come back to the station with us. We have some important questions to ask."

"Again? Certainly not! You can see we're working. If it's urgent, tomorrow morning maybe."

"No," said Thorn, "now."

Thora was trapped. She did not want to offend Paul. Uncharacteristically, she hesitated a moment. "Oh, very well," she said at last, "but we shall stay here, and you can ask us whatever you want to ask in here"

"I don't think that would be wise," Thorn commented.

"I'm not prepared to leave my daughter on her own in the bar, even with Mr Stringer's help."

"Mrs Jefferies," Thorn said quietly, "you may not want your daughter to hear what we are talking about. Among other things, I want to discuss events which took place twenty years ago in Chichester."

Thora was shaken at this. She looked appealingly at her husband, but he was also disconcerted, and could say nothing.

"It would be better," Thorn insisted, "if you came to the station with us."

George took charge. He steered his wife towards the door and said to his daughter, "If you have trouble of any sort, close up. I don't know how long we'll be." Penelope was unconcerned, and the two policemen were aware of the self-absorption of the couple behind the bar. They had discovered a new, enclosed world in which they and their mutual feelings were all that mattered.

The others headed away from the bar. No one spoke until they arrived at the police station. Thorn walked

233

around to take his place behind the desk, Thora Jefferies, her features set in a grimace of distaste, perched on the edge of the chair opposite. Her husband turned to a second chair and made to move it closer to his wife's.

"No," said Thorn. Jefferies stopped moving and looked at him in surprise. "I prefer to interview you separately this time, if you please. By all means stay where you are, Mrs Jefferies, but perhaps Mr Jefferies, you would wait in the next room?"

George Jefferies, his hand still on the back of the chair, hesitated. "We'd prefer to stay together," he said.

"I'm sure you would," said Thorn unconcerned, "but I want to conduct separate interviews." Jefferies still hesitated, then, reluctantly he turned towards Roberts' internal door. Bill opened it, followed him into the sitting room, pointed him to a chair, then returned.

"Mrs Jefferies, "Thorn began, "before we begin this interview, let me save time by telling you we have made enquiries in Chichester, and we are well informed about your life before you moved to the islands."

Thora Jefferies sat unmoved and unmoving, her face still a mask.

"We also have reason to suspect," Thorn continued, "that Matthew Lambert, far from being the total stranger you claimed, was in fact acquainted with you from way back, and, when he arrived on your doorstep, demanding accommodation, it was not by chance. You did not offer him the use of your room because he was a tourist with no hotel accommodation booked, nor did you charge him, as you stated previously, for the use of the room."

"I told you," her expression was still unchanged, "he paid the usual rent but I did not put it through the books."

"I wish it were that simple," sighed Thorn.

"What do you mean?"

"I think you know very well what I mean," said Thorn. "Matthew Lambert came to you that night absolutely certain that you would give him accommodation, that you would provide it without charge, and that you would even pay him whatever he asked in return for his silence."

Still no response, but a glare. Undeterred, the policeman continued, "Matthew Lambert realised that he knew you. But he recognised you not as Thora Jefferies, the wife of a respectable publican, but he remembered seeing you many years ago in Chichester, where his parents ran a dubious club called the Red Diamond. In those days a certain Miss Thora Wright lived in the next street and made a living from…"

"Stop!" The mask cracked at last. The woman sitting opposite him did not, however, break down into a state of nerves or fear. She was staring at Thorn with a look of sheer hatred.

"Where is your evidence for all this? Can you prove Lambert took that room for nothing? How could you possibly know he obtained money from us? And what makes you think we would be so weak as to agree in the face of his claims?"

"We have more than enough evidence that Matthew Lambert arrived without money, drew no money while he was here, yet spent a reasonable amount. We know he probably approached you on the day of his death for an extra-large payment of cash. I'm sure, when our investigations are concluded, your banking records will show a noticeable fall in takings at the relevant times. You must have paid him from the daily takings. We are also aware of your extraordinary degree of protectiveness

235

towards your daughter, and that, in order to keep from her your history as a prostitute, you even tried to persuade her to go to another university rather than to Chichester."

"You haven't any proof, that's what I said."

"Oh, we have evidence of your former – profession, Mrs Jefferies. I've no doubt your daughter can tell us more about your strange attitude to her choice of college."

"Don't you dare bring Penelope into this!" She was on her feet now, blazing.

"I shall do whatever is necessary to arrive at the truth. If that means shattering some of your daughter's illusions about her parents…"

"She wouldn't believe you!"

"She couldn't not believe, if we showed her our evidence."

"You have no right!"

"You keep telling me that, and you may believe it, but I do have the right. Some people might claim it is my duty to the girl to tell her the truth about her own background."

"Pig!"

Thorn was silent for a moment. "Of course," he said calmly, toying with the paper knife on the desk, "if you could simply tell us the truth, we might avoid so much unpleasantness. It would be ironic if you paid good money to Lambert to keep your sordid secret from your daughter, only to have her told by me."

Slowly and deliberately Thorn sat back in his chair and raised his eyes to stare Thora Jefferies full in the face. Once, he thought, he would have felt pity, confronted by such a sight. The once-beautiful face which he had discerned at the first meeting, a little fleshy, but with a classically balanced structure, had assumed an appearance that could only be described as ugly. Anger had brought the blood to the surface and tightened the sinews. The eyes no longer had the clear whites and intensely coloured irises of youth, the cheeks sagged a little, the neck was slack.

"Sod you!" she said. "So, Lambert was blackmailing us. So, what?"

"And where were you at the time of his death?"

"I've told you; we were in bed. We heard him go out."

"And you said you wondered if he had a visitor."

"Yes." She nodded, wondering what was coming next.

"But you already knew he was going to meet Sarah Treduggan at the Standing Stone."

"How could I know that?"

"You heard him make the arrangements when you were in the baker's shop that morning."

"I did not."

"You told your husband, and the two of you followed Lambert to his meeting with Sarah. He waited until Sarah left, then he killed Lambert and you helped him throw his body over the cliff."

Thora Jefferies had regained her composure. "No," she said.

"What would you say if I told you we have a witness who saw your husband there?"

"I'd say you were making it up or lying. Or your witness was. My husband was nowhere near Purley Head."

"What if I told you we have physical evidence you were there: we found a piece of your bracelet. The one your daughter borrowed." It was a bluff, but it might work.

"You're making it up. Even if you had, I might have left that there at any time."

That was the snag, and, try as he might, Thorn got no further. He warned her he had not finished, that she must be ready to answer more questions, that the admission of blackmail was serious, and gave rise to many other possibilities, then he let her go out of the office, and told her to go home while he interviewed her husband.

George Jefferies played the same kind of game as his wife, refusing at first to admit to the blackmail, even when told that Thora had admitted it. At length he did confirm his wife's story, but like her, totally denied he had left the house to follow Lambert. "We heard him go out," he repeated, "that was very shortly after I'd locked up the pub, and we were in the flat. That would be just before 1 o'clock. We hadn't been too busy that night, and I finished early."

At least, Thorn remarked to the Sergeant, they had admitted the blackmail. It was a start.

"Do you really think Job Treduggan saw someone else up on Purley Head?"

"Yes," said Thorn. "Even if he were fit to give evidence, however, he didn't get a good look at the man. I've been thinking: perhaps he saw a woman; Thora Jefferies sometimes wears a trilby. You know, Sergeant," he added as they entered the Roberts' sitting room and prepared to put the preoccupations of the case behind them, "I think we're within a whisker of solving this at last." And he held up his finger and thumb, leaving space between them of a quarter of an inch.

"I hope you're right," said Roberts, heading for his favourite armchair and smiling at his wife. "It would be nice to get back to normal."

Chapter 14

Thorn gazed out of his bedroom window the following morning at the busy harbour and allowed his emotions a little rein. If he could paint, he thought, this was the kind of scene he might try, yet in his present mood it would have been pointless. He felt nothing but obscure irritation at what he saw. The chocolate box prettiness of it all was trivial and did not truly appeal. Tourists who flocked here, (emmets as they were sometimes called, the old word for ants), admired the brightly painted boats, bobbing about on the blue water. It was as though these people had been brainwashed into perceiving a tawdry neatness as a form of beauty. It was not unpleasant to look at, he admitted, but it was no more than a superficial prettiness. It was a dressing-up, a pretence, no more truly beautiful than the costume jewellery beloved by Thora Jefferies.

Underlying this very sour mood, Thorn knew, was the thought that the case was coming to a conclusion. He was sure he knew what had happened that night on Purley Head, when four or five people had made their way in the darkness to the Standing Stone. Of those five, one had met his death that night, a second shortly afterwards, a third had left the world of sanity for a nightmare existence in a mental hospital, and the fourth and fifth, if Thorn had anything to do with it, would soon be behind bars, facing the consequences of their actions.

With the prospect of a successful conclusion before him, it was, he knew, perverse to feel as he did. It was not the conclusion of the case in itself which depressed him, but the fear of what he suspected would follow. For several days now, ever since he had made an effort to accept his fate as an existence entirely bound up with his job, without which he had no significance or purpose. He had been absorbed in the work to the exclusion of all else. He *was* his job, just as Clegg had described himself. If, as he thought, the case was about to end, he would be faced with two alternatives; he could take up the offer already made to him to continue his interrupted leave here (or elsewhere, for that matter), or he could refuse it and return to his own office in York. That might be conditional on his accepting counselling, something he was reluctant to agree to. He had already almost decided he would not stay on in Scilly. The illusion of peace and innocence, which he had allowed to deceive him, when he first arrived, had been rudely shattered by the investigation, and the revelations of those less appealing human failings in the inhabitants and visitors alike. It was as though, when he first arrived, he had seen the islands through the eyes of a primitivist. Now he recognised that perception for what it was, a delusion. These people were like all other people, this island was no more truly, intrinsically beautiful than a northern town seen through the eyes of a Lowry.

But if he went back to work in his usual office, there would inevitably be a time between cases, when all those who knew him would cluster round him, pitying him. What worried him was his own inability to summon up any feelings at all. He would find it appalling to go back to an office and wait for work to come to him; without work he felt he was dead. He was as alive as a machine. His only justification was to work. The end of this case was a kind of death for him.

He turned from the window and went down to breakfast. Tina was singing happily to herself.

"You sound cheerful this morning," the Superintendent observed.

"It's our anniversary," she explained, gesturing towards the mantelpiece. Thorn glanced up and saw three cards.

"Congratulations," he said automatically.

"Thank you." She glided in and out of the kitchen as though she were on casters. No, Thorn corrected himself, it was more like that curious movement of ballet dancers, whose feet move very quickly, yet seemed to be almost detached and the body simply moves smoothly from one place to another. Clearly Tina was happy this morning.

"I hope," she said, brightly, "you won't be wanting Bill to work all evening. We'd like to go out for a meal."

"I'll do my best," said Thorn. "I'd have bought you a card if I'd known."

"Thank you, but I didn't expect one. This is the one that gives me most pleasure." She handed Thorn one of the cards to look at. It was signed Tom and Andrea, and under the trite verse Tina's son had added a few words of his own: "Hope we can come and see you soon. If you and Dad can last this long, maybe we might think of following your example when we can afford it."

Thorn handed the card back and picked up his coffee. The race would continue. The same old rituals and games would be repeated. Other, younger people would fall in love, marry, have children, worry about them. He was no longer part of that world, but that was no reason not to wish them well. For this little family group, which he would be leaving behind, survival was important. He, Thorn, wanted them to survive and, to his own surprise, he realised he did feel something, the faint stirrings of concern, an altogether altruistic hope they would be all right. He thought of Clapton and Mrs Lambert. Maybe their relationship had been strengthened by the experiences of the past few days. Perhaps some good might yet come from this. The realisation confused him. He finished his coffee quickly and went into the office.

"Hallo!" Roberts was looking out of the window at the beach. Thorn could see nothing from where he was sitting.

"What's going on?" he asked.

"Looks as if young Penny is launching her boat."

Thorn joined Roberts at the window. Penny and Paul Stringer were standing near the water's edge as a four-wheel drive vehicle backed towards them. A large, open boat on a trailer came slowly to a halt on the sand. George Jefferies was driving the car, Thora beside him. They both got out and all four began to prepare the boat for the sea.

"Come on," said Thorn. "We need to get the parents back to take fingerprints. We may be able to connect George Jefferies with the burglary with proper evidence. You did dust that monitor, didn't you?"

He had.

"What do you want?" Jefferies was belligerent as ever.

"We wondered if you need a hand."

This resulted in a blunt response, telling Thorn and Roberts to take themselves off in a coarse expression which surprised, perhaps shocked Paul Stringer. He stared at Jefferies, looked at Thorn, then turned back to the boat with a grin. Penny gave her father a reproachful look. Thora Jefferies showed no emotion. She merely stared at the Superintendent.

"When you've finished here," Thorn said calmly, "please step into the office."

"What for this time?"

"I'd like to take your fingerprints, and I'm not satisfied you have told us everything."

"We have," said Thora.

"We'll have a better idea once the divers have searched near the cliff."

"Now what are you talking about?"

"I'm pretty sure they'll find the murder weapon," said Thorn. "These days it should be possible to identify finger prints even after being submerged."

Paul Stringer was listening, as Thorn intended. Thora Jefferies was aware of it, and turned to her husband, but before she could say anything, George barked out a mocking laugh. "Balls!" he said. "You're bluffing."

He was right, but the damage had been done. Paul spoke directly to Thorn. "What's all this about?" he asked. "What murder weapon? What murder?"

"It's all about a man called Lambert." Thora answered, hoping to retrieve the situation." He was staying with us, but he had an accident on Purley Head. He fell off the cliff and died. The Inspector has been hassling us ever since. He has a crazy idea we had something to do with his death."

"Murder?" Paul Stringer was shocked.

Thora turned on Thorn now, blazing with anger. "Do you see what you're doing, you stupid fool? Your hints and innuendos are downright slander. You're destroying my reputation, and all this in front of this young man."

"Judging by what we have found out about your life in Chichester," he said, "your reputation was built on very shaky foundations."

"Chichester?" It was Penny's turn to butt in. "You lived in Chichester?"

Thora looked daggers at Thorn. "Yes," she said, "the same town that Lambert came from. I don't know why there is so much fuss about him. He was no one, a security guard. He left Chichester and joined the Navy. He had a daughter in Hong Kong that not even his wife knew about…"

She stopped. Thorn and Sergeant Roberts were staring at her as though amazed.

"What?" she asked.

"We had better finish this conversation in the police station."

"This is persecution."

Nevertheless, Thora strode towards the office and, after the shortest hesitation, George and Penny followed with Thorn and Roberts. They crowded in.

Thora Jefferies confirmed her earlier statement in which she said she had never engaged in social chit-chat with Lambert. How, then, had she known about Lee Kwang? In an effort to clear her, George incriminated himself. He had, he said, seen her mentioned on the display he had torn down. That was a blatant lie. That piece of information had not been recorded on the wall.

The presence of Penny and her friend, Paul, exerted pressure on Thora. She asked them repeatedly to go, but Penny wanted to know about her former life in Chichester. Paul showed more than prurient interest; he was being protective, his arm round Penny's shoulders.

The room was warm, the air thick with anger, fear and aggression. At times George Jefferies looked alarmingly threatening, but he seemed to find it hard to keep up or understand. The questioning continued, relentlessly. How had Thora heard about the Chinese girl? She insisted her husband had told her.

"Why did this man, Lambert, blackmail you, Mummy?" Penny asked.

"Tell her," Thorn said.

"It was something that happened a long time ago." Thora was squirming, this was the complication she had been hoping to avoid, an explanation she had been paying Lambert to keep quiet about.

"But what?" Penny insisted.

There was no stopping her. She would not be content until the truth came out. When it did, Thora tried to describe her "profession" in the vaguest of terms. She said she was "connected with the sex industry for a while, when young".At last her daughter began to understand. She was thoroughly shocked. "Get us out of here," she said to Paul, and the two of them left.

Thora looked haggard. She was still angry. "Do you see what you've done, you stupid man?" She was shouting at Thorn. Her world was collapsing around her. Her husband made no move to console her.

"You can go," said Thorn, "as soon as Sergeant Roberts has taken your fingerprints. I shall, of course, want to speak to you again. I shall be charging you, Mr Jefferies, with breaking and entering. You may want to get yourself a solicitor."

When the two policemen were at last alone, Roberts asked, "What about Mrs Jefferies?"

"We don't have sufficient evidence to charge her with anything."

"But what about the broken bracelet?"

"Lambert was staying at the Smuggler's. A good counsel would argue the broken piece of jewellery could have fallen into his clothing at any time. No, we don't have enough to charge her with, blackmail or no. This is why we needed a proper team of CID men to check out everything."

"We've been doing our best, sir."

"Yes, Sergeant, but in a case like this I would have expected a team of at least thirty men. This is not a reflection on you. You have done very well. I was impressed at the way in which you got your coastguard friends to help. Incidentally, is the scene of crime still cordoned off?"

"Yes, sir."

"Let's take one more look at it."

Thorn had a guilty feeling. As they walked towards the cliffs at the foot of Purley Head, he was thinking how scantily he had searched. He had looked at the area round the Standing Stone and was reasonably happy about that, but he had failed to do a proper search at the foot of the cliff. The boulders of different sizes left plenty of cracks and spaces. When the policemen, coastguards and others had grouped round Lambert's body, their attention had been on that. He was sure they would have noticed anything out of place, but he knew he should have instigated a more detailed check. He began to make up for it now, working methodically along the stones, starting several yards short of the place where the body had been.

"Anything that fell from the top," he pointed out, "could have bounced one way or another."

"Are we looking for anything in particular?" Roberts asked.

"Anything at all."

"It would be good if we found the knife." Roberts was half-joking. Thorn was not amused. He was too busy kicking himself mentally.

They worked slowly and meticulously. They were well past the central point, and they had found nothing. The storm had washed the stones clean, the sun had dried them. Roberts was at the top of the beach, near the cliff face, and Thorn, nearer the shoreline, stood up to tell him to stop. It was a fruitless task, but he had at last carried it through – far later than necessary. But Roberts had dropped to his knees.

"Are you OK, Sergeant?

"Yes, sir. I thought I could see something."

"What?"

"Can't tell. It just looks odd."

Thorn picked his way up the beach. It would be easy to slip or twist an ankle .Roberts pointed into a crack between two sizeable stones. It might be nothing but an old stick, but there was indeed something almost out of sight. There was no way to reach it without moving the stones.

"Give me a hand," he instructed. The two men heaved and struggled with the smooth stone. It was hard to get a purchase on it, but they were both filled with an almost comical determination, as though succeeding was a test of their manhood. With much grunting and swearing the boulder was manoeuvred far enough to reach the one beneath it. This one was a little smaller. Roberts used all his considerable strength to lift one end far enough for Thorn to reach underneath and grab the object.

"Good God!" he said. He was holding a knife. The blade was narrow, not much wider than half an inch, and about seven inches long. The handle was of black plastic. It looked like a kitchen knife.

The two men looked at one another and grinned, delighted with their find.

"Washed back by the storm?" Thorn suggested.

"No. If it had been in the sea, it would have sunk to the bottom, and it's deep here."

"If it is the murder weapon," Thorn said, "the murderer would have thrown it into the sea, not down here."

"It was dark," Roberts pointed out. "He probably thought he had."

"It's a poor attempt to reach the sea. Even a boy would have been able to throw it further."

"Maybe it fell just a bit short, hit a stone and bounced back."

"Pity about the storm, all the same," said Thorn. "All that rain! There won't be any fingerprints."

"The handle was tucked underneath," Roberts pointed out. "It may have been protected."

"I want you to take this to Exeter first thing in the morning. We'll get a proper test done."

"Right," said Roberts.

"Well done, Sergeant."

As soon as they got back to the station, Thorn set the wheels in motion. The two men were still flushed with success. Roberts led the way into the sitting room, saying, "This deserves a celebration," and stopped dead. Thorn gave him a puzzled look. "Tina!" said the Sergeant; "the anniversary!"

All was not quite lost. There was still time for Thorn to see the couple off for their meal. The Superintendent ate a solitary supper and remembered anniversaries of his own..

Chapter 15

"If it's all right with you," Tina said, as she placed a tray of coffee and biscuits on the desk, "I'll leave you a cold lunch today and ask you to look after yourself. We've been neglecting the allotment for the past week or so. While Bill is away in Exeter and the sun is shining, I thought I'd spend the day trying to catch up."

"Don't worry about me," said Thorn, "I'll nip out to the pub."

"If you're sure."

Thorn sipped his coffee and looked out at the harbour. Roberts would be well on his way by now, probably enjoying the novelty of a day away from St Mary's. If there were any useable fingerprints on the knife, they would provide at best flimsy evidence. The whole investigation had been little more than amateurish. Thorn was used to a team of trained CID men and ready access to forensic laboratories. He had been forced to carry out a third-rate investigation, and he didn't like it. He was far from certain the Public Prosecutor would think it worth bringing the case to court.

The phone rang, interrupting these gloomy thoughts. "Thorn! It's you. Good." It was the DCC. "Good news. I'm sending you some backup, Inspector Howell. Can't send more yet, but Howell's a sound man. You'll find him useful."

"That is good news, sir. I think we're on the verge of wrapping this up." He explained that Roberts was in Exeter with what they believed to be the murder weapon. He also summarised the investigation so far, including the break-in. "If we are in luck, and there are useable fingerprints on the knife, we have at least the makings of a case against the Jefferies. George Jefferies looks like the murderer and his wife, Thora, is an accessory at the very least. There will be a practical problem: if we arrest them tomorrow, we don't have anywhere to detain them. There is only one, rudimentary cell here."

There was a strange, harrumphing sound, and a brief pause. "You'll have to get them to Penzance. I know they have two cells there. Good effort. When Howell arrives, and you have briefed him thoroughly, maybe he can take over from you. You will be needed for the court hearings, of course."

He rang off. Thorn was a little surprised at his own reaction. It would be a relief to hand over this case, or rather, these cases, yet it would be with a strange sort of reluctance. Awkward and unsatisfactory though the investigation had been, it would be even worse not to see it through to its logical conclusion. He carried the tray into the kitchen and rinsed the dishes. He felt ill at ease, restless. It was a sunny day and, from the kitchen window he looked out over the harbour towards Tresco. To the right he could see the long, curving, yellow beach of St Martin's. All at once he felt he had to get out of the house. It was too early to look for a pub lunch. He walked down to the beach and decided to walk as far as the harbour wall. The sunshine felt good, but he had not thought of the dozens of mooring lines which ran from the top of the beach down into the water and out to the buoys. He had to step over them every few feet. He wondered idly how long they lasted before they began to rot. Ribbons of seaweed hung from them like washing, wetted by the sea as they dipped up and down in a rhythm he found calming. He passed beneath the windows of the Atlantic Hotel and wondered where the new Inspector would find somewhere to live. Most of the holiday accommodation was already occupied.

Most of the large launches were about their business elsewhere. They transported locals and tourists to and from the off-islands. At least two of them took sightseeing tours round the Western Isles, where passengers could sit in moderate comfort in the boat to watch birds, seals, maybe catch sight of dolphins. Thorn's only excursion had been to the island of Bryher. The sea had been a little wilder that day, and he remembered standing on the Atlantic side, watching the waves break thunderously against the steep cliffs. It was a grey day, matching his mood at the time. Now, on this quiet beach, which smelled of rotting seaweed, and where the herring gulls wheeled effortlessly in the blue sky, his mood had lightened. He was surprised to find he was appreciating the warmth of the sun and the brilliance of the colours. Reaching the harbour wall at last, he climbed up to the granite paving and looked over the other side to the south. The Garrison rose above him to his left. He was going to miss this, he realised. He made his way to the Pirate, where Ben Jacobs welcomed him with a sarcastic remark about being early. He ordered a pint of cider and a pasty and found a seat by the small window. One or two regulars came in, saw him, and nodded in friendly recognition.

He was reluctant to return to the office too quickly. He decided to walk back to the harbour. The Scillonian was moored at the end of the quay. She would wait for her passengers to board, many of them returning from their trips to other islands. Thorn walked to the end of the wall. He had taken his binoculars with him. He focused them on an open boat, sailing between the islands, its white sail bellying out in the breeze. He recognised Penny Jefferies and Paul Stringer. Thorn knew little about sailing, but this boat was moving at some speed, heeled at an angle to catch the wind. The two young people moved swiftly and gracefully, ducking under the boom as they changed tack.

He began to understand the appeal of the sport, the wind in your hair, the thrill of moving fast, using only natural power, the slap and squish of the water as the boat cut through it.

He was still restless when he returned to the office. No news as yet from Exeter. The phone rang. He picked it up, expecting to hear Roberts' voice, but it was Inspector Howell. He sounded very young. He would be arriving, he said, at 6.30 by helicopter. How did he get to the police station? Thorn told him he would pick him up. He called the Island Council Office and obtained names and numbers of three bed-and-breakfast places which had had last-minute cancellations. He booked one of them for the new Inspector.

At 3.30 Roberts sent a text. "Success. A good thumb print and a match. Back at 6."

He drove to the heliport to meet the Sergeant's flight. There was no time to drive home and go back for Howell, so he warned Tina he'd be late. He'd have to drop Lowell off on the way.

"He'll be wanting a meal," said Tina. "Bring him home first. There'll be plenty for everyone. It's pasta."

He found he wanted to argue, let Howell settle into his lodgings, but he restrained himself. The word 'home' had sounded so natural, so normal: he had grown comfortable here. He was beginning to feel prejudiced against Howell before he had even met him. He also resented having to include the new man in the discussion of the evidence. He was being silly.

Roberts' little aircraft trundled bumpily over the grass and disgorged its passengers. Roberts had only a small bag with him, so had no need to wait. Thorn greeted him, explained they would have to wait for Inspector Howell. They found a seat in the corner of the building, away from the passengers who were waiting for the helicopter to take them to Penzance. Roberts was excited, a little like a schoolboy returning from a rare school trip. He was sure the new evidence was not only important but also would clinch the conviction of George Jefferies. He was surprised at Thorn's scepticism.

The helicopter arrived with a clattering roar. The passengers disembarked and made their way into the building. Inspector Howell was a raw-boned, fresh-faced man in his early thirties. He would, thought Thorn, make an excellent second-row forward. He walked with a swagger.

"Good evening, sir." He held out a large hand which Thorn grasped briefly.

"This is Sergeant Roberts," Thorn introduced him, "Mrs Roberts has invited you to come back and eat with us before we take you to your lodgings."

Howell merely nodded, as though the Sergeant was of no consequence. Thorn looked at Roberts and pulled a face. Howell collected a suitcase and the three men walked out to the Land Rover. Howell walked round to the front passenger seat and opened the door, clearly expecting Roberts, as befitted his rank, to get in the back. But Thorn handed the keys to Robert, telling him to drive, and got in the back himself. Howell attempted to strike up a conversation, asking for information about the enquiry, but it was impossible to talk above the noise of the engine, and he lapsed into silence until they arrived at the police cottage. It was not an auspicious start.

Tina joined the three men and Thorn avoided any discussion of the business. Howell doubtless thought it was in order to avoid a non-professional being part of such a conversation. When, at 9 o'clock, the meal was finished, Roberts announced that he would drive the Inspector to his new lodgings. He could find them more easily than the Superintendent. It took him precisely 20 minutes.

As he shared a nightcap with the Roberts, Thorn was thinking the arrival of the new man was going to make a considerable change. He had begun to feel almost paternal towards the Roberts. He had learned a little of their family affairs and of their conscious determination to remain on St Mary's, where they had friends and a way of life they did not want to give up. Bill Roberts, he felt sure, would have made an excellent senior officer, if that was what he really wanted. He had shown himself to be intelligent, hard-working and resourceful. He was well liked and respected and he could relate to people, gain their confidence, probably make them feel safe.

Howell reported for duty at 9 o'clock, apologising for being late. His landlady had been slow serving breakfast, he said. He had told her he needed in future to be away by 7:45 in the morning. Roberts grinned but said nothing, he knew the lady in question, and knew she would never change her routine, least of all for an emmet. But by the time the Inspector arrived Roberts had already arranged with the Penzance police station to prepared two cells. He had been promised they would "give them a good going over with Jeyes Fluid." And so, at 10 o'clock, the three policemen made their way to the Smuggler's.

George Jefferies was not surprised to see them. He was expecting to be charged with the burglary. Not surprisingly, neither the publican nor his wife was very happy to see the three men come into the bar, although it was almost deserted.

"I suppose you want me to come to the station with you," Jefferies said. "Who is this, then?"

"Inspector Howell," the newcomer spoke for himself, "and we'll want both of you to come with us."

"Two inspectors? A bit much for a case of breaking and entering. I don't need my wife to hold my hand. She'll stay here and look after the bar. Don't suppose this will take long, will it?"

Thorn replied. "It's not just the burglary," he said. He turned to Sergeant Roberts, "Charge them," he said. Jefferies looked startled and puzzled. Sergeant Roberts stepped forward and grasped his arm. "George Jefferies, I am arresting you for the murder of Matthew Lambert …" Thora Jefferies gasped, then, as Roberts continued with the caution, protested loudly. "You can't," she said. "You haven't got any evidence. You know you haven't!"

"But we have," Thorn said gently, and Roberts began to charge Thora Jefferies as an accessory to murder. At this her husband turned and, taking everyone by surprise, aimed a wild punch at the Sergeant's head. Howell moved rapidly, seized the arm and swung it behind Jefferies' back in a half-nelson, forcing the man to double over, face down on his own bar. Thora also became aggressive, but she was soon subdued by Roberts himself. He had brought cuffs with him in readiness, and the two were soon handcuffed together.

The astonished customers were ushered out. Thorn made his way to the private quarters. He met Penny Jefferies and Paul Stringer as they were coming down the stairs. They were obviously planning another day sailing. Instead, Penny had to come to terms with the information that her parents had both been arrested, and, with the licensee under lock and key, the pub would have to be closed. She would have to sort out the mess. Her normally serene composure was shattered, and her inexperience left her in a mild panic. Paul Stringer rose to the occasion, reassuring her that he would help with all the practical problems.

The small group made its way to the police station. Neither Jefferies nor his wife said anything further, except to make a phone call to a solicitor in Penzance. Roberts and Howell took the two prisoners down to the quay later, and accompanied them by sea as far as Penzance, where they were held in police cells overnight. There was a brief appearance at the Magistrates' Court the following day, when they were both remanded in custody and transferred to Exeter prison.

The sequence of events on the night Lambert was killed was not properly established until the trial, nearly a year later. Roberts' familiarity with the lie of the land led Thorn to surmise what had happened. When Thora Jefferies heard Lambert leave his room, she had not yet gone to bed. She had grabbed her coat and her favourite hat, the trilby, and followed. There was no one about, so she was able to follow at a distance as Lambert crossed from the harbour side of the town to the beach on the east. There would have been enough light reflected off the sea to make it easy to follow from there on. George Jefferies must have picked up the knife – subsequently the barmaid identified it as one used when serving food in the bar – and followed his wife. Reaching the top of Purley Head, Thora, followed by George, had circled round to the left in search of cover, and the two of them hid behind rocks. Sarah Treduggan had arrived next, followed by Job. "A fine old game of hide and seek", as Bill Roberts put it. There would have been an onshore breeze, making it easier for the Jefferies and harder for Job Treduggan to eavesdrop on the conversation. Sarah had told Lambert she was going to see the doctor, and Lambert told her he would collect £500 in the morning, so that she could join him. For the Jefferies this was the last straw. When Sarah had left, and had insisted that Lambert should not go with her, just in case

Job might see them together, George had revealed himself. Thora saw the knife in his hand and shouted to her husband. Lambert had been distracted for a fatal moment, long enough for George to do his worst. Between them they had disposed of the body. George had thrown the weapon over the cliff, but he did not know the place well. He was not given to country walks.

Thorn stayed on for two more weeks, until the relief Inspector had been reasonably well briefed, and reports had been written. He would, he knew, have to come back for the trial, but that would be a good many months ahead. Before then, he was needed for two inquests, the one relating to Lambert, the other, more poignant, into the death of young Sarah Treduggan. Her father had by that time already been sectioned, declared unfit to plead, and was confined to a mental hospital. The farm, leased like all properties except Hugh Town and the Island of Tresco, was built on land belonging to the Duchy of Cornwall. The livestock and such implements as were of use were sold. The farmhouse was eventually bought by a wealthy banker, who wanted to escape the rat race. Local builders, including some who came over from the mainland, spent months working on the old buildings, turning them into a smart, but pleasantly authentic home. A large extension at the back made the small farm into a much larger property. Where once the cows had trampled in a muddy field, landscapers laid a large lawn. Shrubs bordered the grass and the new owners explained to the interested locals that they intended to produce a beautiful garden.

The night before Superintendent Thorn left, he insisted on taking the Roberts for a meal in the Atlantic Hotel. He was grateful to them both, and he wanted to tell them so.

259

"Thank you for taking me into your home," he said. "I realise that, when I first arrived, and when I first came to stay with you, you must have thought me bad mannered or at least bad-tempered. There was a reason."

"We know, Superintendent," Tina said softly, putting her hand on his.

"You know? What do know, and how?"

"Inspector Howell, sir," Roberts explained. "He couldn't wait to tell us about the accident, and how you were on compassionate leave because of it. It was quite nasty to hear. If you don't mind my saying so, you haven't really taken to him, have you, sir? And, to tell you the truth, neither have I. He wanted to talk about it – about your private problems, that is, – and seemed to find them just a bit too interesting for me. I was quite rude to him. But I wouldn't be surprised if he spread the information."

Thorn took a few minutes to think about this. His instincts had been correct. The fact that neither Tina nor Bill Roberts had mentioned this to him before, showed that they at least had respect for his feelings.

"Thank you," he said. "Maybe you can understand how the Treduggan case got to me as it did. For a while there, I was in a very bad place, I admit. But St Mary's and Scilly in general have worked a kind of magic on me, I think. When I first arrived, I couldn't see them for what they were. It's since I've been living with you in your home here, that I've come to realise just how beautiful the place is. Whatever horrors take place here, they can never spoil that."

"Maybe you can come back here and have a proper holiday sometime," Tina suggested.

"Maybe. I imagine the trial will be held in Truro, so I shan't be back here for that."

"Once we are shot of Inspector Howell," said Tina, "you really should come back and enjoy the place. We'd love to show you round. You'd be welcome to stay with us again too."

Bill Roberts nodded his agreement and lifted his glass. Further conversation was all at once made impossible. In the bar next to the dining room a large group of men had congregated. They were, Roberts had explained, visiting rugby teams, here for an annual trip from the mainland. The players and followers had been joined by the local teams. They began to sing. It was astonishingly good, if very loud, and Thorn was not surprised later to learn that most of them sang in a male voice choir. The harmonies were splendid, the sound deeply male, powerful. It was like a farewell concert, staged specially for him.

He had time to spare the following morning, long enough to take a stroll round the Garrison for the last time. It was a fine day, just the hint of thin, high cloud. The air was so clear here. There were very few vehicles apart from the old bus that took tourists around the island, a lorry that delivered coal and other heavy goods, and transported them to and from the quay. There was little point in owning a car here, where it was possible to walk right round the island in half a day. There were few people to be seen on the path but, as he neared the southernmost tip of the island, overlooking the conjoined islands of Gugh and St Agnes, Thorn recognised a couple, sitting close together and looking out to sea. It was Clapton and Mrs Lambert.

Clapton spoke. "I suppose you will be leaving soon, Superintendent."

"Today."

"All just part of the job, I suppose, for you. Chaos for the rest of us." There was still a bitter edge to his tone.

"I'm sorry I had to intrude upon your life," Thorn replied. "I do not actually enjoy upsetting people."

"Don't listen to him, Superintendent." It was Mrs Lambert who spoke in a conciliatory voice, "we both know you were only doing your job, and we really ought to be thanking you."

"Thanking me?" This was something Thorn had not expected.

"It made me admit the truth," she said. "And I listened to what you had to say. I was so afraid of losing Peter. I shouldn't have been. That was a big mistake on my part. It is sometimes hard to learn to trust again."

"I'm sure you will be very happy together," Thorn said.

"Oh yes, we will. We are going to get married. Here. The Vicar's calling the banns."

"Congratulations."

"And," she paused for dramatic effect, "if it's not too late, we're going to start a family."

" That is very good news. I really do wish you both the best of luck."

He resumed his walk. At least a little good had come from all this evil. The Treduggan case could never have ended well, but it had not left any legacy, no other members of that family remained to be damaged as a result of the experience. As for the Jefferies, well, Penny would take a long time to recover, no doubt, but in Paul Stringer she had found a young man who would help her through. They were both very young, and it was impossible to foretell whether the relationship would last, but for the moment at least the worst was over, and Penny, with her studies to complete, might look forward to a fulfilling future. And, he reminded himself, he should not forget the

Roberts, their son, Tom, and his girlfriend, Andrea. Tom's parents seemed happy with that outcome, while their comfortable life on St Mary's looked set to continue.

That evening he would be back in York, a city he loved. He had decided to follow the advice he had been given by his own Deputy Chief Constable and friends, advice he had at first dismissed, and accept counselling. He was, he knew, still not right, it would take a long time for life, let alone work, to have the kind of appeal it used to have. But the walk in the clear air, the brief encounter with the couple on the bench, and the splendid vista before him, as he walked down through the Garrison gate to the little town, all fanned a small flame of hope.

THE END